RACE AGAINST TIME

RACE AGAINST TIME

a novel

WILLARD BOYD GARDNER

Covenant Communications, Inc.

Cover design copyrighted 2001 by Covenant Communications, Inc.

Published by Covenant Communications, Inc.
American Fork, Utah

Printed in the United States of America
First Printing: April 2001

08 07 06 05 04 03 02 01   10 9 8 7 6 5 4 3 2 1

ISBN 1-57734-805-2

Library of Congress Cataloging-in-Publication Data

Gardner, Willard Boyd, 1963-
      Race against time : a novel/Willard Boyd Gardner.
         p. cm.
      ISBN 1-57734-805-2
      1. Police--Utah--Salt Lake City--Fiction. 2. Salt Lake City (Utah)--Fiction. 3. Time travel--Fiction.
4. Mormons--Fiction. I. Title
      PS3607.A73 R33 2001
      813'.6--dc21   2001028114
                                                           CIP

For Mom and Dad

PROLOGUE

"Oh, I swear, Owen. Not again. Not now," she grumbled, just loud enough to disturb the other movie patrons.

She was probably the most gorgeous girl I had ever dated. Deirdra was an 8X10 glossy—long and lean, blond and blue eyed, and extremely intelligent. But that's just about where her virtues ended, except for her family money. Big bucks didn't really mean much to me, but it was fun cavorting above my social station once in a while. I thoroughly enjoyed the occasional ride in her British racing-green Jaguar—Connolly leather seats, burl walnut dash, and the distinctive odor of real wool carpet.

"This is our anniversary and I will not . . ." Her voice was now loud enough to get one or two warning stares from indistinct faces in the darkened theater.

I put up a conciliatory hand, "Just let me see who it is first." I contorted my body and reached for my belt to check my pager. Although there was a chance that I'd see a number on the display I could ignore, the chance was remote.

I read the number and began to wiggle into my jacket, catching an icy glare from Deirdra's direction.

"No," she barked, loud enough to get a shush from someone in a seat behind us.

"We'll talk outside." I tried not to sound like I was pleading.

"No," she repeated, but she was getting up and retrieving her things.

We ducked out of the theater and into the lobby where raised voices would merely attract unwanted attention, not drive movie viewers to distraction.

"Who is it, Owen? I can't believe you're doing this. Today of all days. Why couldn't you have just left that stupid thing on your dresser?" Deirdra planted her feet firmly on the multicolored carpet unique to movie theater lobbies, making a final stand right there at the fourplex.

"You know I don't have a choice, Didi. I have to go. It's my job." I felt like throwing a white scarf over my shoulder, proclaiming to return with honor.

"Don't you 'Didi' me, Owen. If you go this time, it'll be your last."

It was not her first ultimatum, but it was her most public. Several popcorn-purchasing patrons were getting us as a double feature, and I thought about calling her bluff.

"I promise to make this up to you, sweetheart. I promise." I was making myself sick.

"No you won't, Owen, you never do. You are always Mr. Responsibility with everyone but me. I mean it, Owen. This is the last time."

Did that mean I could get away with it one last time, or that this was literally the last time? There is nothing worse than an ambiguous ultimatum. Sometimes I'm really glad I don't say what I'm thinking. It didn't matter; she would decide later what she meant.

She squared her shoulders and crossed her arms; this almost always meant something bad.

"I have to go, Deirdra. Let me take you home."

She didn't say no, but she didn't say O.K. either. I tried to take her hand and she snatched it away.

"I'm sorry, Deirdra," I said. "Would you call and cancel our dinner reservations?" I couldn't guess what made me ask that.

"You do it. It was your idiotic idea to come to a matinee before dinner, anyway. It's not natural." Her eyes narrowed.

"What are you saying? Rich people can't watch movies in the afternoon?"

Glaring, she said, "I'm calling someone else for a ride." She turned her back on me and walked to a bank of pay phones in the lobby. A real gentleman would have insisted on driving her home, but I knew how futile that gesture would be. Instead, I took the coward's way out and watched her arrange for a ride. After a feeble attempt at good-bye, I walked out of the theater alone. I felt like an incredible cad. The chilly afternoon air was tropical compared to the frosty atmosphere surrounding Deirdra.

I got in my truck, turned it toward the nearest freeway interchange, and dialed my cell phone.

Several rings later a digital voice picked up, *"You have reached the Salt Lake City Police Department. If this is an emergency, please press one. If you would like to report a crime, please press two . . . ."* I pressed nine and got another set of rings.

"Patrol Division," said a bored voice.

"Owen Richards here."

"Hey, Owen. SWAT has been activated. Ready for the details?"

"Let 'er rip," I said, and accelerated onto the freeway.

CHAPTER 1

Traffic on Interstate-15, north and south through Utah, was strung together like an immense centipede. The Woods Cross exit had been blocked to accommodate a mobile police command center set up under an overpass amidst a flurry of ordered chaos.

Two uniformed Utah State Highway Patrol Troopers hustled between cars, sending angry motorists on to the next available exit while I held a Salt Lake City Police Department badge lazily out the driver's-side window of my new Dodge quad cab pickup. Eventually, one of the troops waved me past and I drove down the deserted exit ramp into the tiny Salt Lake City suburb, Dwight Yokam yodeling at an unwholesome volume from my compact disc player.

On reaching the police Command Post, I parked my truck among a disorganized assortment of familiar-looking rigs, hopped nimbly out of the cab, then hoisted an enormous black canvas bag from the backseat. As an afterthought, I slung a 35mm Canon AE1 single reflex camera over my shoulder. Photography was my hobby.

"Hey, bud," said a voice from the direction where a cop with an overstuffed torso nodded and pulled vigorously on the squat remains of a cigarette.

"Hey." I returned the greeting, not sure to whom I was talking, though his face looked vaguely familiar.

I avoided the command center, which was a converted motor home filled with radios, telephones, and computers. Ranking officers were milling around outside arguing; they were too busy to notice me anyway.

Several hundred yards from the command center, nestled between a set of rusty railroad tracks and a series of backyard fences, stood a group of men in various stages of dressing in camouflage fatigues. This collection of misfits was the SWAT team. They had chosen a secluded patch of gravel near the rail bed for a staging area, and were standing over their black canvas bags pulling out clothing and equipment which was, by this time, strewn about the scrub grass.

I moved toward my group casually, taking in the bracing blast of clean autumn air from the north that had swept away the usual haze of the Salt Lake Valley. Behind me towered the rocky, snowcapped crags of the Wasatch mountain range that edged the picturesque Salt Lake Valley. Growing up here had not hardened me to its charms, and I took every opportunity to appreciate its beauty, wondering what the unspoiled nineteenth-century version must have looked like to the wide-eyed settlers.

Unable to take my eyes off the eastern granite peak glowing orange in the late afternoon sun, I wandered toward my fellow police officers who were conversing in low tones on the raised gravel rail bed.

"Hey, Owen," said Al, a tall, hazel-eyed blond who looked more like a Southern California lifeguard than the Salt Lake City Police Department SWAT team leader.

"Hey, Al," I said, echoing him. I snapped a photo of him with his mouth open—perfect. I snapped a couple of shots of the guys in the background standing in their underwear—daily double. Just about everyone hated my compulsion to take pictures, but I was bucking for an assignment to the Major Crimes Task Force and I intended to pad my resume by honing my photography skills.

Several other greetings, some friendly and kind, and some patently obscene, were exchanged between team members as I neared. I dug into my bag and started to change from chocolate-brown corduroy Dockers and a starched button-down shirt into a set of wrinkled woodland camouflage fatigues that were well overdue for a trip to the laundry.

"Ahhh," I let out a groan of satisfaction. "Now, *that's* comfort," I said as I pulled on the trousers and buttoned the fly.

Lewis, my best friend since childhood and partner in crime fighting, gave me a wink and threw a phantom football across the railroad tracks. I feigned a catch, arms outstretched for the imaginary ball, and everyone cackled as I bobbled and dropped it.

"Get an arm, you hack," I taunted.

Still looking at Lewis, I feigned another pass and gave him the thumbs-up signal, receiving an overly animated version of the same signal in return. Even though our scheduled trip to Kansas City to watch the Chiefs play the Seattle Seahawks on Monday Night Football was a week away, we had been alive with anticipation since Lewis's Uncle Lawrence sent us the tickets.

Lewis's Uncle Lawrence, city engineer of Kansas City, Missouri, had been given six tickets by the mayor of Kansas City and had sent two of these precious items to his favorite nephew. I first met Uncle Lawrence, an intelligent, meditative man with a well-trimmed beard and mustache touched with sterling silver, on a summer vacation trip with Lewis's family when I was fourteen and Lewis was twelve. The highlight of my summer that year was watching the Kansas City Royals play baseball in the Kemper Arena. Lewis's family was big into sports, which never bothered me since I was often invited to tag along.

Lewis and I meant to relive our summer of '84 and had both lobbied for time off work for the trip. We had made hasty plans to camp in my truck on the way to and from Missouri to cut expenses, thus leaving us more money to eat at Kansas City's finer rib joints. It would be my first real vacation in eight years and I was counting the days.

I strapped on my bullet-proof vest, the kind we all wore under our gear, and turned to Lewis. "I'm gonna have to wear this the next time I see Didi."

"A bit unhappy, is she?"

"It was our anniversary."

"That's a legitimate reason to be miffed," he said seriously.

"The six month anniversary of our first date?" I mocked.

"I see . . . keep the vest; lose the girl," he said and shook his head.

Lewis pulled on his load-bearing vest that was heavily laden with equipment. At a healthy six feet three inches tall, 200 pounds, with a long muscular frame and classical tanned features under thick, straight dark hair, Lewis was quite a specimen. His Irish green eyes were the color of seafoam, the product of a dominant family gene, I'd been told. At twenty-seven, he was two years my junior and tried not to let me forget it. His ever-present smile was the natural consequence of the goodness of his heart, a quality that was immediately apparent.

I was a good inch shorter and at least twenty pounds fuller than Lewis. He often assured me, a grin on his innocent face, that I was not fat, just a little dense. My wavy brown hair, hazel eyes, and softer features were qualities that landed me second place behind Lewis in the looks department—but not at the police department. I had joined the force five years earlier than Lewis; he had gone out of the country for a church mission and then finished college at Brigham Young University. When he joined the force, I showed him the ropes. We had been friends for as long as I could remember, and that friendship only intensified as the years passed.

Al was saying something that seemed important, so I turned suddenly and looked at him with a stunned look, earning me some subdued laughter from my teammates. I consciously, but reluctantly, put Monday Night Football out of my head.

"Listen up Owen, I've got a tee time. Let's get this thing done," Al said, tapping his watch in mock frustration. That brought with it a chorus of laughs and friendly insults; it was the team way. I did an elaborate end-zone dance and then continued to change clothes as modestly as I could, considering that my dressing room was a public rail bed, and listened to the briefing.

"At about 1440 hours, a Woods Cross patrol unit saw a car parked on the shoulder of the road just outside the refinery entrance." Al pointed over his shoulder into a relatively small bedroom suburb of Salt Lake City with which all of us were familiar. "The officer traced the license plate and found out the car was stolen this morning from the main lot at Bluffdale Penitentiary. They rebroadcast information on the two guys who escaped this morning." Al turned a page of his loose notes. "The patrol officer spotted the suspects walking into the Phillips oil refinery." He gestured to a site west of the freeway, an industrial area with tall, gray stacks and black pipes rising into the sky. We had all seen it before from the freeway, noticing the tall, thin flames shooting from the tallest stacks, but had paid it little attention.

Al went on, "We are actually in Davis County here. We're the largest SWAT contingent able to respond, so we're really just assisting the Woods Cross Police Department. They have ultimate command over the mission."

There were a couple of grumbles from the team.

"Not to worry," Al said. "They have given command of SWAT over to us, exclusively."

He looked over the group, and seeing heads nod, he continued, "Phillips is huge, covering more than twelve square blocks of pipes, conduits, ducts, tubes, and . . . more pipes, not to mention every shape and size of holding tank known to the industrial world, and towers of all heights, topped with flames," Al said with a flourish. "The suspects—I think I have pictures here." Al fingered a small pile of papers fastened by a paper clip, and retrieved photographs of two average-looking slime bag types, which he held out briefly before stuffing them back into a bursting manila folder. "That's them," he mumbled as his papers flapped in the breeze, reluctant to go back willingly into their neat stack. "Anyway, the patrol officer spotted them walking east past the refinery and they took off through a side gate and fired four shots from a handgun at the officer; he wasn't hurt." Al paused while a couple of us gave silent thanks. "The suspects then ran into the maze of pipes and stacks, here." He picked up a dry-erase board and pointed to an area on an eight-and-a-half by eleven-inch map of the compound. "Patrol has been sitting on it ever since. We assume they've gone to ground in an outbuilding or something."

"Do we know if they're still in an outbuilding?" I asked.

"No, we're not even completely sure they're still in the refinery." Al had a habit of running his fingers through his hair when he got nervous. He was doing that now.

"Woods Cross police surrounded the place as quickly as they could. They have officers at each corner with a view of all the sides. They haven't seen anyone leave," Al tried to reassure us. "But, they don't have enough people to prevent the suspects from making a run for it into one of the neighborhoods. Part of our mission is to strengthen their containment. We have people working on that now."

A few apprehensive looks passed between team members who were just buttoning up, each helping the other to make sure their gear, which mostly hung from their equipment vests, was secure. I was almost ready so I wrapped my camera in a spare shirt and stuffed it deep into my black bag, which would remain at the staging area. I double-checked all my gear and then tuned in for the rest of the briefing.

"We have good identification on these guys," Al began again, trying to focus on the positive. "Ed Harkins, white male, five-eight, about one-fifty, forty-seven years old; he's in for three years on vehicle theft. My guess is that he's not very imaginative. The prison says he's a pussycat, not violent, probably just a patsy." He made another attempt at freeing Harkins's picture from his papers, but gave up as the breeze took a single sheet of paper across the railroad tracks. "Oh well . . . you saw the picture before."

"*This* guy," Al went on, now able to retrieve a photo, "is our bad guy. Raymond Hunt, white male, six feet, one ninety-five and fit, twenty-five years old. He's young and bad. He's in for killing his girl-friend and her mother." A ripple of uneasiness passed among the officers. "He's got prior military experience as a marksman and a criminal history that goes back several generations."

"Foremost, our mission is to keep this thing inside the refinery. Then, we locate these guys and find a way to get our negotiators in contact with them." Al raised his drawing again and pointed to it as he finished his briefing. "As members of the team showed up, I got them in place. Two counter-sniper teams are in place, here and here." He pointed to two red dots on the dry erase board, each with the letter S scrawled by it. "They say they have a pretty good view overall but there are a lot of blind spots because of the number and nature of the structures in the refinery compound." Al ran a frustrated hand over his forehead and into his thick, blond hair. "That's the mission so far," he concluded, scanning the team for comments.

No one had anything to say yet.

"We've got the negotiators here," said Al, "just in case we get a chance to talk these guys into surrendering. The prison psychologist is also here."

"Right," said James, taking notes with an imaginary pencil and pad. "And how do you feel about that?" James often joked around at the wrong time, but we forgave him because of his professionalism on the job.

Al ignored James. "We've got people in place who can see all around the refinery, but we need to get enough teams surrounding the place so that these escapees can't make a run for it."

"Owen," Al looked in my direction and saw that I was checking the action of my Colt AR15 assault rifle, "you, Douglas, James, and Lewis get together and form a maneuver element. I'll decide what to do with your team later," he said with a grin.

Lewis and James were still busy getting their gear together. Douglas was ready and sat quietly on his helmet.

"Your first mission," I said, walking over to him.

He nodded.

"I hope I'm ready," Douglas said with characteristic humility.

"This is where you earn our trust. You'll do fine."

Douglas smiled, and I tucked the wire harness of his cell phone into his vest so it wouldn't get caught on anything.

Al was on a cell phone with the Command Post and was fingering his notes as he talked. He hung up and let out a long sigh.

"So," said Lewis to Al, "what exactly do they do here at Phillips Oil?"

"I've been talking to the senior process engineer. I'll give you the idiot's version."

The four of us were now paying full attention to Al.

"In a refinery, crude oil is distilled into several kinds of fuels. The distilled fuels are collected and either sold or refined into something that can be sold. Phillips produces a great deal of unleaded gasoline, most of which is refined from jet fuel and diesel, which are the primary products of the distillation process."

"So is the refinery shut down now?" asked Lewis.

"Four people are still at work in the control room. The refinery can't be shut down without crude oil and a frightening assortment of chemicals congealing in miles of pipe; apparently that would ruin the place. The rest of the employees are supposed to be out of the compound."

"Great," said James sarcastically.

Al shrugged.

Team members were leaving the staging area in twos and threes to go to their assigned perimeter posts. One of the containment officers, a ten-year veteran of SWAT, retrieved a thirty-round, banana-shaped rifle magazine from his vest pouch and rapped it smartly on his helmet before inserting it into the magazine well of his rifle. With a quizzical look, Douglas leaned over toward Lewis and whispered something in his ear.

James, overhearing Douglas's question, beat Lewis to a reply. "Douglas would like to know why we tap our rifle magazines on our helmets before seating them in our weapons. Anyone?" Several eaves-dropping officers were starting to titter and Douglas's face grew crimson around his freckles.

"Is it A?" James went on, relentlessly. "To check if we're really wearing our helmet? B, to seat the rifle rounds towards the spine of the magazine so they feed reliably? Or C, because the guys on *Apocalypse Now* did it?"

James smiled broadly before launching into a chorus of the Jeopardy theme song. A couple of others chimed in making Al shake his head in disgust.

Douglas, too embarrassed to answer, stood stock still, eyes wide with anxiety. Lewis looked at Douglas sympathetically and started to say something, either to answer or change the subject and get Douglas off the hook, but he cut Lewis off, putting his finger in the air and looking directly at James.

"B is correct," he said proudly. "However, partial credit is granted for choosing C." A muffled chorus of mock encouragement followed, but Douglas quickly threw up a hand to quell the noise. "Except in your case, James, for whom A is the most correct," he said, tapping his knuckles on his helmet. This brought the laughter to a soft crescendo, which made Al grimace over the mouthpiece of his phone. With some sputtering laughter, the other teams of two took their leave. *Good for Douglas*, I thought.

The remaining team of four, of which I was assigned to be leader, bantered about nervously as the others departed, still laughing at James and Douglas. Al busied himself by marking the locations of all the containment teams on his map, and by taking care of a myriad of other details via cell phone while the four of us stood by restlessly.

Al shut off his cell phone and motioned for the four of us to gather around. "I've got a job for you," Al told us. "One of the detectives at the Command Post interviewed the senior process engineer who says there's a series of sewer tunnels under the refinery. One of them leads to the Woods Cross sewer system, which is part of the system for the whole Wasatch Front. There's a good chance we'll lose them," Al said grimly, "if these guys are smart enough to find the tunnels." A pall fell over the four of us as we listened to Al describe our new set of troubles.

"Weren't they born in the sewers?" said James with yet another attempt to reduce stress with humor. No one laughed.

"Do we know where the sewer system connects to the outside?" I asked hopefully.

"Not really. This refinery was built in stages over several years and has seen dozens of additions and renovations. Without an expert here to fill us in, there's no telling." Al massaged the bridge of his nose with his thumb and index finger. "Give me a minute to get the rest of the containment teams spread out and let them know about the new problem. Then I'll see about getting some better information about that." Planting the cell phone in his ear again, he walked a few steps higher on the rail bed.

"Let's get our phones up," I said. Each of us dialed a designated number for the Command Post and became part of a conference call that would include all members of the team, and which would be monitored at the Command Post. We would communicate over the phone this way until the situation was resolved.

Al was talking to someone at the command center on a different line, and gestured to his map of the refinery as if the person on the other end of the line could see him.

He returned to us with an ashen face and mussed hair. "It looks like there is only one way to leave the refinery through the sewer system. If we can block it, I think we can keep these guys from getting out to the city system and escaping. If that's the case, we'll just shore it up and wait them out. The process engineer is on the way with one of the detectives to give us a briefing."

"Does that mean we're going into the tunnels?" James asked, surprised. James could be the team clown sometimes, but he was always serious about his work. He was large and strong and could easily melt you with a smile, or terrify you with a grimace. He used those skills to his fullest advantage as a police officer. After knowing him for as long as I did, I knew he was two parts teddy bear and one part grizzly. He was not, however, a man people toyed with on the street.

Al looked at James and said, "I don't know. Our intelligence on Hunt indicates that he's a real psychopath. Most of our history on him was gathered after he was sent to the walls in Bluffdale. People were always afraid to call the cops on him. Apparently he cleans up and blends into society pretty well. Not your ordinary mouth breather," Al said. "He's been bragging up his escape all week in prison and no one said anything. He was a big guy on the inside." Al shrugged.

As was his habit, Al let the facts sink in, hoping a viable plan would form by way of group symbiosis. "If you guys don't feel comfortable going into the tunnels . . . Al let the rest of the phrase hang.

"Let's go over it," I said.

"O.K.," Al agreed, "the sewer tunnel will be a lot like a hallway in a building, except more difficult to navigate for obvious reasons. This isn't a search and destroy mission; we just need to gain some control over the sewer access to the city. It's just like a lot of our missions; we need to establish containment of an area and control it."

That seemed logical. "Uh huh," I added, nodding.

"You guys think we can place an obstruction in the tunnel?"

I gave up an "Mmm," and then shrugged.

"We don't have much time, guys. The suspects could be beyond our perimeter by now for all we know. How about if you guys take a look at the tunnels and come back with an idea."

All heads nodded, including mine.

"O.K.," said Al. "I'll get on the horn to command and let them know what you're going to do."

While Al relayed the results of our conversation to the Command Post, I turned my attention to our mission: check out the tunnel and come back with an idea for blocking it. Dangerous getting into the tunnel, dangerous staying in there, and dangerous getting out; despite its simplicity, an extremely risky mission.

While we waited for our briefing from the process engineer, we worked out the details of our mission, deciding who would provide cover in the tunnel and who would take measurements. We worked on a plan for the entry. Dropping into a hole required different tactics than the more traditional entries with which we had more practice and experience. Nevertheless, we felt ready, and waited for word from the Command Post. It took only a few minutes but seemed like forever.

We used the time to plan for all conceivable contingencies. What if they give up while we're in the tunnel? What if we take fire? What if we can't block it? What if, what if, what if?

The contingencies exhausted, we sat contemplatively for a few minutes before Lewis broke the silence. "And, what if they should come at us with a pointed stick," he said in the spirit of contingency plans and Monte Python movies. I shook my head; Lewis always asked the same question right before a mission. Some traditions just could not be forsaken.

Before I could utter a response, James quoted the only possible reply, "Run away. Run away." Douglas laughed, but I was not sure if he was laughing with us or at us.

A detective finally arrived at our staging area, accompanied by a very attractive woman wearing an unflattering pair of royal blue, Nomex coveralls with the Phillips 66 logo on the sleeves. She wore a yellow hard hat that was incongruous with her silky, shoulder-length brunette hair. Her dusky brown eyes were the same shade as the turtleneck she wore and revealed a keen mind.

"This is Amanda Meyers, Senior Process Engineer at the refinery," said the detective, "and I'm Erwin Lange. We're here to answer questions about the refinery." I assumed that, but of course part of me was thinking about asking Miss Meyers out for dinner after the mission. For Lewis of course—I think I still had a girlfriend of my own.

"They're halfway to Wyoming by now," said James just loud enough to be heard by Lange. I always cringed when his humor turned sarcastic.

"Thanks for coming," Lewis said politely to take the edge off of James's remark.

Detective Lange, a scrawny man with small, sharp features and very little hair, had a hand-drawn map of the sewer tunnels, which turned out to be extensive. From the sour expression he aimed in

James's direction, I judged that he did not appreciate our kind of humor.

Lange nodded at Al and held up his drawing. "There are a lot of tunnels under the refinery, some pretty large, but only one that needs to be blocked," he said in a deceptively low voice, aiming his remarks at Al, not us peons. "Here." He pointed to a place on the map, or what constituted a map. It was a pencil drawing with a lot of eraser marks and it looked like Charlotte's web. I looked at the map and then at the detective, hoping my face would not give me away. It did.

"Look," he said rather impatiently, "I drew this in a hurry and the tunnels are several layers deep. The fat pencil marks are the first level down and the thin ones are lower levels. We only have to worry about the first level. They are the only ones that have a spur to the city system . . . as far as we know," he added, looking hopelessly at Al.

To the satisfaction of the little detective, I lightened up my facial expressions, and he continued his briefing. He seemed a well-meaning man, despite his demeanor. When his lecture was over, Al asked us if there were any questions for Miss Meyers.

I had one. "Tell me about the men, uh, people still inside the compound. What are they doing and where will they be?"

She looked at me before answering. I wondered if she would go out with Lewis if I asked.

"The only people inside are manning, uh, operating," she teased, "the computers that control the safety systems." Her voice was soft and sweet, just like I imagined for Lewis, but she obviously had some pluck, too. I wondered if she was Mormon, for Lewis would insist on that. "The controllers are essential for safety," she went on. "If a pressure imbalance in one of the systems occurs, adjustments need to be made, or the whole place will blow."

"Bad," I thought aloud.

The corners of her lips lifted slightly, which meant she had a sense of humor. So far, so good.

"The employees are wearing, or are supposed to be wearing, coveralls like mine and a badge," she pointed to a laminated card clipped to her lapel. "They will do anything you ask."

"And, yes," said Al, "before you ask, there are two cops with them in the control room."

"But," Amanda added, "I assured them they would be relatively safe in the control room. And, a lot of the refinery is on camera. Your people are watching, too."

Al nodded.

Very thorough; Miss Meyers was competent and cute. I was giving full reign to my sometimes slightly sexist attitudes. Lewis would like her, I thought. I looked at him to see if he was all starry-eyed. He caught my glance, but his face was impassive and he seemed to be thinking about the mission and not the process engineer. I followed his example and got my mind on business.

Miss Meyers took a deep breath, beginning to show some nervousness. "When we evacuated the refinery, we left things just as they were. In fact, the vehicles within the compound should all have keys in the ignition. It's our policy. If we have to move a vehicle in an emergency, we like to be able to do it immediately. Our employees are in the habit of leaving their keys in their rigs. What that means is . . ."

Douglas interrupted, "They've got wheels if they want 'em?"

"I'm afraid so."

"That's not a bad thing," he said, and then turned to Al. "Are we set up to go mobile?"

"Yeah, the State Troopers are ready for anything that goes mobile. We won't be in that loop. I just hope they steal something slow."

"Yup, something out of gas," James said. "They seem to have a knack for that already." Everyone but Miss Meyers laughed.

"You mean, you want them to have a car?" Miss Meyers asked.

"Uh huh," Al explained. "It's a lot easier to take someone down when they're in a car than in a maze like this refinery. Unless," he continued, "the bad guys take a hostage; then we want it to stay here."

"Oh, and . . ." Miss Meyers paused and looked at the detective who nodded his head slightly as if giving her permission to let us in on a big secret. "We keep a list of everyone on the compound at a given time: administrators, engineers, staff, on-site contractors, and so on. Everyone's accounted for except . . ." She took a deep breath and went on, "Whitney Adams. She's seventeen," she said quietly, "and she runs errands on a bicycle around the compound. She usually works in the afternoons and early evenings."

Great news. The tone of the briefing just took on a new dimension of seriousness.

"We don't know where she is," Al said and he ran his fingers through his hair, two hands now.

"She sometimes goes off the site to get things. You know, to take purchase orders to the store or to pick up supplies. That kind of stuff. She usually checks in and out of the site. But, we don't know where she is right now."

Detective Lange added, "We have a couple of people looking for her in some of the local businesses where she might have gone. We'll let you know."

Al nodded and then there was a prolonged silence.

Miss Meyers looked at us nervously and then changed the subject. "We don't normally allow two-way radios or cell phones on the premises. They can interfere with our radio signals and trigger our shutdown alarms. They can also be a fire hazard if they are not intrinsically safe. Yours are. I checked at the Command Post. Just be aware that all kinds of alarms might go off if you use the phone in there. You might fool a system into reading too much positive pressure. In that case, the pilot lights you see burning at the top of some of those stacks will flare up. It can be distracting if you're not used to it. And," she added regretfully, "the fire alarm is an old air raid siren. It's loud enough to prevent you from talking on the phone. I'm sorry," she said, unnecessarily.

"Amanda," I said, "we need a better grip on the geography in there. Landmarks and stuff." I pointed to a tall, square tower topped with an ever-burning flare. "Like, what's that tall tower there?"

Amanda recovered somewhat at having something to think about. "Uh, that's the catalytic cracking unit." All four team members looked back at her in wonder.

"Excuse me, Miss, but the last time I asked, none of us were rocket scientists," said James.

"It 'cracks' large molecules into smaller ones. That's what we do here: make big molecules small and small molecules big through a chemical refinement process."

More chemistry than that would have given me a headache. We didn't need to know everything right down to the last cracked molecule.

Amanda went on, pointing to a different place on her map. "The smaller flare to the south is a relief flare; it burns off positive pressure, like an emergency relief valve. When that one burns hot, you know you have a problem in one of the systems."

"O.K.," said Al, "that gives us a beginning. We can at least navigate by some of those landmarks."

"And," Amanda went on, "at the far end of the refinery is what we call the west tank farm—six large holding tanks."

"The west tank farm might be a good place to put a guy on top with a long rifle," I said.

"Uh, no," said Amanda, "they don't really have tops on them."

"No tops?" asked Al.

"They contain unleaded gasoline. The tops float up and down on the gas so the tanks don't get full of oxygen. Oxygen and gasoline make for a rather volatile mix. At this time of year the tanks are nearly empty, so if you could see the tops of the tanks, you'd see that the tops are near the bottom."

"All right, no long guns on the tanks." Al took her word for it. "What about some other places where we can get some high-ground advantage?"

"Well, of course you have the refinery offices on Onion Street, and . . ."

"Onion Street?" James found humor in all things.

"Yes, there was a farmer years ago who grew a very healthy crop of onions in a field under the refinery flares. They keep things pretty warm. So, Eighth West has been called Onion Street ever since."

James gave a shrug of appreciation and Amanda went on. "At the far corner of the refinery is the large water tank and the pump house; that's the one with the spider painted on it. The center tower—there are several towers there actually—is the crude area. That's where the crude is distilled. And," she said finally, "the funny-shaped tanks, bullet tanks, are full of butane. Don't shoot those," she added unnecessarily.

"Copy that," said James.

Douglas, who had been very quiet in the presence of Miss Meyers, spoke. "Are there any other ways out of the refinery? Someplace we've missed?"

Amanda thought about that, taking her time before answering. "Well, not really. Crude enters through a pipeline and fuel leaves through lines, but a person couldn't get through those. Trucks come and go, but the entrances are well covered. There's the sewer system," she looked at me, "and hopefully your team can take care of that . . ." She shook her head, "No, I don't believe there is any other way out, unless . . ."

"Unless what?"

"No, no, never mind. He'd die trying. I don't think that there are any other possible ways out." Amanda shook her head.

"Fine." Al vigorously ran his fingers through his hair, leaving it in furrows. "Can you label all those landmarks on my map?"

"Yes, of course." She accepted a black felt-tip pen from Detective Lange.

"Oh yes," said Lange as an afterthought, "Miss Meyers mentioned one other thing about the refinery that will affect us a great deal. I'll let her explain."

"Well," Miss Meyers hesitated, apparently nervous about her next bit of news, "we don't allow firearms on the compound either. Of course, you people will be an exception," she added hastily. "You see, there are a lot of volatile substances in the refinery and one in particular is extremely . . . well, I mean, if you rupture a tank full of hydrogen sulfate, it's pretty dangerous."

"How dangerous?" asked Al.

"A little bit is deadly." Miss Meyers, as pleasing as she was, did not make me feel any better about the refinery environment. "There are H2S signs, yellow with big black letters, but it's still a danger. A bullet goes a long way."

Miss Meyers' knowledge of ballistics was rudimentary, but accurate. James said, "O.K., no shooting at the hydro instant-death tanks."

"Personally, I wouldn't shoot anything in there." Miss Meyers was very serious. "And tanks aren't the only thing. Of course, the pipes are all pretty much full of . . ."

"Wow," James interrupted, as if a light just went on, "you mean, all of those pipes and tanks are full of gas?"

". . . well," said little Miss Meyers, "it's not chocolate milk. If I were you, I would be really careful about how you blow up our refinery."

Miss Meyers smiled for real this time as the team laughed nervously. Even Al had to laugh; James had been bested twice in less than an hour. This woman was perfect.

Detective Lange made a parting comment about his drawings and then offered a sincere vote of confidence and a heartfelt good luck before he escorted Miss Meyers back to the command center.

Once they were out of earshot, Al made a couple of observations. "Let's not worry about the missing girl until we know more. We can deal with the phone problem; it sounds like ours are okay in terms of fire anyway, and you'll just have to ignore the alarms and flares that may go off. The refinery fire teams are standing by. And the local fire department and ambulances," Al added, "are also on scene. The real danger is shooting something volatile, especially the hydrogen sulfate."

"What does that smell like, anyway?" asked Douglas.

"Sour," said Al, "but it very quickly destroys a person's sense of smell, and then it kills you."

"Great," said Lewis, a man of few words.

"People walk around in there all the time. It's not normally that dangerous. What we don't want to do," Al said very seriously, "is to pop a round into any of those tanks. You have to be absolutely certain of your background and target if you fire a round. You may not be able to shoot without risking either a lethal leak, or worse, an explosion followed by the biggest fire you've ever seen in your life."

"Not my rifle goin' off I'm concerned about," said James, patting Douglas on the shoulder. "It's the lunatic in there with the pistol."

***

Al went over our mission before we left the rail bed, making sure that everyone knew his responsibility. We established a rally point behind the water tank and pump house near the edge of the compound; it would be our last secure location before entering the refinery, and the evacuation point in case of a retreat. A large, black spider was painted on the side of one of the tanks. Painted above it was the site safety acronym S.P.I.D.E.R., which stood for the slogan "Safe Performance Initiative Directly Eliminating Risks." How apt.

When we got to our rally point, I gave the signal for a conference before we committed ourselves inside the refinery compound. The team responded by forming a small circle, each of us facing out to protect the team, but close enough to each other to talk.

"Let's go over our tasks one more time," I said, looking out over the refinery. "Lewis?"

"I assume point and cover the manhole as James lifts the lid. I go in first and cover forward down the tunnel."

"James?"

"I cover our flank until we get to the manhole. I carry the long crowbar and remove the manhole cover. I descend into the hole third in line. Once in the hole, I cover behind us down the tunnel."

"O.K. Douglas?"

"Uh, I cover our rear until we're in the tunnel. Fourth down, I measure the tunnel. I'm last out of the tunnel, and then I resume rear guard duties."

"Good," I said. "I cover our flank as we travel and descend into the hole second. Inside the hole, I help with the measurements if necessary. I'm third on the way out. Any questions?" There were none. "Okay. Lets get moving before dark."

"Lessen's yer chicken," said James, announcing our team motto, and we committed ourselves to the refinery compound.

***

The sun was swiftly sinking into the Great Salt Lake in the west, and a colorless dusk abruptly replaced the canvas of orange and red hues that had painted the sky moments earlier. Inside the compound, bright spotlights were mounted sporadically on the corners of massive tanks and on the sides of magnificent cooling towers, silhouetting the landscape between stark, glaring whites and baleful shadows. Ambient light from the refinery spotlights bathed the tall grass surrounding the compound, leaving the ground black around us. The heads of the weeds cast moving shadows on our legs as we walked carefully in formation looking for our manhole.

We knew the approximate location of our manhole cover within the gates of the refinery, and we struck out from our staging area under the cover of two counter sniper units and a number of other officers guarding the perimeter.

We stayed faithfully in formation, Lewis at the point, James and I covering our flanks, and Douglas, armed with a shortened shotgun, constantly looking behind us. I carried an AR15 rifle, a civilian version of the popular M16 rifle that has become a symbol of almost every Vietnam war movie ever made.

Lewis and James preferred the Hechler and Koch MP5 submachine gun, a short, fully automatic weapon that was very effective at close range. They scanned forward, wary of an ambush.

Our route took us into the center of the refinery compound where we navigated between flame-topped towers, and thousands of pipes running by our sides and over our heads. The noise, a 95-decibel hissing sound, was much worse than I had expected, especially near the building-sized furnace, the one that Miss Meyers told us heats the crude. The power bill must be hideous.

Miss Meyers had been right about the vehicles left unattended in the compound; we passed trucks bearing all kinds of company logos, none of them Phillips's, and one rather large dump truck with gravel spilling out the tail end. We skirted these carefully and checked the cabs for the suspects as we passed. Lewis actually cleared each rig, peeking quickly into each passenger area, his MP5 leading the way, and then quietly announced "clear" if no one was hiding inside.

"Entry Team One has reached the objective," I said quietly in my boom microphone as we came near the manhole.

"Copy," said Al, listening to our phone from the tactical Command Post.

James used a long, steel crowbar to open the manhole while Douglas and Lewis scanned for threats. We waited a few minutes after James had flung the cover out of the way, and then threw handfuls of cadmium light sticks into the opening to illuminate the dank hole.

Lewis dropped through first and I followed immediately. At the signal that all was clear, James dropped down, and then Douglas, still acting as a rear guard, followed.

In spite of the light sticks, it was extremely dark in the tunnel, the only other illumination being the pale column of haze washing into the open manhole from above. The first thing I noticed was the stale smell of dirt and wet concrete. The cement walls seeped with moisture that collected on the floor in murky pools. The tunnel was not tall enough to stand in, so we all crouched. Steel reinforcement bars stuck out of the walls at odd angles and tore at my shirt as I hunched near the floor.

I watched while Douglas took rudimentary measurements of the tunnel, fit only for troll-sized people; it was about five feet in height by about six feet wide. Douglas seemed to be doing all right by himself, which left me time to make my own examination. And, I had an idea.

In the cramped tunnel, I unspooled enough silky filament to string loosely across the tunnel at shin level. The key to a good trip wire was to make it loose enough to go taut when a person walked through it, but not so tight that they felt it.

Douglas was done measuring and had begun a hasty pencil diagram of the tunnel and its characteristics; Douglas had a natural inclination to do just a little more than was asked of him. I ripped open one of the Velcro enclosures on my load-bearing vest and took out a small, round canister. I carefully attached the end of my filament to the cotter pin on a pepper-expulsion grenade.

"A little surprise," I whispered to Douglas, "just in case they come this way."

Douglas grinned.

I carefully straightened the grenade pin so that the slightest pressure on the wire would release the spoon and detonate the device, filling the tunnel with the orange-colored irritant. I still had time, so I strung another trip grenade about ten feet further down the tunnel. Redundancy planning was the law of the SWAT jungle.

"Hold up," Lewis whispered into his headset. "Someone's coming."

CHAPTER 2

I didn't hear anything, but I hugged the wall anyway, trusting Lewis. He'd proved his sixth sense plenty of times in the past.

Lewis squirmed closer to the wall, which gave me the feeling that whatever he sensed made him nervous. We all reacted to Lewis's lead, although I'm sure none of us could hear the same thing he did. The tunnel was deadly quiet now that we had stopped moving.

I heard a sound, a soft scraping sound in the blackness at the other end of the tunnel just before the explosive blast of a shot thundered inside, concurrent with the blinding flash of a gun muzzle. Cement chips pelted my face, and a cloud of dust filled the tunnel. Lewis returned fire almost at the same time, apparently able to see and identify the threat. After the confusion of the blasts, I heard rapid footfalls above the ringing in my ears.

"Let's move," I said, not willing to risk my team in the darkness any longer. "Count off." We hastily fell back to the opening in the ceiling of the tunnel.

"One, up," said Lewis to signify that he was present and not seriously hurt.

"Two, up," I followed.

"Three, up," barked James.

"Four, up," said Douglas, his young voice an octave higher under the stress.

Relief washed over me with the knowledge that everyone was still moving and seemingly unhurt. After the count off to make sure we left no one behind, Lewis assumed the rear guard duties and Douglas took point. We left the tunnel in much the same way we entered, just a little more quickly. Douglas rose up as if by levitation and lent an arm to the rest of us. Back above ground, the team immediately postured for another assault as if it could come from anywhere.

As my ears recovered from the blast, a deluge of unnecessary questions swelled from the Command Post. Al answered the flood for me with a string of well-pronounced expletives.

I transmitted a report between gasps. "Took fire in the tunnel. I think we're O.K. Stand by."

Our next task was to move to a secure place and assess our situation. I was about to make the signal to move when I heard Lewis.

"Owen," he said urgently, wiping a small stream of blood into a smear across his cheek. He gestured toward the dump truck we'd passed on the way in. Behind Lewis's raised eyebrows, I read the formation of a plan. With a nod, I gave him the go-ahead to carry on. I patted the top of my head, signaling James and Douglas to cover the open hole we'd left behind.

Lewis re-cleared the cab of the truck and swung open the door. I ascended the truck walls and pulled myself into a deceptively comfortable seat behind a steering wheel the circumference of a hula hoop. The usual controls were present in their usual places—blinkers, throttle, clutch, brake, and even windshield wipers, along with other knobs and levers with mysterious purposes.

I started the loud diesel engine and slowly rolled the leviathan backward toward the hole until I received a hearty thumbs-up from Lewis, whose smiling face in the rearview mirror bolstered my dwindling optimism.

Taking the vehicle out of gear, I pulled and pushed unfamiliar levers with reckless abandon. A few things happened. My seat, which seemed to ride on air, fell abruptly to the floorboards. The seat control, I guessed.

I pulled another set of mystical levers and the bed lurched upwards, sending a shiver through the cab. I held tight to the lever, while the bed raised and tons of coarse rock and dust cascaded out of the back of the truck bed and into the open manhole. James, Lewis, and Douglas heroically channeled the debris down the hole with their boots, and the opening swallowed up the gravel like a California sinkhole.

Once the hole was full, Douglas stood over it with an astonished look on his face, while James and Lewis gyrated their hips like silent disco dancers and high-fived. I killed the engine and climbed down.

We retreated to our rally point where we circled for a conference, all facing outward as before. One by one, we moved to the center of our small circle and examined ourselves for bullet holes; adrenaline could cover very painful wounds and I wanted to make sure that none of us had taken a stray hit while we were confined in the tunnel. No one was seriously hurt, but we all appreciated the chance to check.

Lewis had a nasty gash on his cheek from which I plucked a good-sized piece of concrete. A rivulet of blood ran down his face. "Cool," I said, "now you're as ugly as me."

"Team One to Command. We're code four. The tunnel is impassable," I said to Al over the phone. I would explain the dump truck later. For now, Al would be pleased to know that our mission had been a success of sorts.

"Copy, Team One; move your people to the east, about three-hundred meters, to the parking lot. Stand by as a maneuver element in case the suspect shows himself. Otherwise," Al concluded, "we're going to wait them out."

After having spent a short time in the tunnel, nothing sounded better than an extended siege followed by a short above-ground confrontation. Our mission had changed, but it took only moments to reorganize the team. Assignments were given, and we took defensive positions in the refinery parking lot.

Once situated, the normal tedium of police work ensued. We waited for another hour in the darkness, poised and ready for our quarry to show themselves, while our command staff considered alternative missions.

I looked at Lewis and grinned; a return grin formed and he turned back to his area of responsibility. Another hour passed quietly. We loved our jobs.

***

"Sniper One to Command."

"Go ahead," said Al from the Command Post.

"I've got one suspect eastbound toward the administrative buildings. Looks like he came out of a manhole near the furnace area."

Our sniper teams had much of the compound covered, except for some blind spots in and around the tank farms that speckled the compound. For the most part, the suspects would be within our control as long as they stayed above ground.

"Copy, Sniper One. Details?"

"Copy. White male, balding, prison coveralls. No weapons in sight."

"Received, Sniper One," said Al. Snipers were a strange lot, very cool, and good at giving information quickly.

I looked briefly at the tactical position of my team. They were all taking advantage of available cover awaiting the suspect who was heading our way.

"The other one?" Al inquired over the phone

"Negative. Only one person in our view at this time," replied the sniper calmly.

I could see the man walking, coming right for the lot where we waited. He was indeed everything the sniper said he was.

"He's looking around," the sniper added.

He was skulking through the compound, swinging his head back and forth looking for an avenue of escape, not yet seeing us.

"We'll take him at the edge of the lot," I said in a whisper into my microphone.

He had several steps to go, and with each one my heart skipped another beat. Willing my body to relax, I took several deep breaths, waited for the suspect to reach the edge of the lot, and issued a loud and official-sounding challenge. "Police Department. Stop where you are and put your arms out to the sides." The suspect abruptly stopped, shocked at the voice that seemingly came from nowhere. "Any movement you make not directed by me will be assumed hostile." I repeated the practiced litany I'd said so many times in my career.

The suspect paused and looked as if he was about to acquiesce.

"His name's Ed," said Al over the phone, seeming to sense my needs.

"Turn around and face away from me, Ed," I said more softly. He did it slowly, indecision showing on his face like neon.

"Sniper Team One to Team Leader." I heard the phone traffic in my ear. "Another male has emerged from the manhole. He is approaching Owen's team."

"Owen, you got him?" Al waited for a reply.

"Negative," I answered. I held Ed at gunpoint and tried to sound calm. "I can't see the second suspect from here."

"Sniper One to Command." Sniper One's tone of voice had changed. In his voice, I heard the panic and fear that only a father must be able to feel. There were times when even a professional let the world in. His next words chilled me and cast an icy pall over the entire operation.

"Bad guy number two is holding a young girl hostage."

***

Sniper One reported that Hunt and the hostage had disappeared between buildings in the darkness and they'd lost sight of them. A panic to reposition surveillance teams followed, but the attempt was short-lived and Hunt was not seen again.

Ed Harkins gave up easily, following my commands to the letter until he was secured and interrogated. I wanted to credit my team's decisive action for Harkins's surrender, but he had probably already decided that prison was not so bad after all and that he'd had enough of Raymond Hunt. The pepper bomb in the tunnel that had left its telltale orange dye on his face and neck may have eroded his resolve as well. Whatever the reason, he was now out of the picture; but the picture looked none the better for it.

The perimeter officers, fully briefed about new developments, still occupied the darkest shadows around the confusion of pipes and towers in the compound. Anxiety among the troops had doubled with the news that Raymond Hunt now held an innocent young girl hostage. The siege was in its tenth hour, and fatigue was a danger— second only to the danger Hunt presented. Patrol units assigned to outer perimeter and traffic control were being spelled off as often as personnel would allow.

Our maneuver element was again waiting for the incident to demand something of us. Douglas, James, Lewis, and I retreated to our staging area outside the compound where we were met by Al.

"Maybe we should have pursued down the tunnel," I suggested, rubbing my red eyes with thumb and forefinger.

"You all know better than that," said Al. "That wasn't your mission and it would have gotten someone killed. That's not going to do Whitney Adams any good."

"You're right, Al," said Lewis. "Let's get our minds back on business." Lewis was a calming influence. "Owen, have you got any ideas?"

"If we can isolate him, we might be able to tighten the noose, shrink the containment a little," I said.

"Yeah." Al was thinking out loud. "That would give us a chance to let our negotiators work on Hunt." Heads nodded. "Meanwhile, Ed's been talking to the negotiators. They'll be ready as soon as we need them."

"It doesn't take a negotiator to know that if he doesn't intend to bargain, he doesn't need the girl," James said.

"I guess we need to make sure he has to bargain his way out then, don't we?" Douglas asked.

"Right," said Al, activating his ringing phone. After a brief conversation, he gave us our marching orders. "I need you guys to be ready to collapse the containment as soon as Hunt is located. I want you staged at a central place within the refinery. If he's seen again, and that's a big 'if,' we collapse the perimeter as quickly as possible, trap him in a confined area, and force negotiations."

"Isn't there some way to find him in there?" James asked.

"Sniper Team One has been using the thermal imaging scope, but it's just too hot in there. All they can see is hot and cold splotches."

Al turned and looked at the highest stack in the compound. It was nearly twenty stories tall and centrally located. "I'd like to get a sniper on that." Al turned to me. "We could probably escort a team in. As long as we're going inside the compound anyway, we might as well escort a sniper team in. I don't like those stairs though. Twenty stories out in the open like that." I shook my head.

"There's an old elevator almost all the way, then only one short flight of steps to the very top level," Al said, consulting the map Miss Meyers had made.

"What if he's on the stack, or in the elevator?" I asked.

"I'll have Sniper One scrutinize that stack with the night vision equipment and the thermal. If they can see some of it and give us the go ahead, then I think it's worth a shot."

"If our team stages in the Central Control House, here," I pointed on the map, "that puts the tower right on our way." I must have sounded more confident than I felt. "We can escort the sniper team in."

"So, do you guys feel good about it?" Al was good about letting us commit to missions and not issuing orders. We were a team and he respected our opinions and our feelings about things. Each of us nodded.

"Done," I said, knowing that this was a particularly dangerous mission, but necessary if we wanted to get the girl out unhurt.

"Get ready to go," said Al. "I need to let Command know what we're up to. It'll be a few minutes." Al walked off a few steps and got back on his phone.

I addressed my team. "What do you guys think? Any ideas?"

James was shifting in his gear and Lewis hung his head. They were tired, and had a right to be. "O.K., take about five minutes to loosen up. It's gonna be a long night. Patrol dropped off a case of Power Bars and some bottles of Gatorade, compliments of the city of Woods Cross." No one said a thing, but James was the first one to the food.

Lewis was standing quietly off by himself with his head bowed. It looked like he was praying. Some of the more religious officers did that.

"How ya holding up, Lewis?" He didn't look up immediately and I felt kind of bad interrupting him.

"Fine. Just thinking." He raised his head.

"It looked like you were praying or something."

"Like a monk," he laughed.

"No, but you're as close as a person can get." I made a fist and tapped it on his shoulder. "So, were you?"

"It depends."

"On what?"

Lewis let out quiet laugh. "Do you think we *need* a prayer right now?" He shifted in the gravel and smiled at me.

"It couldn't hurt," I suggested.

Lewis got to his feet. "Well then, put one right here." He poked me in the chest with his index finger and I deflected it. "Consider it contingency planning. You know how important that is."

"I wouldn't know what to say in a prayer." Being something less than saintly and just barely above a heathen on the pious scale, I wasn't all that comfortable talking about religion. Lewis usually kept it low key, and he never talked about religion without a genuine smile on his face.

"You just tell the truth, Owen. That's all."

"And who's going to listen to me, anyway?"

"You never know unless you try."

"Easy for you to say. You've been doing it all your life."

"Got a long way to go, partner," he said.

Al finished talking on the phone. "You guys ready?" he asked.

"What does the tower look like?" asked James.

"Sniper One has cleared the tower visually, but they aren't very confident about giving us a guarantee," Al said. "They suggest you guys be careful moving up the tower. After that, you go to the Central Control House."

"We can clear areas that are semi-open. But a house?" Douglas spoke.

"Catch twenty-two," said Al. "If you stage in the open, you'll be vulnerable. If you clear a building to set up in, you'll have a secure place to stage."

"It won't be a normal building clearing though," James objected; "it will be more like a hostage rescue. What if they are in the building?"

"We'll hit the place fast and catch him blinking," I said.

"Blink and you'll die in the dark," said James to himself.

"The Central House is pretty simple. It's two rooms and a bathroom. Nothing fancy," Al said.

"Let's come down from here," I said, taking Al's map and running my finger along our intended path, "from the refinery offices, across this open ground, and to the side of the building. We stage by that door." I pointed.

While we were staring at the map, Sniper Three arrived at our rally point.

"Hello, men. You too, Douglas," said two human forms covered in camouflage netting.

"Hello Mark, Brian."

Al briefed Sniper Team Three, and we geared up. After everyone understood the plan, we each checked our equipment one last time.

"'Lessen's yer chicken, gentlemen," James said as we set out.

***

We moved through the refinery, careful to stay in the shadows as much as possible. The team moved slowly in the congested areas, scanning in all directions for movement. We crossed open areas with deliberate speed, not wanting to expose ourselves to danger for longer than necessary. We stayed in a diamond formation, each of us responsible for covering ninety degrees of our perimeter as we moved. Mark and Brian walked in the middle of the diamond, looking with educated eyes at the terrain for which they would be responsible after they were in position atop the tower.

The refinery was so full of darkened hiding places that we were especially vulnerable to ambush. That was one reason Al had talked us into securing an inside rally staging area in which to wait for Hunt to show himself.

We'd circled around the outside of the refinery and made our approach to the tallest flare stack where we would deliver Sniper Team Three.

"We're entering the elevator," I whispered into my phone. I pulled the squeaky door of the elevator open, and Lewis quickly peeked inside the dark box. It was clear.

Cracker box on a string, I thought. James was thinking the same thing, judging from the anxious look on his usually placid face.

The lightbulb in the center of the elevator ceiling was conveniently burned out, saving me the trouble of unscrewing it. Hunt would probably know where we were, but there was no sense in advertising our exact location by leaving the light on. "James. Douglas. Cover the base from here. Lewis and I are going up in the elevator with Sniper Three."

James and Douglas took defensive positions while we closed the doors and started the ascent.

The elevator howled and clanked, sending shivers through us in the dark, but it seemed to be moving upward, which was what we wanted. Claustrophobia really could have ruined the ride. The box was pitch-black inside and moved at an agonizingly slow rate, inch by inch, higher into the air. The only evidence of movement was the rhythmic lurch as we passed each floor.

Near the top, I signaled to Lewis indicating that I wanted him to cover the right side. I would cover the left. The elevator stopped. I opened the door quickly and we exited, guns at low ready, button-hooking away from each other.

I turned the corner abruptly and was assaulted by a cacophony of flapping, and a surge of cold air rushing at my face. I leveled my pistol at the noise, my chest constricting, and the muscles in my fore-arms tensing. My eyes didn't even have time to focus on what was hurtling toward me. I ducked, more in panic than as a result of training, as something flew over my head and off the tower. Pigeons. Stinking pigeons. By the time I regained my composure, I heard Lewis behind me.

"Clear," he announced, not finding anyone lying in wait on his side of the tower.

I said the same, and we bid Sniper Three farewell.

The snipers were in a good position, able to command a great deal of ground from their aerie, and they would be able to defend them-selves for a long time with the amount of ammunition they carried. Lewis and I left them and returned to the box for the slow descent.

Neither of us spoke for the first few minutes of the slow ride down. As the elevator neared ground level, Lewis broke the silence.

"Scare ya?" he asked flatly.

I thought about my pride before I answered. "Nope."

Inside the blackened elevator, he didn't need to see my eyes to know the answer to his next question. "Lying?" he asked.

"Yup."

Lewis chuckled.

James and Douglas were waiting for us as we stepped out, and James made an impatient gesture toward his watch.

Our approach route to the Central Control House was through open areas behind the administration buildings. We made good time and saw no sign of Hunt or the girl. When the four of us reached the building, we formed up in a stack, a single file line that put us in order for the building assault. Lewis peeked around the corner quickly and, satisfied that all was clear, led us to the door.

Lewis was the point man, first to go in the door. I took second position. James was third and Douglas was the rear guard. Lewis gave the thumbs up sign, which I repeated to James, who passed it on to Douglas. When Douglas was ready, he squeezed James's shoulder and James passed that signal on to me. When I was ready, I squeezed Lewis on the shoulder. Lewis, who would initiate the action, now knew that each one of us was ready to go.

Miss Meyers had given Lewis a key to the door. He reached carefully over and worked it into the doorknob. Before turning the key, he checked to see if the door was locked. It was not. Lewis did three shallow knee bends, which we all copied in rhythm. That was our silent signal to move. He swung the door open and entered at a brisk "Groucho walk" pace, as fast as he could move and still keep his MP5 submachine gun steady.

We moved through the two rooms and Lewis checked the small bathroom, each of us calling out "clear" as we went. The assault took roughly four seconds.

"Status?" I whispered.

Each of the team members checked off.

"One up."

"Two up."

"Three up."

"Four up."

"Lewis, keep watch out the south window. Douglas take the west window."

Lewis and Douglas took up positions well inside the dark building, away from the windows, but looking out.

All was well. Now we waited for Hunt to show himself to our perimeter or sniper units. Hopefully we'd be in position to intercept.

"Command to Team One."

"Go ahead," I said.

"Stand by for a land line at your location."

"Copy." There was a phone on the wall that rang almost at once.

"Yep." It was Al with an update. "Got it." I hung up the phone.

"Listen up, guys," I said to my team. "Detective Lange has been interrogating Harkins. It's his opinion that the girl's chances aren't very good." I shook my head. "Harkins is convinced that Hunt won't let her live. He was extremely put out by the little gravel incident in the tunnel."

No one said a thing; the gloom was tangible.

"It doesn't change the mission and it doesn't make things any different in a tactical sense, but," I took a deep breath, "lets get this girl back."

Heads nodded and we each resumed our place—and waited.

"It's your move, Raymond," said James under his breath.

***

Fresh eyes were better eyes, so I rotated window duty every ten minutes. Five rotations into our wait we got the signal to move.

"Sniper Three to Command."

"Go ahead, Sniper Three."

"We've got movement near the boiler units. He has the hostage."

"Owen, get your team ready to move," Al said. I could picture Al hovering over a map, deciding which teams to move and in what order.

The dawn light was slowly turning the sky a bluish bronze in the east.

"Sniper Three to Command. Is that a water treatment plant beyond the boilers?"

There was a brief pause before Al answered. "Affirmative, Sniper Three."

"That's where he's going."

"Copy, Sniper Three," answered Al.

We felt relatively safe leaving the building while other units could see Hunt.

"Team One. Go to the water cooling towers and stand by."

"Copy, Al," I said. I gave the signal for the team to move, again in the diamond traveling formation. We moved swiftly until we were in sight of the towers which were not far from the water treatment plant. When we got close, I said, "Sniper Three, you've got the eye."

"Affirmative, Team One, we have 'em in sight. Keep behind the cooling towers. He's studying the settling ponds at the water treatment facility."

"Copy." We moved to the towers and established positions there.

"Sniper Three to Command. He's in the open. I've got a shot." That was the politically correct way to say that you could ear hole the suspect. "No, negative. I do not have a shot," Sniper Three continued. "Butane tanks in the backstop. I do not have a clear shot."

"Copy, Sniper Three," said Al. "Command to Team One. Can you guys move closer and make a challenge?"

"Take a peek; he's facing away from you," said Sniper Three, anticipating my need to know.

I took a quick look around the corner of one of the cooling tanks and saw Hunt and the girl standing by the settling ponds. The ponds were located near the refinery boundary.

"Command, we can challenge." I wanted the man with the big caliber rifle with the nine-power scope to be ready to make sure this guy was not going to hurt anyone.

From the high tower, Sniper Three gave us directions. "Team One, move your team just around the cooling towers and find cover behind a short retaining wall."

"Copy," I said, trying to orient myself to Sniper Three's directions. We moved slowly around the towers and found a short cement wall to hide behind. Sniper Three was on the money. From here, we were much closer to Hunt, who had now moved closer to the settling ponds with the girl.

He held her by the elbow with his left hand, jerking her as he went. She was not resisting, but she was not going willingly either. She was making it just difficult enough for Hunt that he had to pull her along. She was distracting him without antagonizing him. That's just what we wanted.

While I thought about this, my team adjusted into positions of cover where they could see Hunt. Hunt had his back to us and was jerking the girl back and forth behind him, placing her between us. None of us had a clear shot at him.

I could hear Al giving instructions for the perimeter units to collapse on our location. We would soon have this guy trapped in a manageable area.

Hunt was enthralled by something at the water treatment plant. He was scrutinizing the settling ponds; this worried me.

"Team One to Command. Al?" I said into my mouthpiece, "I need more information on the treatment plant."

"Copy, stand by." Al would be talking to Amanda. In the meantime, we watched as Hunt, with his hostage in tow, studied the area.

The treatment ponds looked like those of any ordinary city, only much smaller. They consisted of a series of settling ponds with rotating arms that stirred a brew of wastewater. From the top they looked like huge radar screens with a single sweep running around and around. Cast iron pipes ran several feet off the ground from pond to pond and into a small building that I saw was locked tight when Hunt tried the door.

"Command, where does the treated water go?"

After a second, Al answered. "To a canal through an underground culvert system."

"Copy. How big are the culverts and how far do they go underground?"

"Stand by," Al said. I heard him ask Amanda. "Three feet in diameter; they run underground at least a mile."

"Copy."

I looked at Lewis and gave him a hand signal. I pointed to my eyes and then to the edge of the treatment plant, which was close to the edge of the refinery. I wanted him to get a better look at the culvert that led out of the compound.

He paused for a moment and then moved away to get a look. In the meantime, I watched Hunt, who was still examining the treatment plant, unaware of our presence.

When Lewis returned, he looked worried. "The water drains into three parallel culverts over there," he said, pointing. "The culverts are small, maybe three feet in diameter, running about two thirds full. They're covered by grates. I can't see the end of the culverts or how far they go."

I cursed under my breath. "We have to get to the culverts before he does."

Lewis turned to move.

"Hold on," I said gently.

"Team One to . . ."

"Copy, Team One," said Al. "Stand by." Al must have heard the urgency in my voice and was trying to stay one move ahead.

"Team Two," Al said to another maneuver element, "get outside the perimeter and locate the canal that the culverts feed into."

Team Two acknowledged Al and then he spoke to us again. "Team One, move to check Hunt at the culverts."

We were already on our way. "Copy," I said as we moved toward Hunt and the girl.

Hunt was still focused on the culverts and I watched him jerk his hostage like a rag doll toward them. *That lunatic is going to try it*, I thought.

We were on an intercept course with Hunt. The terrain was open, and dawn was slowly taking the advantage of darkness from us. It worried me that we had not been able to plan for this. Al had made a point to tell Amanda Meyers that we always worked from a practiced plan. Like it or not, sometimes you had to improvise.

Hunt and my team all saw each other at the same time. Hunt stopped abruptly for a second and then bolted toward the water, hostage in tow. We were moving as well.

"Police. Don't move." My commands were smothered by the whine of an air-raid siren and the blast from the flare over our heads, all activated by an errant radio signal that happened to set off the alarms at the worst possible moment. A column of flame shot into the air above us. A wall of heat hit my face and made my eyes water.

Hunt kept running. I went to a knee, hoping to get a clear shot, but couldn't. James had taken a prone position, pointing his MP5 around the side of a settling pond. On his knee, behind a junction of large iron pipes, Douglas had a good angle on Hunt but still couldn't take a shot without risking the safety of the girl. I couldn't see where Lewis had gone.

"Police Department!" I screamed as Hunt neared the foaming current that emptied into the pipes. "Police! Stop!"

Hunt and his hostage disappeared behind a levee near the culverts. I couldn't believe he was going to try to escape through the culverts. They were too small and there was no guarantee that he could get out at the other end. He'd drown the girl.

Hunt reappeared just long enough to plunge into the sluice, dragging Whitney by the hair and using her for a shield. *He's going for it,* I thought desperately, *and he's taking the girl with him.*

Hunt yanked at the heavy steel grate covering the closest culvert. It seemed to break away easily and he tossed it aside.

Whitney's face was visible above the water, her eyes pleading to Lewis who had taken a position closest to the channel and was now in sight. Hunt was up to his shoulders in the water, holding his hostage between him and us. Lewis looked at me; I knew what he was thinking as clearly as if I'd had the thought myself. *No,* I begged silently. *Please Lewis, don't do it.*

Lewis dove into the water near Whitney, whose head was bobbing in and out of the foam. Had she escaped Hunt's grasp? I could no longer see Lewis or Hunt. The surface of the foamy brine exploded into the air as bullets from James's MP5 submachine gun pelted the water where Hunt's head had gone under. Lewis surfaced near the mouth of the drainpipe, holding tightly to Whitney's neck. A shot echoed from deep within the culvert and Lewis's body jerked.

"Lewis!" I screamed. James and Douglas were already running to the edge of the water, firing rounds into the black entrance of the culvert.

"Lewis." His head disappeared into the foam, then resurfaced. He gasped wildly for air, holding Whitney's face out of the water. James was in the current reaching for Lewis; Douglas clung to the bank with a strong grip on James's load-bearing vest. James was thrashing madly for Lewis's hand.

Last to reach the culvert, I held tight to Douglas's shoulder and waist and helped to stabilize him.

James caught Lewis's arm and dragged him against the current toward the bank. Lewis held an unmoving seventeen-year-old Whitney Adams firmly to his chest. The foam around their bodies was slowly turning a sickening pink and Lewis's body was now limp in the water except for the hold it had on Whitney.

James pulled them both onto the dirt bank and held them in his bear-like arms.

"Status! Status!" Al yelled over the phone.

CHAPTER 3

James held Lewis on the bank, just out of the foamy water that flowed around his legs, soaking his pants and boots. Lewis was helpless. I rushed to his side and, taking him from James's grasp, I rested his head in my lap.

Blood mottled the bank where I held him, and I opened his load-bearing gear to reveal a dark red stain just under his left arm. The bullet had missed his ballistic vest by less than an inch. I took a trauma pad from the front breast pocket of his vest and held it tightly on the wound with my palm before looking around to assess our situation.

Douglas had assumed responsibility for the security of what was left of our unit. He had taken a position behind the canal embankment with a clear view of the culvert opening. "I got it covered," he yelled, looking over the sights of his rifle into the dark hole.

James carried the hostage, Whitney Adams, up the bank. She was apparently also hurt and James's fatigues were red with her blood. He sat her on the ground and began a first-aid assessment.

I did the same with Lewis. Pink foam oozed between my fingers, indicating a lung wound. Lewis craned his neck, looking for the girl. "Relax, Lewis, she's okay. James has her. We're gonna get through this, buddy," I whispered to him, silently urging him to fight for life. He took shallow breaths and coughed gently. Each movement forced blood from the wound.

I swore an ill-conceived oath; "Hunt's a dead man, Lewis." But I didn't see vengeance kindled in his eyes like the fire burning in my heart. I looked in Lewis's face for the anger that I thought should be there, but he was peaceful and relaxed.

"No, Owen," he said gently.

I heard a noise behind us and turned to look. Two other SWAT team members descended on the scene. One took up a position next to James and the other barked into his radio, coordinating the approach of the medical personnel.

". . . just a moment." Lewis coughed weakly.

"They'll be here in just a second, buddy. You just hang on."

I pushed on Lewis's wound, but I couldn't check the pinkish froth. "Hold on. They're almost here, buddy. Hold on a few more minutes."

Lewis was our team medic and carried a comprehensive field surgery kit. He had once said he could do almost any field surgery with what was contained in the kit. I tore open the kit that hung on a shoulder strap over Lewis's back. I took out a wad of gauze and placed it over the trauma pad.

Lewis's shoulders and arms began to quiver. "Owen . . ." Lewis coughed, his teeth and tongue bloody.

"Hang in there, buddy. Just a few minutes." I leaned harder on the wound, still unable to stop the flow of blood.

Lewis grasped my collar and pulled me to him. "It's just a moment, Owen . . . a small moment. Have to . . . endure it well."

"What are you saying, Lewis?" My throat constricted and my lungs tightened; I struggled to breathe.

An ambulance tumbled over the rocks through the tall grass along the fence, but it was too late. Lewis died in my arms.

***

An EMT from the arriving ambulance pushed me aside and I stepped reluctantly away from Lewis, leaving his head in the mud. Disjointed events occurred around me, but my mind was vacant except for one desperate thought—Hunt.

"Status, status," I yelled into the bizarre silence. Douglas just looked at me. "Where is he?" I demanded. "Where is Hunt?" Nobody said anything. I bound into the water, running with my rifle aimed into the darkness inside the culvert. "Cover me," I ordered as I splashed toward the opening where Hunt had disappeared.

James and Douglas followed me into the water. I was chest deep by the time they got to me. Douglas was yelling something in my ear and James had a firm grip on my rifle. I wrestled with the force that pulled me away from the culvert. *This was insane,* I thought. Hunt just let the current take him. I didn't understand why I couldn't follow him in the same wash.

"You can't do it," yelled James in my ear, pleading with me.

"I'll follow him into hell if I have to," I said through clenched teeth, diving into the dark opening of the culvert.

By the time my mind caught up with what was happening, James and Douglas had disarmed me and carried me to the bank.

Within moments, Al rushed from the Command Post to my side. He offered me his trembling hand. I nodded, which was all I could muster, and reluctantly accepted his arm on my shoulder.

I tried to speak, "Douglas has the culvert covered and James . . ."

"Shh, we've got it, Owen. You just take a few deep breaths."

The scene around me, which moments before was an intense climax of emotion and reaction, was now strangely tranquil. I wanted to turn toward Lewis's body, but Al gently pulled me away.

"Come on Owen, let's get you out of here."

My stomach twisted with anguish and I thought I would vomit. I fought for control, but my body shook under Al's arm. Al allowed tears to run the length of his bronze cheeks, making no attempt to hide them as he led me back through the compound toward the Command Post.

As we walked, I was aware of only the most mundane sensations: the familiar odor of gunpowder burned in my nostrils; a dog barked incessantly in the distance; a scrap of blue cellophane that once contained a set of foam earplugs lay in the gravel. My mind mercifully allowed me only fleeting thoughts about Lewis, filling itself instead with benign thoughts in an act of self-preservation.

At the Command Post, fresh officers were being dispatched to broaden the search for Raymond Hunt, who had not been found in the canal as hoped. The search would now take on a slower, more methodical pace, involving detectives from various jurisdictions and investigators from the Department of Corrections.

"I need my stuff."

"No, let's let them do it." Al steered me away and nodded to two uniformed patrol officers. "Put Richards's and McCray's gear in the dark green Dodge truck," I heard him say. We went to the hospital in Al's Subaru wagon. I rolled down the window and let the cool morning air blow against my face. Neither of us spoke.

The hospital's emergency room was alive with activity. Lewis's body was partially hidden from view behind a set of thick white curtains, with a host of doctors and nurses hovering over it. The hostage, Whitney Adams, had a serious but not life-threatening injury to her right arm, and the dressings applied in the field were now crimson with blood. She, too, was receiving a lot of attention.

Al was still beside me with his arm around my shoulders, tear stains apparent on his face and neck. Once again, Al turned me away from Lewis's body and escorted me into a vacant examination room. The room was stark and clinical, offering nothing to occupy my mind.

"I shouldn't have sent him. I should've . . ." I began.

"Hey, stop it." Al pulled me closer as sobs racked my body. He let me cry.

Eventually, the tears slowed and then stopped. I wiped my face on my sleeve and took a few deep breaths. "If only I'd . . ."

"If only what, Owen?" Al cut me off. "Lewis has been taking risks like that since the first day he signed on. So have you and I and everyone else on the team." He turned to look me in the eye. "I think you'll always feel some responsibility for this, Owen, but you can't change some things in life, no matter how much you want to. I could sit here and tell you that it's not your fault, that Lewis made the decision himself, that Hunt is the only one to blame, but you and I both know that we'll both always feel responsible because of the plans we made."

"I didn't plan for this, Al," I said.

***

The next three days blurred together and I thought of Lewis's death in short intervals between periods of mind-numbing emptiness. My tears ran so heavily at times and my sobs were so intense that my face and stomach were sore, as if I'd been physically beaten. I spent most of the time sequestered in my condo in the foothills. I talked to my mother and father, who'd since retired and moved to sunny Arizona. They were sympathetic, reacting like any set of parents would, but I felt empty nonetheless. I had an older sister who lived in Seattle. It was nice to talk to her but we'd never been very close. As for my girlfriend, Didi, she tried to be understanding, but she didn't do a very good job of it. I was left alone to mourn for Lewis.

Later in the week, Lewis's sister and her husband came to pack Lewis's belongings in cardboard boxes that smelled of apples. Each box was labeled with the name of a friend or relative to whom the box would be given. Lewis's clothes went in a box for his younger brother, who was nearly the same size. My box was empty as I refused anything they tried to give me.

"I'll start a box of stuff that belongs to the department," I said, uncapping a broad-tipped permanent marker. "All of his SWAT gear is in my truck. I'll have to go through that some other time."

"Fine," said Lewis's brother-in-law, entering Lewis's bedroom from the hall. He stood motionless for a moment by the dresser.

"Here," he said, holding out his hand.

He was holding out the tickets to the Monday Night Football game at Arrowhead Stadium in Kansas City. The game was less than a week away. "Could you just send those back for me? You could give them to . . ."

"No," he said, taking a step closer. "These are for you to use. I was given specific instructions to find them and make sure you had them when we left."

"No. Look, I can't just . . ."

"Yes. The family wants you to use them. They don't want them back."

"Like I'm going to go all the way to Missouri to go to the game now?"

"I know," he said. He was about seven years my senior and I liked and respected him. "The family wants you to have these tickets. They don't know what to do about all this stuff any more than you do." He waved a hand at the half-full boxes lining the hallway. "Do us a favor and take the tickets. You can decide about the game later. Just don't say anything for now."

I finally acquiesced and took the tickets. After the boxes were packed in the back of her car, Lewis's sister gave me a hug and promised to see me at the funeral in the morning. We said our good-byes and I retreated inside the condo where I found a comfortable spot on the sofa and a mind-numbing program on the television. I awoke the next morning in the same place, wrapped in a blanket.

Instead of a formal, public police funeral with bagpipes and a flag ceremony, Lewis's family chose a modest service in a Mormon Church building. I drove there alone despite a couple of offers to go with friends. Inside, a youthful looking gentleman, who apparently knew who I was from my freshly pressed class A uniform, led me through the hallway and into the chapel to a front-row pew next to James and Douglas. The chapel was spacious and opened to the gymnasium, which was lined with rows of folding chairs for overflow seating. There were paintings of Christ on the walls of the modestly decorated hallways, but nothing ornamental in the chapel except for the potted red geraniums lining the aisles. The room was conspicuously absent of religious artifacts—no candles, no statues, and, most notably, no crucifix. I'd been inside a number of Latter-day Saint Church buildings, mostly to play basketball, and was not troubled by the unassuming style and utilitarian amenities.

"Hoops after the ceremony?" James whispered to me and gestured toward the basketball standards in the back.

"I bet we can find a ball under the stage," I replied softly.

Douglas gave us a curious look. I was the only nonmember of the group.

At the front of the chapel, a grand piano and an organ faced each other from opposite sides of the room behind a row of padded chairs and an unadorned pulpit. An elderly man was playing the organ. I was no connoisseur of organ hymns, but I found the music soothing.

A congregation of adults and an unusual number of youth waited reverently in their pews behind a vacant first row reserved for family. I furtively searched the chapel for familiar faces, recognizing a number of police officers who sat in groups near the back. We were all wearing our class A uniforms, our best, which pleased me because I hated dress clothes. I could never match the shirt to the pants, or the pants to the socks, or the socks to the shirt, and the tie to the rest of it all. I was born to wear a uniform.

The row we were sitting in had obviously been reserved for police officers and Al was now being ushered towards us by the same young man who had escorted me forward. Al took his seat beside us, nodded a greeting, and opened a book of scriptures identical in appearance to a set Lewis kept by his bedside. James followed suit, pulling a set from a small black carrying case. Douglas was reading the hymn book.

"Don't tell me how it ends." I nudged Douglas who gave me a "so funny I forgot to laugh" look.

A hush fell over the congregation as Lewis's family entered the chapel behind a closed bronze casket draped with an American flag. The pallbearers walked respectfully beside the casket and positioned it in the front of the chapel. A dignified group of immediate and extended family members took their seats in the front row, and the congregation sang "Be Still, My Soul" under the direction of a tall, elderly woman with silver hair.

I heard some of what was said from the pulpit, but paid little attention; the themes all seemed to center around Lewis's life and God's great plan of salvation. When Lewis's father approached the pulpit to say a few words, he looked at me with the same loving green eyes as his son's. The image was haunting.

Lewis's mother, a tall lovely woman with dark, graying hair, cried off and on during the service. Lewis's youngest brother, an awkward teenage boy who looked just like Lewis, was well prepared with tissues that he produced from his jacket pocket like a magician's apprentice and tenderly handed to his mom.

Only one speaker, a member of the family, piqued my religious curiosity. She was probably only four or five years old and had long locks of curly blond hair. She wore a white lace dress adorned with pink ribbons that matched her cheeks. The pulpit, cleverly designed to raise and lower to suit a speaker's height, rumbled down, and a dark-suited man sitting behind her reached over and pulled the microphone closer to her face before she spoke.

"I know that God loves me," she said with conviction beyond her years. "I know that Jesus loves me." She paused, tears forming in her large expressive eyes. "I know that Uncle Lew still loves me," she choked out the words, "and that I will be with him again in heaven." The little girl stopped speaking, apparently unable to go on. The tears that had formed in her eyes streamed down her cheeks freely. Lewis's sister, who had accompanied her little girl to the pulpit, put her arm out to comfort the child. The little girl took a deep breath and straightened behind the microphone. "Families can be together forever. It's Heavenly Father's plan. I say these things in the name of Jesus Christ. Amen."

She smiled past her tears, and we all smiled with her in that moment. Tears spilled shamelessly from everyone's eyes, my own included. The little girl walked away from the podium, her smile intact, and sat confidently at her mother's side with the rest of Lewis's family.

The faith in the child's words pulled at my heart so intensely that I clutched my chest, hoping no one would notice. So powerful was the feeling that I thought my heart would burst. For just an instant, I felt at peace.

Then, just as quickly, the warm feeling was replaced by a void. For a moment, I had felt pure joy, and now the despair was just as intense. The service concluded with another song and a prayer, and my emptiness intensified.

I drove my truck to the gravesite, passing up several offers to ride along with friends. I hoped to use the time alone to recapture that burning feeling. It didn't come.

Lewis's little niece did not attend the graveside service with her family, and I was strangely disappointed. I stood apart from Douglas and James for a while because I couldn't bring myself to socialize. At the conclusion of the service, I reluctantly met with the others to pay respects to the family.

"How'd you like the ceremony?" I asked Douglas and James quietly, with the vain hope that one of them would mention the little girl's talk.

They both nodded; I don't know what I expected them to say, anyway.

"Lewis's niece was brave," said James. I turned to him, thinking he might say more. It was in his eyes, but he didn't speak. *Say it,* I pleaded silently; *say you felt it too.* But the moment passed and James, Douglas, and I walked slowly to the receiving line near the grave. Al saw us and came, too. He was with Amanda Meyers, whom I had not seen since the day of Lewis's death. Whitney Adams was also there. Her face was scraped and bruised and she wore a full cast on her right arm, but she was alive and smiling, thanks to Lewis's sacrifice.

Lewis's family accepted his passing with grace, and I was relieved when his mother greeted me with open arms in the reception line.

"I'm so sorry, Mrs. McCray . . ."

She put her finger to my lips and smiled, tears forming in her eyes for what must have been the hundredth time that week.

"Police work was Lewis's passion," she said softly. "He'd do it all again." My heart began to burn and I took a deep breath to stave off tears. Feeling like I'd lose control, I smiled politely and continued down the short line, shaking hands or hugging members of the family. I shook hands with Lewis's father. He held my hand in both of his and neither of us had to say anything.

Standing near the end of the line was Lewis's Great Aunt Etta. The McCray's called her their "Utah" Aunt because the rest of the McCray clan lived in the midwest, but Aunt Etta lived in the small town of Ephraim, in her home of sixty-two years. Lewis and I always saw Aunt Etta whenever we passed through on our way to mountain-bike heaven in Moab, further south. She always had an infectious smile and something fresh out of the oven—both of which were equally alluring.

Etta greeted me with a look of intense pity that was quickly replaced by a loving smile. Had anyone else read my mind that way, it might have felt intrusive, but Aunt Etta shared a memory of Lewis that tied us as closely as if she were my own aunt.

I mumbled something in greeting, hoping that Etta would fill in the blanks for me. "Aunt Etta, I . . ."

Etta stepped out of the line and embraced me with frail arms. "We love you, Owen," she said in my ear.

"Thank you," I whispered awkwardly.

"You come see me," she said pulling away. "You come see me. Anytime."

I nodded and forced my lips into a smile to hide the confusion of emotion welling up inside.

Turning away from the reception line was like facing an abyss. There was no place to go, and I was grateful when Al saw me and waved me over.

"You remember Amanda, don't you, Owen?" he said as I walked toward him.

"Nice to see you again," I said to her.

"We're going to get something to eat, if you're interested," said Al.

"Please join us," Amanda encouraged.

"No, really, I've got a couple of things to do. Thanks, though." I waved to Douglas and James, who were talking with Whitney Adams and her family, and said good-bye to Amanda and Al. Cute couple, I thought, and started for my truck.

When I got back home, I checked my voicemail in hopes that Didi had called. A lifeless computer voice told me that I had one new message. When I played it, it was just dead air and the click of someone hanging up in frustration.

Deirdra's boss at the bank had invited her to Washington, D.C., along with an entourage of government muckity-mucks for some kind of financial summit. It was an offer she couldn't refuse, so she didn't. I hadn't been able to catch her by phone since she'd left yesterday, but I was so emotionally drained that I wondered if I even cared. Didi was not universally liked by my family or close friends, although her long, blond hair and tall, slender figure made her quite popular among just about everyone else, including her peers at the bank. What she lacked in warmth she more than made up for in grace and outward charm. By all other accounts, she was the perfect woman, but you could not wade in the depth of her compassion.

I spent the next few hours driving up the canyon east of my condo. The road wound through scenery as colorful and alive as Lewis had been only days before, but I hardly noticed the autumn foliage, and by the time I returned home it was too dark anyway. I wandered into the kitchen looking for something to eat. I was too tired to fix anything. I took a drink of milk straight from the jug, expecting to hear Lewis chide me for slobbering all over it. No one said anything. I carefully wiped the top clean, took a glass from the cupboard, and stood alone staring out the window where I could see the city lights shimmering in the valley like a rippling sea under the moonlight.

"Where to now, buddy?" I sobbed.

***

On the morning after the funeral, I forced myself from bed and made short work of a shower and small breakfast. What I lacked in motivation, I made up for in lethargy and I found myself draped in an easy chair in the living room, pointing a remote at the stereo. I had neither the energy nor the desire to change the station and I listened to a man's voice droning on about politics. My mind wandered. I switched to a CD and realized that it was one of Lewis's; someone was going to inherit an empty CD case. I needed to do something— anything except sit here and think about this.

I loaded a fresh roll of 200 speed film in my camera and threw a 28-50 mm zoom lens in my camera bag. I locked the door of my condo and wandered toward my truck in the parking lot. I passed our neighbor lady dressed in a housecoat and slippers, looking for her morning newspaper.

"Good morning, Mrs. Warneke."

"Good morning, Brother Richards."

A lot of people around the condo called me "brother"; I'd never liked it.

"Owen," I reminded her for about the billionth time. I found her newspaper under the stairs and tossed it up to her.

"Thanks, Brother Richards. I wish the paperboy could aim as well as you," she said as she turned and shut her door.

"Any time," I said. "And, it's just plain old Owen," I added, but I don't think she heard me.

I looked at my watch before I climbed into my truck. It was eight-forty and too late to catch the best morning light for pictures. I started my truck anyway and rolled out of the parking lot. I had to go somewhere, if only to get away.

I had driven almost to the cemetery entrance before I was able to convince myself that looking at a dirt spot was only going to depress me more. Wherever Lewis had gone, it wasn't there.

I drove away from the cemetery, giving Lewis's gravesite only a cursory glance. I found myself on the southbound lane of Interstate-15 headed toward the point of the mountain. Why south and not north or east, I wasn't sure until half an hour or so later. As I passed

Provo and left the most populated area of Utah behind, it became obvious that my only destination south of the metropolis was Ephraim and Aunt Etta's.

Etta met me at the door with a hug. "Owen, well, what a pleasant surprise." She was small and frail and had tightly curled white hair with that sort of grandma-looking purple cast to it. Even as old as she was, probably in her eighties, she bore her rounded shoulders with the vitality of a much younger woman.

"Hello, Aunt Etta. I was just driving through." Etta took a look at me and graciously declined to ask me where I was headed.

"Come in, Owen. I'd like to talk . . . if you have time?" she said a little playfully.

"I just wanted to get out of my place for a while," I said as we walked together into the kitchen. The smell of brown sugar and cinnamon brought a wide smile to my face. I hadn't felt like eating for days.

"You know," she said, as she pulled out a chair for me, "I got up this morning and had a notion to bake. Who would have known I'd have company?" Her eyes were the same Irish green as Lewis's and they twinkled when she talked.

Etta's home was comfortable. Lewis and I had spent hours listening to her spin tales about her ancestors while eating frosting-drowned cinnamon rolls fresh from the oven; she knew how to captivate an audience. I once brought Deirdra here, hoping that Deirdra would enjoy Aunt Etta's company as much as Lewis and I did. Etta had been her cheerful and accommodating self, offering homemade pastries and fresh milk, but Deirdra never asked to go back.

"I'm glad you remembered your way here," she said.

"How could I forget? You just follow your nose. There's a whole lane of traffic on the freeway taking the exit toward Ephraim right now."

"You're a charmer, Owen."

Etta lived in a spacious brick house that had been built sometime in the late thirties. It was just across the street from one of the hundreds of Mormon Church buildings in Utah. The decor had not been changed substantially since her husband had remodeled in the fifties. In the kitchen, where Etta entertained, the counters were topped in bright yellow, and the cupboards were plain white with chrome handles. Etta had not updated her chrome dinette set since before the death of her husband in seventy-one; the yellow plastic covering on the chairs was split in places.

"What are you going to do with yourself?" asked Etta as she shuffled from the oven to the counter to tend to a fresh lot of hot cinnamon rolls that I eyed greedily. Etta dressed like a grandma too; she wore dresses of polyester, usually some kind of conservative floral pattern, and black leather shoes that laced. Her attire was not particularly fashionable, but very functional.

"Don't know. The department has me on administrative leave for the next two weeks. I guess my little stunt at the culvert has them concerned about my sanity. I have to see a shrink in a couple of weeks. I can't stand just sitting around." I was paying more attention to the rolls than I was to the question, not an uncommon state of affairs.

"Do you really want to go back to work so soon?" She poured me a glass of milk.

I looked up. "Nope," I said. "But I gotta do something. I'm not going to be able to sit around my apartment for two weeks." My voice betrayed a hint of emotion that I covered by coughing and taking a long pull on the cold glass of milk.

"You ought to do something," she said matter-of-factly as she deposited a cinnamon roll drenched with white frosting in front of me.

"Yea. I think I'll just hover around your back door waiting for more rolls," I said before shoveling the delicious pastry into my mouth.

"There's always room for little Owen at my kitchen table," she laughed.

"Mmm," I said through busy lips.

"You should go to the game," she said hopefully.

The suggestion was unthinkable. But in Etta's green eyes, I saw no mockery; I saw only her deep and sincere wish for my emotional recovery.

She said, "I'm sorry about Lewis. This must be hard for you."

"It is." I couldn't think of anything else to say. Lewis was not only a friend, but a person for whom I had so much respect that I actually watched him, the way he acted toward people and situations, and I tried to emulate him. These were things that I could never tell anyone, under any circumstances. How could I possibly put him behind me? I wanted to say something to Etta, but I found that all I could do was sit with my head down, now close to tears.

"We lose people in this world," she said gently, "and it's never easy."

I knew she was talking about her husband, whom she lost before I knew her.

"Doesn't it ever get easier?" I asked, lamely.

She looked at me and smiled. "Sort of," she said. "Easier, but not easy. I still cry myself to sleep some nights."

"Etta, at the funeral there was this little girl and she . . ." I was not sure I even wanted to ask the question. "She gave a little talk, and she said something about seeing Lewis again. Is that what Mormons believe?"

"Yes it is, Owen." She smiled. "And that little girl is my niece. Great, great, or something."

"Do you . . . do you believe that?" I stammered.

"Yes I do." Etta smiled. "I know it. Lewis isn't far away. He's a lot closer than we realize."

My heart swelled, just a little this time. These were new experiences for me, but there was no mistaking the same feelings I'd had at the funeral. As before, however, the feeling faded. To cover the emptiness, I asked for another pastry, and one was promptly placed before me.

"What about it?" she asked.

"About what?"

She stood by me with folded arms. "Going to the game. I know what a big trip that was to be for you two."

"We two," I emphasized.

"That doesn't mean you can't go, Owen."

"The point of the game wasn't really the game."

"Well, you're right. You'll just have to come up with another point."

I knew Etta was trying to say something or teach me something, but I really lost her point in all this talk about points. I was going to ask her what the point was, but I didn't, because I wasn't about to be flippant with Etta. I had too much respect for the woman and she would never put up with an ill-tempered remark from me. I think that was one reason I drove all the way to Ephraim. Everyone else was letting me get away with pining and feeling guilty and angry. I knew Etta would not. She had seen too much of the world to let me whine about it.

"Another point?" I asked politely.

"You know, when my husband died, I thought I couldn't live without him." Etta took off her apron and sat down across from me. "I had to discover that I could. We were very close. We were soul mates, our lives very much intertwined. It wasn't easy coming up with a purpose for living."

"It's apparent you did. And, you've done it well."

"No, that's not quite so. I have to do it every day, whether it's easy or not. I didn't just turn a switch and discover a new purpose for living. I have to struggle to make each day purposeful, to endure to the end. And, not only endure, but endure it well. And, in a way, we all have to do that every day. It's just easier when everything seems to be in its proper place."

I nodded. I knew she was right; she certainly had the credentials to talk on the subject. My heart was not as easily convinced. The game was four days away, and I hadn't even considered going without Lewis.

"I'm not saying that you have to go to a football game to give your life purpose, Owen. But don't let Lewis's death take away more than it has to. You do still have to go on." She smiled at me and got up slowly to check to make sure her oven was off.

"You mean go to the game?" I asked.

"It might help. Sort of a send-off for Lewis."

"I don't know. I can't go back to work anyway. I could use a little time away. Maybe I will," I said, slapping my knee.

"Now that we've settled that," she said, "I want you to do me a favor."

"Anything for you."

"You should probably ask what it is first."

"Aunt Etta, nothing could give me more purpose in life than doing something for you for a change."

Etta laughed. "Oh, Owen, I think you should ask what it is before you ingratiate yourself into a corner."

"You ask; I come through for you. Shoot."

"You're such a nice boy."

"Now who's pulling whose leg?"

"All right," Etta said. "You remember Lewis's cousin, Julianna?"

Did I remember? Julianna was the kind of cousin who made me wonder about the stability of Lewis's genetic makeup. She must have been about seven the last time I saw her, and I was glad that it was the last time I saw her. Julianna the pest.

"Sure, I remember Julianna."

"She stayed in the valley after the funeral. She wanted to spend some time with a college friend of hers."

"Julianna has friends who go to college?"

"She's twenty-two."

"Oh." Could she be twenty-two? I wondered if she was still sticking her tongue out at people.

"She needs a ride."

"She's here?" I grabbed the sides of my chair reflexively.

"No, she's in Provo, visiting her friend at B.Y.U. for the day. But she is staying here." I'd been a police officer for too long not to recognize a con. Etta was pulling a fast one on me.

"But, she needs a ride back," Etta continued, undaunted.

Okay, a few hours in a small, enclosed area with an obnoxious red-headed pest wouldn't kill me. "Consider it done. I can be to Provo and back before dinner."

"Well, that's not it," Etta said slowly. "She needs a ride back to Kansas City."

CHAPTER 4

I spent the rest of the morning absorbed in Etta's wisdom. She was right, of course; I needed to get away from Salt Lake for a while. If I could do a favor for the McCray family by taking Julianna to Kansas City, so much the better.

We said our good-byes and Etta gave me a long hug, like I was one of the family. I left reluctantly. When I got back to my condo I packed a duffel bag and went to bed early. I woke at four A.M. and hit the road back to Ephraim before the morning traffic backed up on I-15.

Driving and thinking about my destination was an exercise in nerve control. I had not seen Julianna since her childhood when she communicated her feelings by sticking her tongue out at me on a semi-regular schedule. I heard she'd had it pierced; nothing could repulse me more. She was a little waif of a redheaded thing, Missouri's version of Pippy Longstocking with an extra measure of irritation added. Even Lewis, who loved everyone in the world, was prone at times to frown upon his little cousin Julianna from Kansas City. She seldom visited Utah, but the memory of her red hair and freckles endured long after her departures. I shook off the fearful memory of her from the summer of '84 when I went to Kansas City with the McCray family. I decided to withhold further judgment; she had grown up, after all.

I pulled into Etta's driveway for the second time in two days, set my parking brake by force of habit, and jumped out of the truck. There was room enough in the backseat for one, or maybe two, small bags. Anything else the imp wanted to put in the truck went in the bed, rain or no. I wouldn't admit to having spread out my stuff to fill the rear seat of my extended cab in hopes that Julianna would have to throw her expensive flower-festooned luggage into the bed of my truck, but I certainly took no pains to pack tightly.

I practiced my best disinterested gaze and rapped on the large oval leaded glass of Etta's double doors. What had been cheerless trepidation quickly turned to raving panic when I saw the figure inside the entryway making her way to the front door. Her image was slightly distorted by the glass, but what I could see of her was a testament to how things can change.

The woman who answered Etta's front door was gorgeous and composed. The years had lightened her carrot-orange hair into a striking honeyed auburn that framed her face gently and cascaded over her shoulders and down her back. Her eyes, long ago the color of strained peas, were now the bright, confident, beautiful green of the McCray family. When she opened the door and smiled, I was reduced to a stammering clod.

"Hello, Owen. I'm so glad to see you," she practically sang in her melodious voice. "You look great. You've hardly changed."

"Julianna?" I remembered her in baggy denim overall shorts that exaggerated her bird legs and knobby knees that were the same shade of white as her rubber-toed sneakers. The oversized overalls had been replaced by a pair of olive-green leggings, and she wore a velour turtleneck tunic of the exact same color. Her freckles had disappeared too, leaving a complexion that was creamy and flawless.

"Yes," she grinned. "Come in."

I thought I was going to trip on the threshold, but I navigated that dangerous area without incident. "Where's Etta?" I croaked. I needed backup.

"Bless you," she replied as if I'd sneezed. "I'll go see where Etta is." She turned gracefully and walked toward the kitchen; her long slender legs were very definitely not bird legs anymore! "Make yourself at home," she called over her shoulder.

I slouched in a heap on Etta's burgundy camelback couch with my face in my hands until she returned with Etta. A few important points were made during our introduction, most of which passed me by like a speeding locomotive. The only thing that really stuck in my mind was Julianna's firm assertion that I had not changed a bit. Oh, great.

The next thing I recalled clearly was leaning over the bench seat of my pickup, hefting my bags out of the cab to make room for—who could have imagined—conservative, tapestry luggage. Julianna assured me it was not expensive and could easily make the trip in the bed of the truck.

"Oh, no trouble. I really meant to pack this stuff . . . ugh," I grunted as I pulled my heavy canvas SWAT bag over the seat, "better, so that . . . ugh," another big bag came over, "you could fit some of your . . ."

"Really, Owen, it's not that important. This is a really nice truck. I like how these back doors open," she said, opening the suicide door of the cab. "You could get some of that from here. It looks easier."

Smooth, Owen, I thought as my face reddened. I finished unpacking through the rear doors of my truck and placed an appropriately sized suitcase, a matching overnight bag, and a split leather satchel on the back seat where Julianna could get to things she needed. *Deirdra would have had a ton more luggage,* I thought, with not a small amount of resentment.

"Okay, I think that's everything," she said and leaned against my truck.

Her eyes were incredible and I caught myself looking at them often, too often, and I think she caught me a couple of times. I said some stupid things in my own defense: "Gee, I can't get over how much you've changed." Quick thinking. Julianna just smiled with graceful forgiveness, but Etta did not. She kept giggling like a schoolgirl and winking at me, without the slightest attempt to hide it from Julianna.

After ten years as a cop, I discovered that I was not immune to complete discomfiture, and Etta dangled that fact like a carrot in front of me. She really had a good time. In fact, Julianna was so graceful about the whole thing and Etta was having so much fun, I wondered how fair it was that I was miserable. At the same time, I was practically walking on air about the whole thing—so much so, that when we had said our good-byes and given our last hugs, I started the truck, and then started it again, disturbing the neighbors with the sound of flywheel parts being ground to shavings under my hood. Etta just about cried with laughter.

Smooth, I thought again. *Smooth.*

***

Our relationship for the first few minutes on the road was awkward. After the weather, which was mild but rainy in places, there was nothing to talk about. You can only say so much about mild weather, but the rainy places offered me something more to say.

"Rainy here."

"Uh-huh."

As we headed east to Denver, we quickly left the yellow barren landscape for the rugged pine trees of the Rocky Mountains.

"So what have you been doing since you were seven years old?" I asked.

"Let's see. I got my permanent teeth, and . . ." She laughed.

"No, really."

"Well, right now I'm finishing an MBA at the University of Missouri in Kansas City, I teach piano on the side, and I'm the Activities Coordinator for our ward."

"What was that last one?"

"I help plan the activities for our ward."

"Oh, yeah. I get hauled to those things once in a while. I suppose someone does have to organize those."

"Yes, they do."

"So, after your degree, then what?"

"Oh, I don't know. I figured that now was a good time to further my education. But I don't know if I'll ever even use the MBA."

"No specific plans, huh?"

"Maybe I'll be a curator at a museum," she said. She told me about her interest in early U.S. history and the history of the first Mormons. She seemed to know a lot, not that I was a good judge. I didn't know anything about Mormon history but I suppose the pioneers had to come from somewhere.

She laughed a lot and I liked it.

"Or, maybe I'll be a country western singing sensation," she said from out of nowhere.

"You sing, too?"

"I like to sing in our ward choir," she said.

"I couldn't carry a tune in a bucket."

"Oh come on, it couldn't be that bad."

"Well, I like to strum my guitar and hum along, but you won't catch me singing in the choir."

"Maybe not," she said with a grin.

The conversation became so comfortable as the hours wore on that we talked like old friends. We stopped for gas and lunch at Grand Junction, just inside Colorado. On the way out of town, Julianna pulled a licorice rope out of a brown paper sack. She let it dangle from her lips.

"Want one?" She pulled another one from the bag.

"Sure."

"These were my favorite when I was little."

"Really," I said, thinking about the old Julianna.

"Remember when we played truth or dare with the neighborhood kids that summer you came to Kansas City?" Julianna asked after a pleasant silence.

"Yeah. And you never did do our dares."

"Yes I did."

"No way. You did not." I had her there. "Remember when Lewis and I dared you to eat a worm? I'm recalling an incensed, carrot-topped dervish screaming to her mama and . . ."

"Enough, enough, enough. Eating worms is beneath the dignity of a charming copper-headed young lady. Besides, I'm sure you had second thoughts about a few dares in your day, Mr. Richards."

"No. I can't recall any. If I said I'd do it, I'm sure I did."

"In that case, truth or dare."

"What?"

"Truth or dare," she insisted.

"Truth," I said with some trepidation.

Julianna shifted in her seat and fixed her big green eyes squarely on mine. The bottom dropped out of my stomach for an instant and I held my breath. I knew that eventually we'd talk about Lewis, but I didn't want it to be now.

"So," she said, her lips softening into a gentle smile, "why did you become a police officer?"

I caught my breath and a cool wave of relief washed over me. This was the kind of question for which all police officers had a series of stock answers prepared. Every person I had ever met asked me why I'd become a cop and if I liked it, and sometimes people would even ask me to tell them an exciting story from work.

Relieved that Julianna had lapsed into a pretty standard question, I responded with my favorite answer, which was conveniently close to the truth. "To drive fast and shoot guns."

She laughed, which was the desired response. "No, Owen, you're doing it again. Truth or dare, remember?"

"That's the truth," I insisted. "Anyway, it's hard to say why someone chooses to be a cop. I think the job sort of chooses you."

"You must like it."

"Sure, I like it. I like it some days more than others. I can say that I've done an awful lot of strange things as a cop. No two days are ever the same." I was quickly running out of stock phrases.

"Well, Mr. Truthful, what do you like best about it?"

"It's a toss-up between shooting guns and driving fast, but I guess I'd say driving fast." I looked at her and smiled but she didn't smile back. A myriad of other quips about cops passed through my mind, but none promised to quell Julianna's scowl.

I settled for something more truthful. "I guess I like solving problems."

"Solving problems?"

"Yeah, I get in my car each night and my dispatcher sends me to places where people are having problems. I go there and help solve the problem. Sometimes it involves arresting a bad guy and sometimes it doesn't. I guess I just like to be the guy who helps solve the problem."

Julianna nodded and looked out her window for a moment. "I suppose that qualifies as an honest answer, for the moment." She flashed a killer smile at me over her shoulder and I almost ran off the road. "But, this is the real question I wanted to ask."

"Bad form, Ju, you've had your truth."

"No really, I want to know." She twirled a lock of her honey-kissed hair on her lithe finger. "What would you be if you weren't a cop. Is it okay to say cop?"

"Yes. And, that is an easy question. If I weren't a cop, I'd be a photographer."

"Photography," Julianna said excitedly. She straightened in her seat and faced me.

"Sure." I picked up my camera off the floorboard at my feet and dangled it in front of her, keeping one eye on the road.

"That's fantastic. You never really think of cops being interested in real things."

I'd heard that before, usually just before I said something sarcastic about being born wearing the uniform. I looked at Julianna's excited eyes and let it pass. We talked some more about my interest in photography. I told her that I bought my first really nice camera just after I graduated from high school and that I'd had one with me ever since. I was making points with this girl.

"Your turn. Truth or dare?" I said.

"Oh, truth of course."

"Did you really pierce your tongue?"

Julianna blanched and then just as suddenly blushed to a very becoming shade. I smiled, inside.

"I went through a few trying times when I was in high school," she said. "But, I can say that I never, ever, actually went through with having my tongue pierced. See," she said, sticking her tongue out at me.

"Hey, that's not the first time I've seen that thing. It hasn't changed much since you were seven."

She blushed again, a more subtle shade. In the back lighting of the afternoon sun, she looked very beautiful.

"We're not done yet." She fixed me with a determined look.

"Oh?"

"Truth or dare?" she asked.

I really didn't want to play anymore, but I really, really couldn't say no to Julianna.

"Dare, then." I had nothing against the truth, but she had shown a propensity to want the actual truth, which made me a bit nervous.

"Hmm. I'll have to think a few minutes. I was expecting you to avoid a dare so you wouldn't have to welsh." Her smile was disarming.

"Welsh," I spat. "If there is one thing I don't do, it's welsh."

"Whatever you say, Owen. Whatever you say. I'll let you know."

"You'll let me know. Dare me now, Ju. Dare me now."

"Okay, okay, when I think of something I'll . . ."

"Who taught you how to play this game?" I blustered. "First a double truth and now a delayed action dare."

"Would you like some cheese with that whine, Owie?"

I shook my head in mock disgust and then we both laughed until we cried. What would it take for Didi to be more like Julianna, I wondered?

"You and Lewis must be pretty serious football fans," Julianna said, breaking one of the many comfortable silences between us.

"Pretty much. I was surprised your dad would part with his Chiefs tickets. I thought he was such a big fan."

"He's a pretty big fan, but this was something he wanted to do for Lewis."

"I know. It makes me feel kind of funny using the tickets like this," I said, broaching the subject of Lewis's death for the first time.

"Dad never went to the games much. Sunday is a busy day for him. He's the bishop now." Julianna politely diverted the conversation to safer ground.

"What?" I gasped. "I thought he was the Kansas City Engineer."

"He is," she laughed. "He's also the bishop of our ward. So," Julianna went on, "we don't go to football games on Sunday."

"No, I suppose not. Come to think of it, Lewis was pretty busy on Sundays, too. But," I pounded on the steering wheel for emphasis, "he never missed a Monday Night Football game, except for work, in which case we'd videotape."

"So, when my dad got tickets for a Monday game at Arrowhead, who do you think he thought of?"

"Me," I said, and Julianna laughed.

"Of course. I'm just glad you decided to include Lewis. He's my favorite cousin."

"You know," I said, lapsing into nostalgia, "I remember once when we were playing stickball at your house in Kansas City . . . I'll never forget that first trip there with Lewis when I met your family. Anyway, I was probably about thirteen or fourteen. One of the neighborhood kids hit a ball through a window on your street. Everyone but Lewis ran when the window broke."

"I remember that." Julianna's eyes lit up.

"Yeah, and Lewis went to the house and settled up with the owner. It cost him his summer allowance."

"You probably would have done the same thing."

"No, I ran away," I confessed.

"You probably *wanted* to do the right thing," Julianna patronized.

"That's just it. I might have wanted to; I might have wanted to do a lot of things."

Julianna nodded and our afternoon faded into evening.

We enjoyed more conversation as our easterly route on Interstate-70 through Colorado took us into some of North America's most beautiful country. I found myself fascinated with the metamorphosis of Julianna and ignored a lot of the scenery and most of the points of interest, including our approach to Denver where we had planned to stop over.

"It might be a good time for dinner," she hinted, as we passed another exit that promised Denver's best food and lodging.

"Oh, yeah." My pledge to eat when and where I wanted on this trip, and not let pesky little Julianna drag us to burgers and fries, was long forgotten. "I bet you *are* getting hungry," I said.

I took the next available exit and slowed to a crawl along a restaurant row that offered just about any kind of food. "What sounds good?"

"Anything sounds good. Whatever you like," she said politely.

"You choose," I insisted.

"There," she said, pointing a long, elegant finger in the direction of a seedy-looking building painted sunflower yellow with dark red trim, that advertised Mongolian fare and karaoke on a worn marquee. The "K" in "karaoke" was a lowercase "L" disguised with black electrical tape. Julianna looked at me, those green eyes proposing an adventure. I pulled my truck into the parking lot and aimed it at a parking spot. I would have worried about door dings, but mine was the only vehicle for six spots.

Walking through the parking lot, I could smell ginger and curry, which was somewhat reassuring. I intended to inspect the board of health certificate posted inside, nonetheless.

As we entered the small, dimly lit restaurant, a cloud of steam rose from a huge, steel griddle located in the front. Two white-coated cooks walked in circles around it, throwing sliced vegetables, noodles, and meat into the air with flat wooden spatulas. The food was tossed deftly around the grill and then swept into large porcelain bowls decorated with Chinese characters.

A plump, happy-faced girl who spoke broken English directed us to our table.

"You eat here before?"

"No," we said together.

"Watch her," she pointed to a petite young Asian girl standing at the food bar. "She very good."

We watched as the small girl filled a rather large bowl with fresh vegetables and raw sliced meat until it was heaped. She then placed both of her hands on the top of the food and pushed until her feet came off the ground, compressing the contents of her bowl. Then the process of filling her bowl started again.

"That's a lot of food," I told Julianna. "She'll never eat all of it."

"Maybe she'll take some home. You know, make the most of her date."

The girl's date was politely filling his bowl with a moderate amount of food.

"After you." I gestured toward the food bar, and Julianna forged ahead.

There were a couple of dozen kinds of vegetables to choose from, along with sliced beef, pork, or chicken, and a gigantic pan of soft noodles at the food bar. I put cabbage, sliced carrots, mushrooms, and a whole bunch of little cobs of corn in my bowl. I heaped on noodles and topped it with sliced pork. The choice of sauces at the end of the food bar had me in a quandary. The plum sauce sounded good and I reached for the ladle. One of the cooks saw me and shook his head. He nodded at the Mongolian sauce, and when I picked up the ladle he gave me a fat smile which revealed a missing tooth. I poured several ladles of Mongolian sauce in my bowl.

"More," Julianna said.

"Huh?"

"The sign says six to eight ladles for a bowl that size. More," she ordered.

I complied and gave the cook my bowl. He threw the contents onto the grill sending a plume of steam into the rafters. Whatever his extracurricular pursuits, the man was handy with his bamboo paddle. Julianna waited beside me with an eager smile while we watched our dinners going up and down and all around the grill. We were both hungry.

A few other patrons were sitting at their seats using various authentic Mongolian culinary tactics to get their dinners successfully into their mouths. Julianna and I took our bowls to the seats at the outer edge of the excitement and settled in for an experience. The karaoke machine, as advertised, sat dormant on a three-foot, miniscule stage smaller than the grill, near the back of the dining area.

"Good choice," I said just before stuffing a wad of noodles into my mouth.

Julianna nodded, mouth full and eyes bright. "I've never had Mongolian food," she answered between bites.

"Me neither." Every few minutes another customer's food was tossed onto the grill with a sharp sizzle.

The fashion in which I was forced to eat was not going to make Miss Manners's top ten list, but I found that Julianna was graceful even with chopsticks.

"So, what happened to the Julianna of my youth?" I asked.

"I was just wondering the same thing about you. Egg roll?"

For a moment, I thought she had just called me an egg roll. I took one and regretted starting my next sentence with a mouthful of it. "I don't feel like I've changed much. Still the same ol' Owen."

"Even after all that's happened?" she asked.

So far, we had avoided talking about Lewis's death. It had been an unspoken agreement, and this transgression made me uncomfortable.

She broke the short silence. "You might not have known, but Lewis and I grew very close over the last few years. He was more than a cousin to me. He was my friend, too."

The room was getting smaller and I wanted to excuse myself, to drive back to Salt Lake City. "I'm going to miss him," I said with a little more forced bravado than I intended. "But, he's gone and I have to get past that."

She looked at me for a long time then, and I feared what she might say next. I was not yet over occasional fits of sobbing and I was determined to hold myself together in front of Julianna.

"It's time," she said without explanation. Our hostess walked by just then and Julianna stood to whisper something in her ear.

My anxiety turned quickly to anger. Where did she get off telling me it's time to forget Lewis? I was about to say something when she turned to me again, her face alive with a smile that turned my anger to curiosity.

"It's time, Owie," she said again as if I would know what she was talking about. There was some movement behind me at the small stage where the karaoke machine sat and I caught Julianna's eyes darting playfully from me to it and back.

"Your dare, sir." She pointed her long, pretty, finger—longer now by a mile—at the karaoke machine that had been brought to life by the hostess.

I started to hedge. "Not on your life," I growled. "No way."

Her eyes got wide, the whites showing. "I see," she proclaimed, "big, tough cop? Rough and tumble Owen? A man who backs out on a debt, a welsher!" And there she left it, wide green eyes staring me in the face. The karaoke was making some kind of noise in the background, but the back of my neck was heating up and I was blushing, not so much in embarrassment as in terror. I thought of a few names I could have called her, worse than Pippy Longstocking or Little Orphan Annie.

In that moment, my pride argued with my honor in a pitched battle that sent chills down my fevered neck. If it were the last thing on the planet earth I did, I would get her for this. Under normal circumstances, I could resolve to say no and mean it. But, with Julianna staring at me and after what I had said to her, I could no more back down than fly to the moon.

"I'll get you for this. You know that."

"But, Owen, you always follow through on your dares," she jested.

I think she read the terror in my eyes as I resolutely pushed my chair out and stood up. The small stage now seemed twelve feet high, and suddenly there were a lot of people in the restaurant, if you looked from the vantage point of the stage. I stared dumbly out where far too many eyes were staring back at me in expectation.

I reluctantly, but bravely, took the cordless microphone from the hostess who was in collusion with Julianna and raised my chin. If I was going to make a fool out of myself to all of Denver, I was going to do it big. The selection had been made for me, obviously at Julianna's request, and the prelude to Nat King Cole's "Unforgettable" claimed the attention of the crowd. Curse this place, curse Etta for tricking me into this trip, and curse the beautiful redhead who was laughing her guts out at our table. Curses.

***

I vowed never to forgive Julianna. We stopped for the night at a hotel near the freeway that catered to professionals. No frills, but very nice. As we were checking in, Julianna hummed a few bars of "Unforgettable" and giggled. Our rooms were on the same floor, several doors apart. I scowled and carried her bags to her room.

Julianna practically skipped ahead of me, her eyes twinkling. I trudged along behind with the bags. She unlocked the door and waved me inside. I hoisted her bags onto her bed.

"Oh my, I haven't change for a tip," she said. I smiled sarcastically.

"Five-thirty?" I said, testing her stamina.

"Five-thirty it is," she said cheerfully.

I turned away reluctantly and walked toward the door, wondering what it would take to get an invitation to stay for a while.

"Owen," she called to me at the threshold.

I spun on my heels. "Yes?" I answered hopefully.

"Thanks for dinner. It was . . . unforgettable," she teased and pushed me out the door.

I stomped down the hall, entered my room, and slammed the door for effect. "I didn't want to stay anyway," I told myself in the floor-length mirror on the closet door. *I couldn't even convince myself*, I thought as I plopped on the bed.

I turned on the television and called Didi at her swanky Washington, D.C., hotel. She was out. I was actually relieved, but I left a halfhearted message anyway. Before I'd left Salt Lake City, I'd told her that I was taking one of Lewis's cousins back to Kansas City as a favor to the family. She was uninterested. I should have introduced them first; Didi would have taken one look at Julianna and developed a healthy interest in my vacation.

And, just what was my interest in this trip? I clicked off the television and rested my head on a pile of starched pillows. I fell asleep humming "Unforgettable" and thinking about the green-eyed girl down the hall.

In the morning, bright and early, Julianna met me at the door to my room. She was pretty cheery for five-thirty.

"My bags are already downstairs at the checkout counter," she almost gloated.

I shook off my early morning attitude and forced a smile.

"You look pretty good, considering the hour."

"Oh, thanks. You look . . . Uh, did I tell you my bags were already downstairs? If you give me your keys I can put them in the truck while you get another three minutes of beauty rest."

"Good one."

She laughed and sauntered down the hallway in front of me, waving her long red hair.

The hotel's free buffet breakfast saved us a good hour of tooling around looking for a place to eat, and we were back on the road heading east shortly after six A.M.

Not long out of Denver, the Rocky Mountains gave way to foothills and then to the wide, long prairie where we drove and talked, Julianna taking turns at the wheel. It was probably a mistake to let her drive, not because she was a menace to the road, but because it gave me too many opportunities to stare at her.

"Owen, can I ask you something?" she said as she checked her blind spot and made a lane change.

"Sure."

"Did Lewis suffer much? I mean, they told us how he died, but not really." Her timing took me by surprise, but I expected Lewis's death to come up eventually. "The newspaper stories didn't really say much," she said. "And neither did Aunt Monica or Uncle Trace."

The family had been given a polished account of the incident, just a little more information than the press release. The raw details, the kind you didn't burden family members with, belonged to the officers who were there.

"I don't think he suffered." I remembered the peace in his eyes just before he passed away.

Julianna stared through the windshield. The look on her face said she wanted to know more, but wasn't sure how to ask.

"Did he . . ." she hesitated and then shook her head.

"You can ask," I said. I hadn't wanted to talk about it, but I sensed in Julianna a deep need to know.

"Did he say anything to you?"

"You mean about dying?"

"Well, yes. I just wondered . . ."

I turned a little in the seat, as much as my seat belt would allow. "He didn't say very much. He didn't have any famous dying words, if that's what you mean. In fact, it was really different than all that. Lewis was so calm. He didn't seem . . ." I started to say something, but struggled to think of the right words. "He wasn't even angry. After what this guy did, Lewis wasn't even . . . I don't know."

Julianna was silent for a long time. She stared through the windshield at the long straight road ahead. I fixed my gaze at the horizon, a flat line hundreds of miles long. My heart swelled in anguish but I fought it back.

"I guess I'm not surprised," she said without looking at me.

"Yeah, I don't know. I haven't found any benevolence for Raymond Hunt in my heart. To me he's just an animal." In truth, I hadn't thought much about Hunt in any specific terms since my little scene at the culverts. I wasn't ready.

"Does that bother you, that Lewis wasn't angry?" she asked in a way that suggested that it shouldn't.

"Yeah, darn right it bothers me. Doesn't it bother you?"

"I don't know."

"He was pretty quick to forgive his own killer," I snapped.

"Is that so bad?" She was getting a touch accusatory.

"It is when it's your best friend," I barked, "and he dies for no reason."

Julianna recoiled slightly, probably not expecting my intense reaction. "I'm sorry," she whispered. Tears began to slide delicately over her cheeks and drop into her lap.

"No, I'm sorry. I didn't mean to . . . I haven't really talked about Lewis much since he died, except for a few minutes with Etta."

I reached out and touched her arm with my finger. "Pull over," I said softly.

The shoulders were wide with gravel and Julianna stopped the truck well off the highway.

Julianna closed her eyes and took a deep breath. She was trying not to cry and she dabbed her face gently with her shirtsleeve, but tears formed in her eyes and her shoulders began to shake. It proved to be too much for me. The anguish and sorrow I'd been fighting all week erupted and I began to cry like a child. Sliding over, Julianna put her arms around me and held me.

"I'm sorry, Julianna," I managed between sobs.

She squeezed me tighter. "It's okay, Owen, it's okay."

"Just before he died," I told her, "he told me that it would be just a moment, and something about enduring it well." I pulled away so I could look at her, but held her hands. "I'm not sure what he was trying to say."

"Well," she said, "maybe he just wanted you to know that things that happen in this life are really just a moment in the big picture, by the Lord's reckoning."

"So, to you guys, Lewis's death is just a small thing? I mean," I added quickly, "I'm not trying to be sarcastic or anything. It's just an interesting way of looking at life."

"I don't mean that Lewis' death is a small thing, but it helps when you understand that life on this earth is a part of something bigger."

I let that sink in and remembered Lewis's composure as he died.

"Man, the guy had no fear."

"No, he had nothing to fear. There's a difference." She smiled and then looked thoughtful for a moment before going on. "'My son, peace be unto thy soul, thine adversity and thine afflictions shall be but a small moment. And then if thou endure it well, God shall exalt thee on high; thou shalt triumph over all thy foes.'"

"Where'd you get that?"

"Joseph Smith received that revelation when he was in prison. I'm sure Lewis knew that scripture by heart."

"That's just like him."

"What?"

"Lewis wasn't talking about how to die. He was talking about how to live," I said.

We endured an awkward silence together and I felt a mixture of relief and embarrassment as I let go of her hands and wiped my face.

"And, the most important thing is that he still exists," Julianna said. "He's doing what he's supposed to be doing."

I thought about that and wondered if I had the faith to be certain of it. "I don't have to convert to believe all this stuff, do I?"

She smiled. "You don't have to convert, but it sure would make it a lot easier." We both laughed.

The rest of the day we spent talking about our mutual friend Lewis, his life, not his death, and by late afternoon we found ourselves staring at the Kansas City skyline.

We'd made an early start out of Denver with plans to make Kansas City in time for dinner. As we neared the city, I mentioned that Lewis wanted to eat at a certain rib joint. I couldn't remember the name, and Julianna just smiled.

"Say no more," she said. "Drive."

I followed her directions to a neighborhood that looked a little less than hospitable to strangers, but Julianna assured me that I was going to be eating the best barbecue ribs in the midwest and, quite possibly, the world.

"Where are you taking me?" I wondered aloud. "Are you sure this is safe?"

"You want the best?"

"Yes."

"Then drive where I tell you and don't make trouble."

"Yes, Ma'am."

Arthur Bryant's restaurant was on the ground floor of a bulky, brick building fronted by a white awning under a red and white sign. It was dinnertime and there wasn't an available parking space anywhere near the front door. We finally parked around the side of the building against a two-story brick wall with no windows and, suspiciously, no graffiti. I'd kept my fanny pack, which concealed my pistol in a hidden holster, under the seat for most of the trip. It was now firmly fastened around my waist as we walked around the corner to the entrance. I stopped dramatically at the corner and pointed my remote entry at the truck, clicked it and activated the alarm. The truck honked once and the headlights flashed; Julianna rolled her eyes.

"This is the best in the world?" I asked, always the skeptic.

"Ab-so-lutely," she assured me.

I opened the door for Julianna and she graciously entered with a smile. The smell of roasting meat and barbecue sauce taunted my growling stomach. Small square tables surrounded by chairs upholstered in crimson vinyl sat beside a long line of patrons. The ceiling was unfinished and you could see hot water pipes running in a matrix overhead. No maitre d' and no tablecloths and, thank heavens, no karaoke.

"I want the biggest order of barbecue ribs on the menu," I said.

"You better look at the menu first, big man," she said, pointing to a red and white marquee on the wall.

"Me just want ribs."

"Let's order then." Julianna moved comfortably to the back of a line of local folks waiting to place their orders. A man in a red checkered shirt that fit snuggly over his potbelly, stole a glance at Julianna. I nicknamed him Joe Bob; he looked like the kind of guy who knew the neighborhood and had seen a few ribs in his day. I wondered how long it would take for Joe Bob to steal another look. It didn't take long.

A line longer than ours ran along the other side of the seating area from which patrons were coming away with frosted glass mugs of beer.

"Hold my place," I said as I stepped toward the beer line.

"You're going to the wrong line." Julianna furrowed her brows at me.

"No, I'm not. I'm getting a . . ."

"You're going to the wrong line," she said, pulling me by the arm back to the food line.

"No, I was just . . ."

"Not if you're with me," she growled.

I cowered and then, under protest, went back to the food line. When we got to the counter, Julianna ordered ribs for both of us. A cook in a stained white apron used a thick slice of homemade bread to pick up a side of barbecue-coated ribs and slap it on a plate. He left the barbecue-smothered bread on the plate.

We carried our food to a table by the wall, away from the lines, under a huge picture of President Jimmy Carter with his face full of ribs and sauce dripping from his chin. This was quickly becoming my favorite rib joint. My chest tightened when I remembered that I should have been eating this meal with Lewis.

"Kansas City is an interesting place," I observed through a mouth ringed with sauce. Julianna smiled politely and finished a bite. I asked, "So, how does a nice Mormon family like yours find itself in Missouri, of all places?"

Julianna stared at me for about a minute. "You haven't been paying attention, have you?" she finally said.

"What do you mean?"

"I mean, never mind." She shook her red curls. "I just thought that some of the history of Utah would have rubbed off on you. Apparently not. I was actually born in Utah. We moved to Missouri when I was about five. My father took a job out here with the city."

"That explains it. There can't be many LDS people out here. Didn't they all ride out in covered wagons or something?" I wanted to show that I knew some Utah history.

Julianna furrowed her brows in what was either pity or disgust. "How long have you lived in Salt Lake?" she asked accusingly.

"All my . . ."

"I know," she interrupted, "and that is the sum total of what you know about the Church? Pioneers in covered wagons and lots of wives," she mocked.

"Well, I never really . . ."

"Didn't Lewis ever talk to you about it?"

"He never browbeat me with piety, if that's what you mean." We forgot our ribs for a moment. "But it's not as if he never told me anything about his personal beliefs. We just never got into the covered wagons and where they came from."

My voice betrayed my defensiveness. Julianna's lips curled into a sweet smile and she picked up her last rib. She examined it thoughtfully and said, "Perhaps it's time someone told you where those wagons came from."

I shrugged, not completely uninterested. Julianna could probably make paint drying interesting.

"Next to Utah, Missouri is probably richer in Mormon history than any other place," she said. She worked on her last rib and then carefully wiped her mouth.

"Well, you can't spend ten minutes in the Valley without hearing about pioneers singing and walking, and walking and singing," I said.

Julianna ignored the jibe. "Well, the first Mormon pioneers didn't really come from Missouri. Not directly, anyway." Julianna cleared our table while I got a last look at Arthur Bryant's world-famous Kansas City rib joint.

We walked away with full stomachs, and Julianna suggested a tourist itinerary. "Okay, tomorrow is Saturday, so we'll drive out and get a look at some of the important historical sights around Kansas City. I'll give you the royal tour. And," she added, "you can take pictures."

"How can I refuse?"

On the way to Julianna's home, I got a short course in Mormon history, which in all fairness was pretty interesting.

"My ancestors were in Missouri in the early days of the Church. They went through a lot out here."

"Tar and feathers," I said glibly.

Julianna didn't laugh. "Yes, some were tarred and feathered; some were treated even worse."

Some of the hardships and religious persecutions Julianna described sounded like blatant exaggerations, but I kept my opinions to myself, knowing that Julianna would never intentionally mislead me.

***

The next morning, a wet autumn Saturday in western Missouri, I steered my big Dodge diesel towards the rolling line that sufficed for the horizon. The landscape was dramatically different from the towering mountains that surrounded my Salt Lake City home. Here the trees were mostly deciduous and were losing their colorful leaves, and the tall grass rolled on for miles and miles, interrupted occasionally by thick stands of barren shrubbery. The change in scenery satisfied me, despite the rain.

We spent most of the day visiting historical sights, and Julianna was really quite a good tour guide. As if it wasn't enough to watch her brush locks of burnished hair out of her green eyes, she also gave a concise and informed lecture at each spot. As indifferent as I was to Mormon history, I found some of it fascinating.

"Mormons experienced vicious opposition as well as unprecedented growth in Missouri," she said as if reading from a textbook. "The Mormons who settled this area were run out of the state on a number of tragic occasions."

"Run out?" I said.

"This area," we had stopped and were looking at a large open bluff, "was once Far West, one of the largest towns in northern Missouri. It was home to over five thousand people, mostly Mormons. They were burned out and massacred after the governor ordered their extermination."

"Extermination?" I wrinkled a brow.

"The official extermination order wasn't repealed until nineteen seventy-six," she said. "It didn't pay to be a Mormon in Caldwell County in eighteen thirty-eight."

"It's a wonder they survived to cross the plains in such numbers," I remarked, hoping to sound somewhat informed.

"A wonder, indeed, Mr. Richards."

"So whatever happened to those people who made life so miserable for the Mormons?"

"They assumed much of the Saints's property and went on living in Missouri—the pukes."

"Whoa, Julianna McCray, your language!" I exclaimed, amazed at Julianna's new vocabulary.

She straightened in her seat. "Forgive me, but the term is a well-documented, historical epitaph for Missourians of that period."

"Okeydokey, artichokey," I said, shaking my head.

We continued driving east on a two-lane highway. I was admiring the undulating landscape and wondering why they didn't stay and fight for what was rightly theirs.

"Like it?" Julianna was looking out her window at the rolling, forested prairies.

"Sure. It's nothing like Salt Lake City."

"Rolling prairie. That's what I like about it."

"It's a change of pace," I said, wishing there were a mountain somewhere. "How do you tell which way is north without the mountain range for orientation?"

"Oh, yes. There's a trick that only we Missourians know about."

This would be interesting; I liked to hear about the local lore.

She went on, "Behind those clouds there's a big fireball in the sky."

I started to look out the window where she was pointing.

"That fireball usually goes from east to west each day." Her face was deadpan.

So was mine, until she started to laugh and couldn't stop. I eventually joined her.

We drove north for about half an hour and then east a couple hundred feet down a gravel road.

"This is it," Julianna announced as we entered a clearing cut by a small creek. "It's right over there, somewhere," she said pointing down a gentle slope to a small wooded valley.

"And what would that be?" I asked.

"My great, great, great grandfather was born here. The exact location and the incredible story about his birth is recorded in his mother's diary, and that is a story in itself, but things have changed too much for me to find the actual spot. I'll show you where I like to imagine it is."

I stopped the truck and we both got out. It wasn't raining at the moment, but the air was brisk.

Julianna walked around the truck to meet me. She glanced at my feet and wrinkled her nose in amusement. "You're still wearing those ridiculous thongs?"

"No. Flip-flops. What about it?"

"Never mind, Tourist Boy." She walked past me shaking her head and smiling. "My favorite spot is through that brush down along the creek bed," she said.

My camera hung on my neck, as usual, and I grasped the body with both hands to prevent the lens from swinging around as I slid down the embankment. Sticks and twigs pulled at my sweatshirt as I parted the thick brush.

Julianna waited above in a long sleeved T-shirt, apparently enjoying the fresh, brisk air.

"Take a picture," I heard her yell.

It was the golden hour, that hour just before sunset that photographers await, when the sun is low in the sky and its light is diffused in a golden, flattering hue. The fact that the cloud cover ruined all that bothered me not a bit, considering the intended subject of my photo shoot.

"Walk that way," I gestured. "I see the perfect picture. I want you in it."

The brush along the depression was impassable in places and the daylight filtered in through it. I wanted just the right angle, so I forced my way through the brambles to find the perfect place to stand. The branches were stiff and clung to my shoulders as I clawed my way through. What a stupid time to be wearing my flip-flops. One unfriendly branch took me across the face, hitting both my eyes. I suppressed a curse, owing to the uncommonly pure company I kept, and squeezed my eyes shut. Tears formed to quell the sting and I blinked them back.

"I'm blind," I yelled, making a joke of it in case she'd seen me walk headlong into the branch and start crying. She didn't respond.

"Give me just a few seconds," I hollered up into the clearing. My eyes had stopped watering, but were still blurred. I closed my eyes and gently rubbed them before I raised the camera and made a rudimentary aperture calculation. I wanted enough exposure to bring out the shaded areas and not wash out Julianna's face. I played with the settings, waiting for her to show up in the frame. She made her way down the slope to the edge of the creek and made a couple of modeling gestures before settling in for the picture. I took a little extra time gazing at her through the lens, pretending to make minor adjustments. Oh man, she was beautiful.

"Okay, say . . . rutabaga."

"Rutabaga?"

Holding the camera firmly, I eased down on the shutter release expecting to see a momentary flicker. Instead, the frame turned black for a moment as if the shutter was stuck. When the shutter finally snapped back, a different woman was centered perfectly in the frame, and Julianna was no longer there.

"What the . . . ? Excuse me," I said, peeking over the camera.

The woman wore a long, calico dress with a full skirt and a knitted wool shawl over her shoulders, looking like she'd just stepped out of an old-time sepia photograph taken at a county fair. She had one hand to her face, brushing at the wisps of red hair that spilled out from under a wide-brimmed bonnet while her other hand clutched at the shawl. Her hair was just the color of Julianna's, and there was something of Julianna in her eyes as well.

Her face was fair and she wore a pained expression, just short of tears. Reflexively, I snapped another photo and lowered the camera.

"Uhh, hi," I said. The woman did not answer, but stood in front of me, looking furtively at the camera and then at the bank as if she didn't know what to do. Whoever she was, she was scared.

"I knew I'd find you," she finally murmured.

I took a step in her direction before hearing what I unmistakably recognized as a gunshot. The sound of the shot echoed through the evening air and over the distant hills, but the report was not far off. I dropped the camera, letting it fall to my chest, and pulled the zipper on my fanny pack to expose my pistol. The handle of my gun went firmly into the web of my hand, as it had done thousands of times before. Pulling it from its hidden holster, I lunged for the woman and shoved her to the ground in the shadows of the thick brush.

"Where's Julianna?" I asked, but got no response.

Another shot broke the evening air as the sun dropped below the horizon, leaving only long shadows on the Missouri countryside. This shot was much closer.

"Hurry," said the trembling voice of the woman beside me. "It's my brother. They're killing him."

CHAPTER 5

"Stay down," I ordered the woman. I lunged up the bank toward my truck but didn't see Julianna anywhere. I yelled for her, hoping she'd hear me, "Get in the truck and lock the doors." I scrambled back down the bank to where the woman was obediently waiting.

Cautiously, the woman and I crept into the shade of the brush, which offered some concealment, and made our way toward the sound of the shots. I held my pistol in both hands, letting go periodically with my left hand to feel for the woman following me. I scanned the foliage, ever wary. The idea that I was a fool crossed my mind more than once, but it was overridden by the intensity of the woman's plea for help; this wasn't my first experience with pleas for help, nor with foolishness.

I was several hundred yards from my truck when I heard the unmistakable moans of an injured man. I turned to look at the woman. She was clearly desperate; tears streaked her dirty face and her jaws were clenched against her brother's laments. Her beseeching eyes tempted me to call her Julianna, but I knew it wasn't her. She crouched behind me, a fistful of my shirt in her hand. I wanted her to stay close, so I nodded and she made a curt nod back.

Slowly I arose and she followed. I backed up abruptly to avoid the barren branches of a tree, and my body bumped hers. I recoiled slightly and looked at her stomach. The woman was pregnant. She read my questioning face and ran her palms over the pleats of her dress that spread out neatly to cover the roundness of her stomach. The center of my chest burned with the increased anxiety.

I turned back to the noises and took short careful steps toward them. I located a small depression where there was enough brush to conceal our movements, but every step was still a risk. I picked each footfall deliberately, sometimes moving a twig or branch with the toe of my flip-flops to make sure not to step on anything noisy. It meant dividing my attention between what was on the ground and what was out in front of my pistol, but stealth was crucial. Again, I thought about what a bad time it was to be caught in my flippies. I relaxed my toes as I walked to prevent the back of my thongs from flipping against my heels at each step.

The sounds I heard up ahead were voices, angry and taunting, and I heard an occasional stifled moan. The familiar sound of someone being beaten registered in my head. We worked our way out of the depression into a narrow strip of forested land that ran parallel to the creek. I could move faster now, confident that the voices I heard would cover our approach. We took cover behind a thick tree at the edge of a clearing where I saw three human forms taunting and attacking a writhing figure on the ground.

"My brother," the pregnant woman whispered as we crouched behind the tree.

The figures administered vicious kicks in turn, and then one delivered a cracking blow to the fallen man's head with the butt of what looked like a flintlock rifle. The woman behind me flinched, grabbing my shirt and almost pulling me off balance.

The most foul and filthy human I had ever imagined was on the other side of the low-growing branches. His hair fell wildly past his shoulders and stopped somewhere behind his fat back in long greasy strands. His misshapen face was wider than it was tall, as if his head had been shortened in an apple press. Its configuration made his mouth wider than normal so as to cover the considerable space between his cheeks and ears. His face was covered with weeks of grime, and his facial hair was an outgrowth of fine whiskers that could only loosely be considered a beard. He wore a torn and soiled thin jacket over trousers too short by about six inches. A shirt that had at one time been white hung out under the jacket.

The fat-faced man spat sounds through rotting teeth and leered maliciously at the prone figure lying in the dirt below him. His speech was slurred and difficult to understand, with something of a drawl.

"He's a dead man," he spat, as he rolled the boy's body over with his boot. The woman behind me gave a soft gasp, not loud enough to be heard by the others, as the swollen face of the wounded man was revealed.

"Let's jes maim 'im an' send 'im back whar he come from." The second suggestion came from a tall slender man, similarly dressed and groomed with only slightly shorter hair, and teeth that showed only slightly better care.

"He come from hell. He's hell spawned." The fat-faced man obviously enjoyed what he thought was a clever rejoinder and emphasized his glee by placing another bone-jarring kick in the fallen victim's back. The figure on the ground rolled over slowly, now seemingly indifferent to the beating.

I reflexively aimed my pistol at the most immediate threat—the fat-faced man nearest the body. The three men jeered and pointed their antiquated rifles at the head of their victim who was, by now, far from caring.

"Come on. Let's git this done and git outta here," pled the third man, a nondescript medium-sized man who seemed apprehensive about the beating and had acted with relative reserve so far as I had seen.

In response to the last bit of advice, the tall man stepped closer to the body and pulled back the hammer on his rifle, the mechanism making a loud click. He pushed the barrel into the cheek of the beaten man who stirred at the new stimulus, opening his eyes and peering up at his tormentor.

The woman crouched behind me with her hand over her mouth, suppressing sobs. I should have fired by now, or least challenged the three men verbally, but the next series of taunts astonished me.

"Say it, Mormon boy. Say you ain't Mormon, or you'll wake up in hell," the tall man said.

The boy, for so he appeared now with tears in his eyes, responded slowly through teeth clenched in pain. "I will not."

The third man, who hadn't seemed to enjoy the game as much as the others, shifted back and forth and murmured urgently, "Let's git. The boy ain't gonna do it."

"Do it," screamed Fatface, showering his captive with saliva. "Do it, fool."

The youth did not yield.

My pistol was in hand, at low ready, but I didn't shoot. Instead, I did what years of police training and experience demanded: I challenged.

"Police department," I yelled in a practiced authoritarian voice, "Don't move, don't speak." The verbiage was a product of habit and while it may not have been the most appropriate phrase, considering the situation, it was highly effective in getting the unmitigated attention of the three squalid ruffians.

After several stunning seconds, when the surprise of my challenge wore off, Fatface spoke. "County Militia. We found one trying to leave the mill."

"Leave him there," I said for lack of anything more convincing to say. It almost worked and I could see the apprehension in their faces as they looked at each other. The tall man who had been holding his rifle on the boy turned from stunned to skeptical.

"Who are ya?" he said, his confidence inspiring his cohorts. "Show yerself or I'll put a ball in ya." He raised his rifle in my direction, and the others followed his lead even though I doubted they could see me hidden in the shadows behind the tree. I had heard two shots as I neared their location and was confident that at least two of the rifles were not loaded, but I was understandably hesitant to test my hypothesis.

Police training clearly forbids the firing of warning shots, despite what generations of armchair cops learn from watching police dramas on television. Under my current circumstances, however, I aimed my pistol at a thick tree limb directly over the head of the fat-faced hillbilly who was still spitting commands at the beaten form lying on the ground.

My reaction was a breech of training and common sense, but it seemed like the right thing to do. I wasn't sure that the scene I witnessed wasn't part of an elaborate hoax or even a historical reenactment put on by the locals. This was, after all, a place of historical significance to millions of Mormons. My eyes darted around quickly for an eager cast of spectators. Seeing none, I loosed six well-aimed rounds at the beefy tree branch directly over the heads of the three men. The noise was tremendous and the consequences of shooting the tree were far better than I could have imagined. Chunks of tree bark ranging in size from little specks that flipped into eyes and caused spastic blinking to fist-sized projectiles flew in every direction.

My challenge didn't get the attention of the ne'er-do-wells, but my shot placement did. The three men vacated space with the speed of Olympic sprinters, or in the case of the tall gangly one, with the grace of an Olympic gymnast. I watched them flee and waited until they were well away from us.

Before moving from cover, I scanned the area for additional threats. Seeing no one, and wanting to get to the injured man quickly, I hurried into the clearing where the drama had taken place, the woman still close behind.

The figure on the ground looked to be a teen, not really a man but more than a boy; the bright luster of youth shone on his face despite the beating he had taken. He was cognizant enough to thank me, but he was in no condition to travel under his own power.

"Mostly superficial," I told the boy's sister as I performed an initial survey of his injuries. "Contusions and abrasions," I said, hoping to console her. I ran my hands up and down his arms and legs looking for broken bones but I was more worried about internal injuries that might not manifest themselves until it was too late.

"Will he live?" she asked.

I started to say yes, but under the circumstances, I wasn't sure. "We need to get him some help," I said judiciously.

She nodded. "To the mill," she said.

He was semi-alert and breathing steadily, but more extensive first aid would have to wait until we were in a safe place.

"This place may not be safe for long. We need to get him back to my truck. Who were those guys?"

"Militia." She shrugged. "Clay County, perhaps."

"Militia?" I said as I pulled the boy upright by his shoulder. "I bet the local cops love these guys," I said.

"Cops?" she asked.

"Yeah, the police. I bet they'll know who those guys were."

"Police," she repeated. "Sir, this is not Boston or New York City."

Her tone was bitter. "This is Missouri, the Western Frontier, and we are Mormons. There is no law here."

Definitely someone who needs a tinfoil hat, I thought, thinking about all the nutsos I'd dealt with on the street over the last ten years. A lot of them wore tinfoil hats to protect them from space aliens. Hey, whatever works.

I took a fold of his coarse pants in my fist to support him. The boy moaned softly as we took a few apprehensive steps back toward where I'd left my truck.

"You go ahead," I said to the woman, gesturing in the direction of my truck with a nod.

"Elias, I'm sorry," she whispered to the hurt boy through a stifled sob.

"Lead the way, Anna," the boy said. The three of us moved as swiftly as possible, considering the boy's condition, the woman's big belly, and my footwear. I stopped every twenty yards or so to reestablish my grip on Elias and to wriggle back into my flippies. Anna scouted a few feet ahead for the surest path. By the time we were back to the clearing near the truck, twilight had faded to blackness, deepened by intermittent rain.

The banks of the creek made for a well-protected place to set the boy down. He grimaced briefly and then relaxed as I propped him against the hillside.

"You stay here," I said to Anna. She nodded and turned her rain-streaked face towards the boy's.

I crept forward, up the bank, and peered through the brush at the truck. There was no movement. I scanned the perimeter of the clearing, but saw nothing.

My survey of the area around the truck was limited because I didn't want to get too far from my wards until I was sure the Militia, or whoever wanted the boy dead, was not waiting in ambush. Using the growth around the clearing as concealment, I made a semi-circle around the truck, stopping often to listen. There was no sign of the militia, and no sign of Julianna.

There was an empty feeling in my chest, as well as a burning panic. I nearly called out for Julianna, but decided not to give away our location to the three angry men hunting the forest for me. Warily,

I walked to the truck and looked inside. Julianna's fleece jacket was still draped over the headrest and her purse was tucked in the gap in the split bench seat.

The brush was too thick around the clearing for me to see the highway. The clearing looked different than before. Everything looks different in the dark, I reassured myself. I took slow, deep breaths and focused on quelling the fire of anxiety still blistering my chest, so I could think about what to do with the injured boy. Julianna would be standing out at the highway getting help, I was sure. First, I needed to tend to the boy.

I opened the cab of my truck and pulled my day bag from the back seat. My day bag contained trauma first aid equipment, some food in the form of military meals—ready to eat, light rain gear, enough ammunition to start a small war, and a pair of binoculars. I always carried wool blankets in the truck, so I tucked those under my arm. I had several two-quart bladder canteens on the floor of the rear passenger compartment and I slung them both over my shoulder by their straps. I took two steps toward the creek bank then about-faced in my mud-caked thongs. I definitely needed to change my footwear. I exchanged my flippies for a pair of thick socks and insulated, waterproof leather boots.

I remembered Lewis's field surgery kit, but decided not to bring it along since it was meant for more serious injuries and I wouldn't know what to do with it anyway.

I descended the creek bank and found Anna and her brother where I'd left them, Anna hovering awkwardly over the boy to keep the rain out of his face.

"Here," I said to Anna, handing her the blankets, "tuck these around him. I want to take a good look at him and then I'll drive the truck over."

"Thank you, sir," she said and went to work. I unrolled a camouflage rain poncho and handed that to her. "Cover him with this. It'll keep him dry," I told her. She briefly examined the green and black pattern and unfurled it over the boy's body.

I poured some water into the boy's mouth and he drank as much as his swollen lips would allow. I took two tablets of Ibuprofin from my day pack and held them in front of the boy's face, waiting for him to open his mouth. He did not, so I gently plied open his mouth and set the tablets on his tongue.

I lifted his head slightly and poured a slow stream of water past his lips. The boy gasped and gulped the water, swallowing the tablets with a painful grimace. Anna watched without speaking. He slowly opened his swelling lips, letting go of another soft moan.

"His name is Elias," Anna spoke for him.

"My name is Owen, Owen Richards," I said to the woman absently, thinking more about the boy's injuries than introductions. The rise and fall of Elias's chest was deep and even and he appeared restful. I touched his shoulder and spoke gently to him. "Elias, my name is Owen. Can you tell me what hurts?"

He roused, not to a state of full comprehension, and said a few incoherent words of thanks either to me or to some higher power—I couldn't tell.

"We need to get him to a hospital," I said to Anna.

"You have saved his life. He said you would."

"We need to get him to a hospital," I repeated, ignoring her. "I'll bring the truck over and then we can move him."

"I fear that moving him will cause more injury," she said. "He needs to rest."

"I know," I said, a little frustrated. "But we need to get him to a doctor."

"We can get help at the mill, but the woods are too dangerous. They will be looking for us everywhere."

"Let's get on the road. Where's the nearest town?"

She paused and gave me a slightly baffled look. "The road is too dangerous. The mobs will be watching it. Elias and I were travelling to Far West when we were accosted by the mob. I fear my brother placed himself in danger so that I could escape. He told me I would find you."

"How would he have . . . Far West?" I said, bewildered. Julianna and I had been there earlier in the day. It was nothing more than a prairie and a few large stones once intended as a temple site. Beautiful, but barren. No doctors.

"There's nothing at Far West." I announced.

"Nothing?" she gasped. "What has happened?"

"I don't know; there's just nothing there. Your brother needs medical attention."

"If there is nothing left of Far West," she sighed, "We must go to the mill. It is the closest help.

"Where is the mill? How do we get there?"

"It's back the way we came. About a mile, but it may be farther."

"Okay, you stay here while I make room in my rig. I only want to move him once. I'll be right back."

Bewildered and more than a little troubled, I climbed the embankment once more and walked warily toward the truck. I covered about twenty meters without seeing any evidence of the road, or Julianna.

Had Julianna moved my truck off the road? Perhaps she had been trying to escape and . . . I was letting my mind run unbridled. My stomach ached and my pulse quickened.

"Slow down," I told myself aloud. I took a slow, even breath and did my best to prioritize. I simply couldn't leave the area without Julianna, yet the boy desperately needed more care than I could provide. Perhaps, I thought, Julianna had gone for help. I would probably find her by the road.

The engine turned over smoothly and the headlights illuminated the tall grass and trees before me. The rain was heavier now and I peered past my windshield wipers into the sheen. I'd left the truck on a firm dirt road, but it was now sitting in a clearing surrounded by grass and mud.

I rocked forward about a foot before my wheels started to spin. I shifted into four- wheel drive, locking in the hubs, and lurched forward again. Now all four tires spun together, digging holes in the soft mud. I cursed aloud and opened the door to inspect the damage. The front tires were only inches deep, but the rear tires had been sitting in mush and were now buried to the axles in mud.

I hopped from the cab, and the sludge sucked at my boots as I examined the mired truck.

I conducted a pattern search for the road by walking a square about twenty yards per side. I found nothing, not even the shallow dirt ruts leading to the highway. I increased the scope of my square to take in just under a hundred yards to a side and found little more than before. I was sure I'd turned south from the highway, but I checked all sides with equal diligence. Nothing. I scrambled down the slope to where I'd left Anna and the boy.

"Anna? Do you know where the highway is?" I asked.

"Highway? There is a path, a road, that leads from the mill to Far West. It's mostly along the creek."

"I can't seem to find the highway I drove in on. I think it's north of here."

"Not north of here, sir. There is very little north of here."

"Right." I clenched my teeth in frustration. I climbed the hill to the clearing and looked again.

I made the same search as before and found no highway. In fact, my search taught me that the countryside in which my truck was now imprisoned was impassable by vehicle owing to abrupt knolls, deeply cut gullies, and occasional stands of thick forest, all neatly bogged down in mud. Even if I could free my truck from its current location, it would find the same fate in all directions. Each of my boots carried about a pound of the Missouri countryside as evidence.

I debated whether I should call out for Julianna and risk bringing the locals to me unnecessarily. They hadn't seemed too friendly and I doubted they liked me any more than I liked them. I decided to risk it, pistol in hand.

I walked to the far side of the clearing opposite the truck before wailing Julianna's name into the darkness in several directions. There was no reply. Deciding that the rain was just drowning my voice, I quit yelling and started thinking.

I stood there in a stupor: truck marooned in a two-hundred-acre sty, gorgeous red-head missing, injured boy and his overly pregnant sister waiting, huddled by the creek, and a trio of mouth-breathing hillbillies on the loose.

I checked my pistol, reloaded what I'd shot and threw an extra magazine of seventeen rounds into my fanny pack. As an after-thought, I slid a can of pepper spray in the front pocket. I pulled my camouflage Gore-Tex® coat over my shoulders and made the short journey back to the creek and my new friends. When I got to them, Anna was weeping quietly over Elias.

"What's wrong?" I asked, feeling Elias' head. I could tell immediately that the fever was getting worse. Anna said nothing. I dug in my gear for the Ibuprofen tablets and held another one in front of him.

"Tell me, what is that and why must you give him more?" asked Anna.

"Oh," I looked at my watch, "you're probably right. Eight-hundred milligrams of Ibuprofin. He won't need more for a few hours." I put the pill back in the bottle, Anna watching curiously. "I don't know what's happening here but we're running out of options. I was going to suggest that we stay in the truck until morning, but we need to get this boy to a doctor."

Anna nodded.

I gathered Elias up by the arms; he was limp and too sick to walk. "I'm not sure how far I can carry him," I told Anna as I gave her my day pack. She looked at it and put the straps over her shoulder as she'd seen me do a moment before.

"Put this on," I said, handing her my jacket.

Anna examined the coat, running her hand over the material and watching the rain bead up and run off. "Thank you," she said as she put it on and drew the hood over her head.

"How far is the mill?" I asked.

"Less than two miles, I think," she said. "Due south."

"We'll take it in sections," I said as I hoisted Elias to his feet. Anna helped me wrap Elias in wool blankets under the poncho.

We slogged through the mud and range grass for just over a mile before Elias's weight became too much for me, and my thighs burned with each step.

"Let's stop and rest," Anna said, seeing my fatigue. She helped to get Elias situated in a comfortable-looking position. "You cannot go on." I was glad she said it first. I didn't want to be bested by a pregnant woman.

"I just need to rest a minute."

Anna toyed with the zipper on my coat, running it up and down rhythmically. "Wondrous," she said, "I've never seen anything like it." She brushed some of the beaded water off the arm and shook her head. "Wondrous."

"Gore-Tex. Greatest thing since sliced bread," I muttered.

I found the rest of the walk along the creek in the rain anything but pleasant. Elias managed only a few discordant moans between rest stops, and I was in a great hurry to get him to the doctor and return to my truck and find Julianna. We turned east at Shoal Creek and made the last part of our trip to the mill as the rain let up and the sky cleared. We traveled faster now by the moonlight that peeked through broken clouds.

The settlement, when we reached it, was more like a Boy Scout camp than a town. In the ambient light, I could make out only dark shapes. A log building no bigger than a garage rested on the banks of the creek. Anna and Elias told me this was the mill. A handful of smaller dwellings, well spaced around the rolling prairie, surrounded the mill. Behind a thin stand of trees, I thought I saw the outline of a covered wagon. We would find no hospital here.

The mill settlers apparently took their security very seriously and we were challenged before reaching the settlement perimeter.

"Who goes there?" I heard before I saw anyone.

Anna answered. "Elias is hurt. Please help us."

The sentry apparently recognized Anna by the sound of her voice and emerged from the brush, flintlock rifle at low ready. He was dressed a lot like Elias and when he recognized Elias's limp form, he came quickly to our aid. There was no one else about at that hour, and all of the cabins were dark. We passed into the middle of the settlement, apparently intent upon a specific residence that I hoped would lodge a doctor. Anna rehearsed the events that explained Elias's condition to the eager ears of the sentry. He said very little, grunting under his load.

We reached a small log home, and the sentry rapped on the door, which was opened moments later by a squat but formidable man in his late fifties. Holding an oil lamp in his hands, he ushered in the sentry and Elias. Anna and I waited outside. There was some commotion inside and I could only trust that someone there knew how to treat Elias's injuries.

"So," I said, "he'll take care of your brother?"

"Yes, sir. Elias will be well cared for."

"Good. I'll just wait a few minutes until I hear the good word from the doctor."

"That is very kind of you."

We were standing just outside the cabin when, out of the darkness, a young girl appeared. She approached hesitantly.

"Good evening, Sarah," said Anna graciously.

The girl returned a demure greeting and joined us.

"Sarah, this is . . ."

"Hello, I'm Owen Richards," I introduced myself. Sarah was young, probably no more than seventeen or eighteen years old. She had long dark hair with a natural curl, and dark eyes that glistened even in the night.

"Pleased to make your acquaintance, Brother Richards," she said and offered her hand. I took it and shook it gently before she pulled it back.

"Oh, it's not really 'brother,'" I said, trying to explain that I was not one of the members of their Church.

Anna quickly interjected. "Oh, yes, Brother Richards has been so very kind."

"We are all very obliged, Brother Richards," Sarah said, bowing her head slightly. She turned to Anna. "How is Elias? We were so worried when you left. We just heard."

Anna shook her head. "He's not well, Sarah. Why don't you go inside and help? I'm sure they can use you."

Sarah's eyes lit up. She took her leave politely and went inside.

"Friend of Elias's," I said with a grin.

"Why, yes. In fact I believe she's set her cap for him," Anna said. "Pity he can't see the lines of concern on her face."

"It won't do him any harm to have her around about now. Will it?"

Anna nodded and looked at me.

I was certain I had lines of concern on my face, too. I was worried about Julianna.

Anna and I stood in front of the cabin for a few moments before she broke the silence.

"Mr. Richards," Anna said, "pardon me, but you would do very well to accept the title of brother when in the company of the Saints. You will find our people skittish of strangers not of our faith."

I shook my head. "I have to ask, Anna. What kind of society is this?" I posed the question as tactfully as my curiosity would allow. "I mean, I heard the men calling Elias 'Mormon boy' and I live in the heart of Mormon country. I don't quite understand."

I must have caught her off guard because she said nothing and offered me a queer look instead. I went on gently, "I respect what you're doing here. It must be tough, though."

Still nothing, so I decided on an easier question, "How long have you and your people been living like this?"

This question was apparently more to Anna's liking and she answered. "I've been here, in Missouri, since I was twenty. Four years ago we left Boston to come west to meet the Saints."

"Boston," I said with interest, "Sox fan, then."

She looked at me without understanding, as if I should elaborate. "Sock fans?" she asked.

I changed the subject. "You came with your family?"

"No," she said, casting her eyes away. "I came with my husband and two brothers. One brother died two years ago; my husband died six months ago of the fever." Anna spoke softly. Obviously these were hurtful things to talk about, but she went on. "The rest of our family, just an aunt and uncle, did not support our becoming Mormon and we were obliged to leave Boston." Anna rubbed her large belly. "It took us three months to walk from Boston to Kirtland, Ohio, only to find that the Saints had moved here, to Missouri," Anna said wearily. "I fear that another move is imminent."

"Why? I mean, I can see you're having problems, but, why don't you get help from the police, or the feds for that matter. From what I've seen, these three Missourians don't pose much of a real threat and they've obviously crossed the line into malicious harassment of your people."

Anna raised her head and looked me in the eyes. "You don't know anything about what has gone on here, do you?" Her tone was not accusatory. "How long have you been in Missouri, Mr. Richards?"

"A couple of days. I was quite fond of it until tonight."

"Missouri is my home. I walked what seemed like a thousand miles to be here among the Saints. I'm not fond of the treatment we endure, but the land is ours."

"You said that before. You walked? You literally walked from Boston?"

"Indeed. We walked a great portion of it. We had no money for stock or wagons and we found little work on the barges to pay our board. So, we walked, worked, and then walked again. We became very close, my brothers and I."

"He was older, the one who died?" I imagined he was.

"No," said Anna sadly, "he was eight when we left Boston."

I didn't say anything for several seconds, almost disbelieving the very believable woman before me. Somehow, this forgotten section of Missouri was still fighting a war that had ended more than a hundred years ago according to my new knowledge of Mormon history.

"The mob," I asked, "is it more than the three guys out there?"

Anna nodded. "It seems at times to be almost the whole of Missouri."

I knew that could not be true, but perhaps to Anna and the Mormons here it seemed that way.

Anna looked me in the eyes and said, "Elias is a message carrier from Far West. He came to the mill to deliver a warning, and," she said lovingly, "to take me back to the safety of Far West before the birth of my child. Elias said it was not safe to travel by day, so we left here just before dusk. I'm not to speak of Elias's duties except to a few trusted friends."

"Why are you telling me?"

"I do not know, except that Elias seems to have taken you into his trust. In fact, Elias said you would help us. Just before the mob captured him, he sent me ahead to find you."

"Me?" I was skeptical. "I've never seen Elias before tonight."

"At first," Anna went on as if I hadn't spoken, "I assumed he knew you were waiting for us. Now, I am not sure."

"I can assure you, I've never met Elias before."

"I see. Sometimes Elias just knows things. Thank you, nonetheless."

"I knew a guy a lot like that," I said, thinking of Lewis.

Anna smiled and ran her fingers through tired wisps of red sun-bleached hair. "I must look a sight," she said. The dim glow of the stars enhanced a set of classic features that were dirty and sunburned. She was a stunning, graceful woman whose lifestyle had left its mark on her young face. But her hardened features magnified her beauty, which was further enhanced by a dazzling set of sea-green eyes—eyes I'd seen before.

"I need to go," I said reluctantly, pulling my gaze from her face. "I hope Elias is alright."

"You saved his life."

I was a little embarrassed and I smiled at her in the darkness under the cabin eaves.

The door to the cabin opened and the burly man stepped outside. "He needs his rest, Anna. And so do we all." He turned to me and put out a hand. "He was badly beaten, but he will live. Thank you . . ."

"Owen Richards," Anna said.

"Thank you Brother Richards," he said.

Anna introduced him to me. "This is Brother Harry Liddle, our doctor."

"Pleased to meet you, Brother Richards."

I shook his hand, remembering what Anna said about letting people call me brother, and then turned to leave the settlement.

"Owen Richards?" Anna pulled at my sleeve.

"Yes?"

She took off my coat and handed it to me. "Please be careful. And," she said as an afterthought, "God be with you."

***

I wasted little time hiding from the likes of the three amigos who seemed bent on Elias's demise, but I was wary and checked my back regularly on my way back to my truck. Two miles was an easy trek without a grown man on my shoulders, and I was back before midnight.

I was still worried about mobbers finding me in the night, so I stopped by the clearing and examined my truck from a distance. There was no sign of local militiamen and no sign of Julianna. I hoped she hadn't fallen into their hands. The thought was too terrible to entertain, so I convinced myself that she had gone for help, and focused on my more immediate problem.

My truck was still mired in mud and I couldn't imagine how I would get it out. But, even if I could get unstuck, I'd have to find the highway.

I repeated the pattern searches I'd made before, but had no luck. I made two long forays into the wilderness, one to the northeast and one to the northwest. I walked at least three miles each time and found nothing but prairie. As a last resort, I probed south and a little west, knowing what I'd find. By the time I got back to the truck I was exhausted. I warmed up the heater and tried to think.

"Stay where you are," I muttered. "Any three-year-old knows that's what you do when you're lost."

The trouble with my theory was that I wasn't the one who was lost. Or, maybe I was. I tried to eat a Power Bar that had been rattling around in my jockey box for who knows how long. I ended up spitting it out after one bite. I wasn't that hungry anyway.

My cell phone, I thought suddenly. I couldn't believe I hadn't thought of it sooner. I took the device out of my SWAT gear and turned it on. The battery was charged but it registered as a no-service area. Go figure. The hills of northern Missouri were little more than bumps, but I thought I might get better reception if I walked uphill.

I headed northwest, where I thought the highest ground was, and watched the readout on the face of the phone for a blip that meant I could call out. Nothing happened. I must have walked several more miles, and by the time I got back to my truck it was getting light.

I decided while walking back that I would head for the nearest city at first light. Anna talked about a Far West, obviously a different Far West than the one where Julianna had taken me yesterday. Anna had said it was west along the creek. That's where I would go.

I left a note for Julianna under one of the wiper blades that said I'd be walking to Far West for help and would return before dark. WAIT HERE! I ordered in capital letters.

I put my day pack on the hood of my truck, draped my raincoat over it and made one last venture into the brush to answer nature's call.

From my secluded vantage point in the brush, I watched with dismay as Fatface and his two friends wandered into the clearing; when they saw my truck, they began cursing, obviously intrigued with my truck. Unseen, I crouched and watched.

"Well if that ain't some pumpkins. What is it?" Fatface demanded. There were a couple of grunts in response as his two friends examined my truck from front to back. One of them spat on my windshield. Gross!

"Looky at this coatee," the tall blond said, picking up my three-hundred-dollar Gore-Tex coat and trying it on.

I shook my head. "Someone needs to teach these mouth breathers some manners," I said under my breath, "before one of them messes with my truck and there's real trouble."

I made a tactical retreat into the shadows and formulated a plan.

CHAPTER 6

My plan was hastily conceived and just a bit juvenile, but perfect for the three Missouri derelicts dithering around my truck. I backed away from the creek bank soundlessly and skirted the clearing to get a better angle. They were arguing in muted voices—I couldn't tell about what—so I was relatively certain they would neither see nor hear me. Still, I was careful to adhere to proper tactics.

Without taxing my tactical movement skills, I was able to position myself close enough to discern their losing battle with basic hygiene. They were perhaps the dirtiest humans I'd ever seen. Fatface had a ring of grime around his face that glistened with spittle as he spoke. He was pointing and gesturing at my truck and walking back and forth. The other two seemed subordinate to him. One was the tall man who had delivered a vicious blow to Elias's face with the rifle stock. He stood looking at my truck, not talking. The third man, the nondescript man with straight greasy hair, grunted randomly at what Fatface was saying.

Three flintlock rifles rested upright against the fender of my truck. Any assurance I felt that they would take proper care not to scratch the paint on my rig disappeared when one of the miscreants prodded at the hood inquiringly with the pointed end of a long fixed-blade knife. This activated my vehicle security system, which resulted in an earsplitting rhapsody of horn honks and flashing lights that sent the three men into a hilarious panic. To say they were startled would be the very essence of understatement. The greaser with the knife ran for the other end of the clearing, taking steps of approximately six or seven feet per footfall. The tall man fell to his knees and stumped away from the truck with his hands clapped against the sides of his head so tightly that I thought he would give himself cauliflower ear. Fatface made me come close to giving away my hiding place because I had to choke back snorting laughter as I watched him. His first response was inaction, except that his eyes snapped open and his large mouth froze into an oval. This lasted for only a moment and was followed by random lurching; apparently he was so unsure of which way to run, his mind chose to try all directions at once. The result was fascinating. I switched off the alarm with my keyless remote, and the threesome, now standing some distance from the truck, slowly regained their composure.

I managed to suppress what should have been a good belly laugh and, after a short period of mourning for the paint job on my new truck, I forced my attention back to the rifles that were still leaning against my rig. The dark orange crust covering the lock mechanisms was probably a bad sign, and the rust visible at the breech might even inhibit the accuracy of the weapons. In all, it seemed that the three of them cleaned their rifles about as often as they bathed.

Had I not witnessed their brutality with Elias, I would have thought these idiots completely laughable. I reminded myself not to underestimate them, although I was about to pull one of the oldest tricks in the book and I fully believed it would work.

I'd collected several fist-sized projectiles, known to the layman as rocks, and piled them by my feet. I was about fifteen feet back into the scrub brush around the clearing. About five feet away, there was a sort of natural trail leading away from the clearing that ran past my position. With luck, they would notice it just as readily as I had.

I was nearly ready to put my scheme into action. Thinking it through earlier, I'd laughed about the likely outcome; now I was apprehensive. My idea was simple: draw the Missourians away from the clearing by throwing rocks into the trees and making enough noise to force them to go investigate. If my luck held, I could reach my truck and grab some equipment while they combed the bushes in search of me.

Before I started throwing rocks, I wondered whether I had under-estimated my opponents. Fatface had finished jibbering, and a smooth brown stream of tobacco juice escaped his lower lip and clung to his chin. He tried to wipe it off and succeeded in flipping it back into his face. He cursed under his breath and rubbed the sludge into his face. The others watched and didn't seem to mind; one of them blew mucus out of his nostril as if to make my point for me. No, I hadn't underestimated.

Had I considered every contingency? Probably not, since one couldn't hope to foresee all the things that could go wrong. I could always run away, or, in the worst case scenario, I could stand tall behind my pistol and take my chances against their hopefully inaccurate and poorly cared for muskets.

I unzipped my fanny pack and drew my pistol with my right hand. With my left hand, I picked up one of my rocks. The front pouch of my fanny pack was open to allow me easy access to my pepper spray inside. My breath was coming more quickly now and my heart raced, but these were all-too-familiar symptoms of a pending drama. I rather liked it. I took a deep breath and got to work.

I threw my first rock into the trees near the opening in the brush. It rattled the branches and made a loud thud when it hit the ground. Fatface turned slowly, his mouth hanging open loosely. He'd obviously heard it, but it didn't seem to bother him. He looked at the treetops with mild interest, scratched the seat of his pants, and then rubbed his chin. His face regained its earlier stupefied expression, and then his brain returned to neutral. The other two men were as ignorant to the sound as fence posts. I threw the second rock harder and more directly at the trees. It thumped around and caused about the same reaction from the men.

I threw another couple of rocks and was unable to get the attention of my newest buddies. It didn't matter because the next thing that happened effectively killed my plan. The man who had discovered my security system still had his knife in his hand. Bravely, he looked at his two friends and placed the tip of his knife on the door of my truck. He drew the knife along my door and even from my distance, I could see a thin strip of paint curling at the tip of the blade.

"Contingency plan," I hissed through clenched teeth. I picked up a rock and threw it directly at the man with the knife. I missed. The next one struck Fatface on the thigh. The Missourians looked around in a panic and reached for their rifles. My third rock struck the hood of my truck, leaving a nasty dent.

I burst into the clearing and fired three more rocks at the befuddled men. I got the complete attention of all three men and a new plan had developed; I ran like the devil.

With Larry, Moe, and Curly in pursuit, I dodged and ducked through the brush. My face and body were whipped torturously by tree branches, and I fell several times on the slippery grass. My mind was racing for an alternative plan. I passed up several locations for a final stand because that wasn't the plan I preferred at the moment.

I could hear my pursuers, but I couldn't see them except for movement in the trees behind me. Their shouts were a mixture of bravado and curses. I hadn't noticed if they had thought to bring their firearms with them. Probably, but I was sure they'd have their hillbilly knives. What hick didn't have a knife?

I wanted to put some distance between me and them so I could take some reasonable defensive position, but their pursuit was relentless and I had to keep track of each one of their paths and take evasive action as necessary. Even under such distress, ducking and running through the Missouri forest, I had time to tell myself that this had been a stupid plan. So far, only half my plan had come to pass—I'd drawn my foes from the clearing. Brilliant.

Eventually I made some ground. I could only occasionally hear the yells of the three Missourians, and I believed they thought they had lost me. My jeans were soaked and muddy, which slowed me down appreciably. I found a thick clump of brush and went to ground in it. It had been a bad choice because the branches bore thorns, but I was hidden in its brambles.

I caught my breath and assessed my situation. I had been running in a southwesterly direction, for the most part, and I thought I saw the creek several times during my escape. I estimated I'd run about a mile and a half from my truck.

I took advantage of the pit stop and rested, still listening warily. I heard some noises far off and dismissed them. I might have left some sign in the mud—it was inevitable—but I decided not to worry unless they got too close.

One eventually did. I heard some scrambling and saw the flickering shadows of movement. I couldn't tell which one it was, but the form moved slowly as if hunting something. I reached for my Glock and the pepper spray. My breathing had slowed, but now it accelerated, hastening out of control. I didn't know how much more chase I had left in me.

"Fellers! Fellers!" the man closest to me called out. Anna had suggested that these men were part of a local militia, but they certainly didn't seem fit to be part of a real military outfit.

"Down the hill?" I heard another yell from far away.

"Naw," the nearest one said to himself. "That Marmon is right," he took a few steps in my direction, "over," he came even closer and bent to look into the clump of brush in which I was cowering. "Here!" he screamed suddenly, seeing my eyes.

His next sound was likewise a scream, but not of victory. When he crouched over to look for me, eyes wide and searching, I held up my little can of pepper spray and pointed it through the branches. Just after his exclamation of success, he took a deep breath and that is precisely when I chose to activate my spray. Total and complete hosedown.

The Missourian reprobate was making howling noises befitting his breed and dancing in circles with his hands over his face.

"Durn skunk," he wailed, "durn Marmon skunk."

I slowly backed out of my hiding spot and drifted away from the temporarily blind Missourian. His friends came from the far corners, but I skulked away quietly and eventually made my way even further west. For whatever reason, I neither saw nor heard any more that day from my playmates. To be safe, I abandoned plans to return to my truck. Running from those three had given me a strong head start and I made good time toward the Far West that Anna had told me about. But dang, I was sure going to miss my coat.

***

Anna had enthusiastically described the trail to Far West and I found it lying east to west paralleling Shoal Creek. Walking during the day was risky, but I encountered no further hostilities. I did see an occasional farm that I discreetly avoided.

I was a person in fair physical condition, running fifteen miles a week religiously and doing an occasional push-up or sit-up once or twice in between. Still, due to my wet and tired condition, by the time I reached town, it was past midday.

To my horror, there was no McDonald's, no 7-Eleven, not even a telephone pole; there was no sign of civilization in Far West. The city, which was indeed larger than the mill settlement, as advertised, was a well-plotted community of several hundred log cabins, sod huts, and a few plank houses, surrounded by canvas covered wagons and livestock. But, Far West might have been more appropriately called Old West.

Anna had assured me that no highway existed north of the mill. That information had to be weighed against her equally unbelievable claim that the only roads west of Far West were Indian trails. I was awfully sorry to learn she was right about the highways north of the mill, and now suspected she might be precisely on the money about what lay west of the city.

Although disappointed, I rather liked Far West. It was a city on a hill with a commanding view of the miles of surrounding prairie and light forest. There were no trappings of modern civilization and I thought that one could get used to the solitude.

The first street I came to developed from a path, to a trail, to a series of parallel ruts, and then to a full-fledged dirt road lined with well-spaced log structures. I could see in the distance that the street itself emanated from a large town square reminiscent of a bygone era. There were a few plank buildings nearer the square, and log huts and canvas tents populated the outskirts.

Far West was at least as antiquated as the mill settlement, but larger and with a more varied industry, judging from the hanging shingles of several well-situated proprietors.

Knowing that paranoia reigned in the area, I approached carefully and was pleasantly surprised to walk unchallenged up the main road. There were people about, all dressed like *Little House on the Prairie* folks, who either walked purposefully up and down the dirt roads or engaged in pleasant conversation in small groups. I thought I was at a pioneer village in an amusement park. One group of passersby gave me a visual once-over and a friendly nod, but the locals mainly paid little attention to me.

My first significant contact in town was with an elderly gentleman, smartly dressed in black tails, walking by himself up a side road that intersected with the road I was on.

Feeling underdressed in mud-caked jeans, I approached the man and asked, "Excuse me, is there a phone nearby?"

"Good afternoon, brother. Lodging is being arranged in the square. You are certain to find assistance there," he said warmly and then turned abruptly on his heel.

"I just need a phone," I called to his back. He nodded and kept walking, eager to be about his business, I guessed.

Another passing gentleman gave me the same sort of instructions. My third friendly conversation was more enlightening.

"Excuse me, sir." The gentleman addressing me was clean, polite, and handsome. He was humbly dressed in a worn brown jacket and pants, and one of those ties that looked like a scarf. Over it all, he wore a dirty black duster. His friendly greeting belied intelligent and suspicious gray eyes neatly assessing me from under a wide-brimmed, low-profile fedora.

"Yes."

He was about my age, if not slightly younger, and in good physical condition, judging from his bearing. He was just under six feet tall and wore a dark mustache and goatee. He was overdue for a shave and his face was tanned and showed signs of a rugged, outdoor lifestyle. His prematurely graying brown hair was thick and slightly wavy, and just long enough to hang over his collar. He was handsome to the point of excess and bore it with the confidence of a highly competent man.

"May I assist you in any way?" he asked. "You are new to Far West, yes?" He was smooth. Along with his good looks, he spoke with the hint of a foreign accent that gave the entire ensemble an exotic finish.

I got the eerie feeling that he knew well and good that I was new to Far West. I deemed excessive congeniality was the prudent course.

"Yes, I am," I said, "My rig got bogged down in the mud outside of town and I'm looking for a telephone."

He looked at me for a moment. "You'll find little in the way of accommodations in Far West. As you must know, we are having a great deal of trouble accommodating those seeking sanctuary here. However, all are invited to the safety of the city."

"I'm not planning on staying, I just need a . . ."

"Brother, I am Brother Bart LeJeune." He introduced himself before I could ask any of about a million obvious questions. "At your service, sir."

The title "brother" still made me cringe, but it seemed wise to let it go at this point. On the other hand, 'Sir' was a title I'd heard often enough as a police officer, but it sounded antique jumping off LeJeune's tongue. LeJeune attended me politely, except for one moment when his eyes darted sideways awkwardly and a small, darkly dressed man at our flank scurried in and out of a shadowy alley as if by command.

"Owen Richards," I responded, trying not to let on that I noticed the man. I was feeling a bit like prey. "I'm from Salt Lake City," I added, trying to earn extra points. LeJeune did not seem to care.

"You are traveling?" He raised a brow. "Might I ask . . .?"

"Oh," I said, anticipating his question, "A vacation. I just need a phone and the number to a good wrecker." I hoped he would tell me that I was standing in the historical district and that there was a pay phone and a burger joint around the corner.

He didn't.

"A sojourner. Is that so?" His raised brow furrowed skeptically.

"I suppose so," I answered, now wary. "I was traveling with a girl and I really need to find her."

"Refugees arrive each day, it is true. Saints from all four corners of the earth. Yes, en masse." He strode around me, looking me up and down. "Men wandering alone through Clay County? Not often." He punctuated the *not often* part in such a way as to politely tell me he thought I was a big, fat liar. I disliked the courteous disputations when a sarcastic "not" would have made his point in a less passive-aggressive way.

"I wonder," I said, trying to gloss over LeJeune's latent challenge, "is there a phone nearby?"

Throwing his hands out in a what-are-are-you-talking-about sort of way, he said, "You have me, Mr. Richards. What is it you need?"

"A phone." Nothing. Not a synapse seemed to fire in LeJeune's head. "A telephone." I used the whole word as a last resort. I put my thumb in my ear and mimed into my pinkie.

He furrowed his brow and shook his head. "A traveler, as you claim to be, must realize that this is not New York City, nor is it London or Paris. This," he said smartly, "is the aptly named city of Far West, Missouri. We boast no telegraph machine here."

LeJeune's superior demeanor was mitigated by the return of the small guy in dark clothes who approached as quietly as a mouse and appeared at LeJeune's side. Excusing himself politely, LeJeune strode out of earshot temporarily. I was sure I was not free to leave, no matter how pleasant LeJeune was acting. Furthermore, I was sure that the fellow in dark clothes had been watching me, for how long I could only guess, and I cursed myself for not having noticed.

LeJeune finished his secret tryst and approached me with a broad, genuine smile. "Mr. Richards, my apologies. Had I known your true identity, I would have welcomed you straight away." LeJeune's shadow man disappeared again while I was wondering what the sudden change in character was about. LeJeune went on, "Brother Liddle sent word and vouches for your presence here. You must understand our present concerns." He gushed his apology and nearly got it all over my shirt.

Impressive, I thought. Either Liddle had a phone hidden in his dark cabin, or someone had followed me all the way from the mill.

"How did you . . ."

LeJeune interrupted, "You saved the life of one of my men. One of my best men. When you disappeared from the mill, Brother Liddle had you followed—with the intention of returning the favor, of course." He said this all very quickly in explanation.

I was followed all the way from the mill—what a dolt! And hey, where was this follower when I'd needed him at my truck?

"My apologies, but we must be ever vigilant," said LeJeune.

I silently accepted LeJeune's apology and I agreed with his notion of vigilance if Far West faced the same problems that existed at the mill.

I examined LeJeune and bet myself a staggering sum that nothing happened in this part of Missouri that LeJeune didn't know about. This was his town.

"Come with me, Mr. Richards," he said with a broad sweep of his arm.

"How could I refuse?" I answered with a smile. Indeed, could I have refused?

***

LeJeune tried to disguise a disparaging look at my clothes—mud covered and still wet—and escorted me to a building of brick and plank construction where the smell of fresh bread made my stomach growl like a she-bear.

I was shown into a two-room house, not much larger than Harry Liddle's cabin at the mill settlement. The windows were larger and allowed more light inside to reveal a sparsely decorated, but tidy interior. Two women worked over a kettle of stew simmering over a wood fire in the stone fireplace. A butcher-block table situated to one side of the first room was covered with cubed meat and vegetables destined to be a new batch of stew.

"This is a friend, Owen Richards, just recently in Far West." LeJeune made a small flourish with his arm, and two elderly ladies greeted me.

"Very nice to meet you," I said. The two women were apparently tasked with the feeding of the needy, who I learned were streaming into Far West to escape mob persecution. I was handed a bowl of watery stew and a thick slice of bread.

"Thank you," I said politely and with great sincerity.

"You are welcome, brother," said one of the women. "Already been blessed." Her smile was as warm and inviting as the homemade bread. She reminded me of Etta and, in fact, I could see Aunt Etta filling their role if she were here.

The other woman looked as if she was going to say something but LeJeune interrupted her, taking me by the arm. He led me out of the building, stew and all, bidding a curt farewell to the cooks.

Outside, LeJeune said, "We are feeding a great number of refugees, as you know. The logistics are a nightmare." He waved a hand at the city.

Far West was indeed a busy place. We were still near the center of town, near the large unoccupied city square.

LeJeune seemed intent on offering me the two-dollar tour, but I had other things on my mind. I took another healthy bite of bread, followed by my last spoonful of stew.

"Mr. LeJeune," I said, swallowing, "I was traveling with a girl, uh, a woman, Julianna. When I returned to my truck, she was gone. I don't mean any disrespect to you or your people—this is all very interesting—but I do need to find her and a phone. Just point me in the right direction and I'll be out of your way." I wanted to ask if there was any civilization nearby, but I thought it might be rude to imply that what LeJeune and his people were doing wasn't civilized.

LeJeune bit his lip and ran a finger across the brim of his hat. He said nothing, but it wasn't for lack of concern about my presence.

I tried a new tactic. "Is there a police department here?"

"Am I to understand that your companion, Julianna, is alone outside of Far West?" LeJeune asked in a distressed tone, ignoring my question.

"Well, yes. I mean, no. I don't know. I assume she went for help when I went to help Anna and Elias. She's probably looking for me, actually."

"You underestimate the danger in Caldwell County at present. A woman alone is in grave danger. Reports of mob raids in surrounding settlements arrive daily."

I cursed under my breath; I had to find Julianna.

After a short silence, LeJeune said, "I owe you a great debt, Mr. Richards. Anna, and Elias," he added as an afterthought, "mean a great deal to me. When did you see your companion last and exactly where?"

"She was at my truck, just north of the mill settlement. It was just before sundown. I assume she walked north toward the highway."

"There is no route north of the location you describe. However, if she went north, as you believe, she may well have skirted the danger." LeJeune touched his moustache. "There is no conceivable reason for mobs to be north of Jacob Haun's mill." LeJeune's mind ticked away at the problem. "Tell me, is your companion, Julianna, familiar with this area? I realize you told me you were simply a passing traveler," he added with a touch of sarcasm.

"Yes, she is very familiar with this area. In fact, she studies Mormon history and we were touring historical sites. She's a Mormon," I said to gain points.

LeJeune didn't say anything; he just looked at me with questioning eyes. He was a smooth interrogator.

"Excuse me," he finally said and turned to one of his minions who materialized like magic. They walked out of earshot and LeJeune spoke quietly in his ear. The other man nodded, turned on his heel and left. LeJeune walked casually back to me, tipping his hat to a passerby as he did so.

It occurred to me that I was surrounded by otherwise intelligent, industrious people affected by a mysterious communal ignorance about the modern world. Maybe they just chose to shut out the world.

"I am prepared to present your cause to my superiors, Mr. Richards."

"Shall I wait here?" I asked, probing.

LeJeune assumed an indignant expression. "You are free to explore the city as you feel necessary," he said.

I smiled and nodded; a cold breeze passed between us.

LeJeune excused himself to tend to more important matters, leaving me free to explore the city on my own. But freedom in Far West, it seemed, was a relative thing. As long as I chose to stay in Far West, I was sure I would be followed, and more savvy about this possibility now, I discovered my "shadow" almost immediately. After a short game of cat and mouse in which I would scuttle innocently down side streets and wait for him to catch up, I settled on a bench situated on the main thoroughfare.

I thought, as I looked out at the City Square, that I should be able to walk in any direction and hit a main highway. I knew there was a highway out there somewhere. I'd driven in on it. I'd go north, and from there I could hitch a ride and find Julianna in Kansas City—hopefully.

I wanted to lose my "tail" before leaving the city. The last thing I wanted was someone following me into the woods and making trouble.

He was behind me, in a predictable place, skulking on the shady side of a log dwelling. He wore a dark suit of coarse cloth with the jacket open in the front and no tie, and he was middle-aged with fine, stark features.

I stood up and started walking away from him. I took about twenty steps, stopped abruptly, and turned about face as if I'd forgotten something. Caught leaving his shadowy post, my tail paused for a moment and then turned to walk away from me at an angle. It made me smile. Tailing a suspect is easy as long as your suspect moves away from you. A foe that walks right at his tail really throws a monkey wrench in the works.

It was like herding a sheep. I walked in the direction of my pursuer long enough to get him moving away from me, and then I cut between a woodshed and a cabin and doubled back. When next I saw LeJeune's man, he was standing in the City Square with a puzzled look on his face, no doubt dreading the cursing he'd receive from his boss.

Too easy, I thought. I looked north and found a path that looked like it would take me straight out of the city. I followed it through a series of widely spaced cabins that gave way to less substantial dwellings of sod construction as I neared the city's outskirts. Further out, the people were living in temporary shelters of everything from tent canvas to lean-tos.

Near a worn wagon, a small girl sat on the ground, her legs sticking out from a dark brown, full-length dress. She looked at me with big, brown, fearless eyes, and addressed me as "brother." She was as cute as a little brown bug.

"Yes, darlin'," I answered.

"May I," she pointed with a shard of charcoal to the board on her lap and a small stack of rough-edged paper, "sketch your portrait?"

"Sketch me?"

"Yes, brother. My mother encourages me." A wan woman mending something looked at me with a warm, approving look.

The innocence in the little girl's dirty face and the sincerity of her smile won me over, and against my better judgement, I asked, "Does it take long?"

I was enchanted by the girl, but I still had Julianna to think about as well as Bart LeJeune. I didn't think he would hold me in Far West against my will, but he made me uneasy, and I didn't want to be spotted again by one of his men.

"Not long, only a moment of your time, sir," said the girl with a smile as she unveiled a fresh paper. "May I?"

"Hush, girl," her mother chided. "Sir, you need not be bothered by her insolence."

"No, ma'am. I would be honored." I looked around for LeJeune's men, and, not seeing them, I decided to model for the girl.

"What would you like me to do?" I asked, indulging the young artist.

She looked me over with an artist's eye, taking in elements I could only guess at. "You mustn't posture, sir. I can paint you by memory in whatever pose I choose. You need only stand for me to get a good look at you."

"Very well," I said as I adjusted the fanny pack at my waist and straightened my shirt. If I was to be immortalized, I didn't want to look like the village idiot.

"You like to draw, huh?" I asked, realizing too late that this was a silly question.

"Yes, sir," she answered, not looking up from her work.

"If I come back and bring a beautiful woman with me, would you draw her too?"

She looked up, excitement glowing on her face. "Yes, sir."

"It's a deal then. I'll bring you back a real model, as soon as I find her."

The little artist went back to her work, smiling.

"This is enough," she said. "You may come back this evening for the finished sketch."

"I'm leaving now, but if I do get back this way I'll collect my drawing. Perhaps I'll make it a gift to my friend. Now, what do I owe you?"

The little artist looked pleased and said, "I don't accept payment, sir."

"We'll see about that." The little girl and her mother both smiled. I dug into my fanny pack and pulled out a five-dollar bill. The little girl's eyes were wide. Digging deeper, I found a ten spot and gave that to her instead. She looked at it and gave it to her mother who examined the currency critically and stuffed it into a pocket in her dress.

"It will be finished this evening, sir," said the little girl.

I nodded and went on my way.

Having learned my lesson, I watched my back even after I'd made good distance from Far West. A tail was unlikely, but LeJeune seemed like a competent intelligence officer and fully capable of running Far

West as if it were Leningrad. His trustworthiness was a different matter; because of our amiable alliance, it was difficult to distinguish which of us held the other in the greatest contempt.

I escaped from the city, passing a bored-looking sentry who gave me only a cursory glance, and trudged across the grass. Not only was I wary of someone following me, but I kept a close eye on the horizon for the three Missourians who beat up Elias and chased me with the same intent.

I kept mostly to the open areas whenever possible, and hurried past the congested areas. The first two miles were uneventful, as the terrain changed very little. I discovered no highway and wasn't accosted by anyone.

As happens when one is engaged in a mundane task, I became more relaxed and began to think. *What had happened to Julianna? Had Elias survived the terrible beating? Who was Anna and what were her people all about?* Those questions and dozens more danced through my mind as I walked, and I conveniently pushed thoughts of danger out of my head. I kept telling myself to pay attention, but after the first few miles, I had completely convinced myself that I would soon find the highway and return to the real world. This was all so incredible . . . and unforgettable. My thoughts returned to Julianna. *Where was she?*

***

It was still early in the day and I was confident that I would be back to civilization before dark. I purged all thoughts that something dreadful had happened to Julianna and convinced myself that she was just as troubled about me as I was about her, and was waiting for me in Kansas City.

The prairie was like a giant quilt with patches of sod interrupted by picturesque little forests. Actually, some of the forested areas were vast expanses thick with trees. The grass had yellowed, despite the October rains, and most of the trees were brown and without foliage. As an idyllic landscape, it was peaceful and easy walking; as a tactical environment, it was perilous. The wide-open spaces left me vulnerable, and the density of the forested areas offered opportunities for ambush.

I had long ago measured my stride and calculated the average number of steps I took to the mile. It was a good way to estimate distance traveled by foot. However, it required the traveler to make an accurate calculation and then retain the number of steps per mile in his memory. Since I had not done either of these things, I took a wild guess that I'd gone about three miles due north. And, I hadn't found the highway.

My route north was ill defined; I hoped only that if I went far enough I would surely hit the highway and find the rest of the world thriving in spite of this lost civilization hidden in its midst.

The field grass was still wet with last night's rain and I carefully high stepped through it in a losing battle to keep my pant legs dry. The battle was soon lost and I trudged onward, demoralized in wet pants. But my feet and body were dry, which was no small consolation.

Relentless rain, as on the night before, might have made my circumstances less bearable and I was thankful for the relative warmth of the autumn sun. *Thankful to whom?* I wondered. Lewis had been so sure about things like that.

I crossed a great deal of territory, letting my mind wander, but for the majority of the time, my thoughts were of Julianna. I rather liked her.

She was obviously a practicing Mormon, but it gave her an innocent quality. She was thoroughly intelligent and stubbornly confident, which gave her an inner strength. And, she was attractive in the extreme. Her most appealing quality, what I liked best about Julianna, defied description. It was this quality that I thought about as I walked the prairie, still doggedly pursuing an east-west highway somewhere to the north.

What was it in Julianna's character that I liked so much? Was it poise, conviction? Perhaps it was her utter confidence in religion or her belief in a higher purpose to life. Maybe it was simply the product of her healthy self-esteem. Whatever the source, the quality was apparent every time she flashed a smile or raised her eyebrows at me. I was pacified by that thought, and I was confident that she hadn't panicked when I left her in the clearing to help Anna.

I was walking in an open area, slightly downhill, skirting a thick stand of trees to my right and thinking of Julianna when an ominous presence ran its icy fingers down my spine. *Get down.* I halted briefly, wondering what to do. *Get down. Get down.* I found myself unable to resist the strong, unmistakable admonition, and I lunged forward onto my stomach without another thought. At the same moment, a small gray plume billowed from the tree line fifty yards to my right. I caught a glimpse of it as I tumbled forward. I had buried my head in the grass by the time I heard the concussion of the rifle and the whip of a passing bullet. I heard a few distant whoops and hollers followed by the sound of baying dogs and the pounding of horses' hooves closing on my defenseless, prostrate form.

Plans for escape and evasion turned quickly to a plan for a peaceful surrender, followed by a plea for clemency from my attackers. The filthy Missourians I was expecting didn't show; instead, I was taken roughly into custody by smartly uniformed professional soldiers. They tied my arms behind me, draped a black sack over my head, and tied it tightly around my neck with a length of cord. My hands were efficiently tied behind my back. The bindings on my neck and hands were tight enough to hurt. I barely resisted claustrophobic panic.

The few glimpses I got of my attackers before I was bound corresponded to the rest of my experiences in Missouri. These men, too, were dressed in antiquated uniforms and carried vintage muzzle loaders. These firearms, however, were well cared for.

Curt orders were snapped out and a flurry of "yes sirs" followed each. I was hoisted heartlessly to the back of a sweating horse that reeled in a circle upon feeling my weight, thus conveniently confusing my sense of direction and making me nauseous. I couldn't even tell where I was being taken. Man alive, was I getting tired of these Missouri pukes!

CHAPTER 7

I was thus transported by horse for what felt like days, but what was more likely a matter of several hours. Lack of food might have made a grump of me, but lack of water left me too weak to complain. When I was finally jerked from my perch, I struck the ground hard, shoulder first.

I felt a searing pain that was replaced by a hot tingle after a few moments. With my hands still tied firmly behind me, it was difficult to determine the severity of the injury. Nothing felt broken, but it would certainly make a timely escape awkward.

I was dumped in a heap and given a firm order to stay put—I did it without argument. I waited in vain for the sack to be ripped from my head to reveal my whereabouts. I'd have no such luck. Not that it made any difference in what I could see, but I closed my eyes to better sense my surroundings. It was getting colder and I assumed it was late evening or nighttime. The camp smelled of horses, wood smoke, and the faint aroma of roasting meat. I hoped some was for me. I heard the jovial voices of men. I could hear fragments of several conversations, but they shed no light on my fate. Out of the din, I picked out the punch line to a ribald joke, a tale of wifely woes, and a lonesome song on a harmonica: typical soldier noise. Over those sounds, I could hear the unmistakable clanging of metal utensils on tin plates. I was in a camp.

I tried to sit up, but the stabbing pain in my shoulder left me nauseated from the effort. In the discomfort department, my chafed legs ran a close second to the pain in my shoulder. After several attempts to find comfort on the inflexible ground, I gave in and rested fitfully on my good shoulder, as the sound of dinner gave way to the sounds of a camp going to bed.

I suffered a long and sleepless night and was in no better mood when I heard the soldiers stirring, and smelled a revival of the wood smoke. The unmistakable smell of bacon reminded me that I hadn't eaten since the morning before. I'd have traded the bacon, however, for a precious drink of water.

Morning had me wondering about my fate, but nothing was revealed to me concerning my ultimate destiny until the camp was alive with sounds and everyone's fat belly was filled.

I was finally addressed by a rude, but cultured voice. "Get up," it said, heedless of the fact that I had not been able to accomplish that kind of feat without the use of my arms since junior high.

"Get up." This time I was compelled to do so by the assistance of a strong hand around my injured arm that had me on my feet faster than the blood could catch up to my head. I stood dazed for a moment, grimacing under my head cloth.

"This way," the voice said more sympathetically. I attempted a response, but my mouth was too dry and all that came out was a cough. I was led, blindly stumbling over the uneven ground, to a new place to sit that was no better than the first.

A new voice issued the command to unveil my face. I blinked back the sunlight as the sack was pulled off my head, and I squinted into the dark eyes of my interrogator. He was stout but not fat, large but not tall, and his clothing was well fitted and expensive looking, despite being a couple of hundred years out of date. His dark hair was streaked with silver, and he wore a well-trimmed beard of silver.

"I am Captain Samuel Bogart," he said as if his reputation was universally known.

I was anxious to tell my tale and be released, but I decided to say just my name. "Owen Richards."

"Yes." I did not know if that meant he already knew my name or if he was simply acknowledging me. "Recently of Far West," he added. "What was your destination yesterday?" he asked. He was polishing a silver and brass telescope and he looked at it rather than at me as he spoke.

I hoped that this might be a good time to let go with my story, but I decided that discretion was in order.

"Look. I was just passing through and got my rig stuck in the mud. I'm not part of any of this."

"You Mormon?" he asked directly, and then went back to his telescope.

"No," I said a little too quickly, although my sympathies lay squarely with the religious settlers. He met my denial with a disbelieving grimace.

"I see. What was your business in Far West, Mr. Richards?"

"Like I said, just looking to get my truck out of the mud."

"And you enlisted the aid of the Mormons as a first resort, after the unwarranted molestation of members of my militia? Is this what you want me to believe, Mr. Richards?"

I waited too long to answer and he took it as an admission of guilt. "I'm not a part of this," I said, my eyes icy. I'd had enough of this guy.

Completely disregarding my version of the truth, he bombarded me with the same kinds of questions with which my interrogation had begun. Where were you going and with what information? To whom do you report? And a host of similar questions were asked that left no doubt that Bogart considered me a spy.

It was a first for me, and I wondered what feuding Missourians usually did with spies. The prospects were grim, so I concentrated instead on repeating my denials, as futile as that turned out to be.

Bogart showed no outward signs of ire or frustration during the interrogation, but I suspected that he was inwardly raging. His eyes were a contradictory mix of vacancy and animation without kindness, empathy, or humanity, and were alive with amoral depravity and malignancy. The force of his leadership was obvious, and his people either respected or feared him. Perhaps both.

I matched him stare for stare, using the precious moments to take in what I could of the camp. The soldiers around me were well uniformed and obedient; they were a stark contrast to the other Missourians with whom I was acquainted. There were a few yokels wandering about the fringes of the camp, but, like second-class citizens, they deferred to the professional soldiers among them.

I was sitting outside a drab, brown canvas tent like most of the others I could see, but much larger. Bogart appeared to have his own staff and a lot of equipment. His clothing and personal effects were collected along the side of his tent in pine boxes with rope handles. In one such box was my fanny pack, unopened. *I'll never see it again*, I thought.

"Take him back," Bogart said calmly. A rough hand grabbed me by the hair and pulled back my head. Another set of hands was forcing the sack over the top of my head.

"Separate him from the others," Bogart barked.

I jerked my head to the side, avoiding the bag.

"Others?" I asked, glaring.

Bogart simply smiled and nodded to his henchmen, who bagged my head.

I was brusquely dragged away and placed unceremoniously back on the ground. I wanted desperately to know who the others were. In fact, knowing I was not alone was a minor victory and did much to lift my morale. I learned by listening to soldiers' gossip that the unit that had efficiently and swiftly kidnapped me was part of the Missouri Militia. They were clearly antagonistic to the Mormons, thus the rampant paranoia in Far West. I learned nothing about the other prisoners.

The problems I'd witnessed so far took on staggering dimensions when I thought about the number of loyal Bogartites collected here. I was now certain that the intense religious harassment, if exposed to world scrutiny, would rival any other international scandal currently under popular press investigation.

I spent the rest of the day in a pile on the ground—ignored. I moved occasionally, hands still tied, to work out the stiffness, and although my instincts told me I was under guard, there was no actual evidence to corroborate my suspicions.

My tongue swelled from dehydration, and when I thought I could hear the din of lunch, I croaked into the blackness for water. I was rewarded moments later by kick to the gut, just forceful enough to take the wind out of me. I reeled on the ground as quietly as I could and decided that silence was probably my best course of action.

I longed for my fanny pack. It had been stripped away immediately after my capture, and the thought of it among Bogart's possessions made me forlorn. It contained a folding knife, a flashlight, pepper spray, a leftover chocolate brownie from an MRE, and, most importantly, my pistol. Wish in one hand and spit in the other. I hadn't the spit to spare anyway.

I mentally patted myself on the back, though, for memorizing what I could of the camp while I could see. I visualized the camp and tried to place key features in my mind. Tents spotted the area, at least a hundred, and maybe more. They were strung in haphazard lines at the base of a long steep hillside on a gentle slope that led down toward the steep mud banks of what I had overheard was Crooked River. The river ran in a deep ravine, mud on both sides. Tall grass and trees grew from the ground water on the banks and followed the river as it meandered along less than a hundred yards from camp. There was no real cover from a hillside attack except the banks of the river, which would have made a natural defensive battlement had Bogart placed his men on the southern side. A frontal attack and a flanking maneuver from either side of the river bottom would see the camp in ruins. Now all I needed was the cavalry.

The tactical disadvantage of the site was obvious and I wondered what unseen motive had persuaded a man as seemingly capable as Bogart to rally his troops in such a vulnerable place.

The men carried weapons that were at least a hundred years out of date. Those who had no rifles were armed with curved cavalry swords, ancient pistols, and wide-brimmed hats; the lot of them looked fit to harass only defenseless settlers, which seemed the order of the day. I assumed from the activity I could hear in camp that small patrols and sentries came and went; it was a pattern that would make escape more difficult. The camp seemed organized though, however antiquated it was.

Why me? was a sentiment I'd grown out of as a child (perhaps as a young adult), but my subconscious dredged up vestiges of these emotions and marshaled them for a mental parade. I would have liked to brag that my years as a police officer could see me through dire circumstances, making mere kidnapping, bound arms, and starvation pale in comparison, but I could not. My mental litany went something like this: *Oh my shoulder; I'm hungry; I can't see; my wrists hurt; Where's Julianna?;* and so on until the pattern had repeated itself several thousand times. Between plaintive sighs, I wondered if I would shrivel to death from lack of water, or drown in self-pity—it was a toss-up.

The day passed, and night replaced it. I slept in snatches and woke, as I had the day before, to the sounds of the camp waking up. This morning though, I was not taken for interrogation. I was beaten.

The militia men who worked me over left no kind of brutality neglected. The cloak over my head was much like a small black pillowcase kept in place by a tightly wrapped hemp rope. The sack prevented me from seeing my assailants, so I could tell neither who nor how many participants amused themselves at my expense. I thought to keep track of voices, but that option extinguished itself as survival instincts took over. By the time the last boot sent stars running across the horizon behind my closed eyes, I could remember little except my own inward pleading for the torture to stop. I pled silently to Lewis's God, since he seemed like the only God I really knew, albeit vicariously. I thought about the little blond girl at Lewis's funeral and about her faith. But she was only a child. How could she know? I put her out of my mind and prayed while my body was brutalized.

Whether the beating had been the result of malice and opportunity or a disciplinary event sanctioned by the camp authorities, I had no idea. I'd been struck with fists, clubs, and mostly boots. Vile threats were made, the veracity of which was manifest by the intensity of the battering. My clothes were rent to expose my body and I felt the warm sting of urine splatter over my body. Hurt and demoralized, all I could do was pray.

The answer to my prayers came at the end of the thrashing in the form of my still-beating heart. The battering had been so thorough that I couldn't tell what hurt or where, and I ached fiercely. My tongue was so swollen that I had begun to chew it, yet I found myself mouthing a prayer of gratitude. I was still alive.

I lay all day as if dead, and no sympathetic hand wasted the time to check for a pulse. Panic allayed itself only long enough to allow my senses to clear, at which time I realized that another beating would likely kill me. I was powerless to prevent it: blind, injured, and tightly bound. Physical exhaustion, dehydration, and hunger sapped what was left of my strength after the severe beating and with it, any resolve to escape.

The second beating, of which I was only marginally aware, occurred in the dark of the night, long after the sounds of the retiring camp turned quiet. It was less severe than the first, and began abruptly with a kick to my ribs that roused me from a confused stupor. Again, I turned a moment of panic into resolve through fervent prayer, an image of the faithful little girl at Lewis's funeral burned into what was left of my shattered memory. Curling into a fetal ball, I gave myself as much protection as I could.

The beating ended and the night became quiet again. I heard sobbing and it took me several moments to realize that I was the one crying. I felt disembodied—numb, and I was sure that death was near. I lay like that for what could have been a hundred hours or a hundred years. I didn't care.

"Water?" a whispering voice softly breached the solitude. I ignored it. "Water?" I felt a careful hand under my neck. I had not the energy to acknowledge it. Gentle hands tipped my head back, and cool water was poured though the sack. I sucked up all that soaked through.

"Thank you," I rasped, regaining my faculties.

"Remember, Owen, this is but a small moment. Endure it well." The voice was low and soothing, as soothing as the water.

"Thank you," I said again.

"Fear not," he whispered.

He poured more water and let some spill on my neck. It stung where I was rubbed raw, but it cooled the worst of the pain.

I thanked him again and despite trying hard not to, I started to sob quietly in his arms.

He took me by the hand. "Our prayers are with you, and we are many."

I'd felt it no more than twice before: a sweet burning in my chest. It was strong this time, much stronger than before. It was so strong in actuality that I thought it should hurt, but it was pure comfort and I basked in it like a warm bath, letting the feeling wash over me.

"Lewis?" I finally asked, but he was gone. It couldn't have been Lewis, could it? It just reminded me of him.

I was left lying on the ground much as before, except the anguish of numerous injuries was miraculously gone. I lay back again, wondering if my visitor was of heaven or of earth, and not much caring which.

***

I wasn't sure if I first heard shouting or the report of a rifle, but by whatever stimulus, Bogart's camp became a hive of activity and panic as a score of far-off rifles shattered the night's silence. Curses and the rattling of ramrods into hot rifle barrels followed. A voice, infused with rage and vengeance, bellowed an order to charge. By the sounds of their hurried footfalls, it seemed that Bogart's troops quickly retreated into the river bottom and established a line behind the natural breastwork. I imagined that the attacking force made a line as I heard another volley exchanged. During a lull, a voice rang out in the valley, "God and liberty."

I tried to get up and fell. I pulled at the ropes binding my hands but was unable to free myself. I stopped and told myself I could think my way out of this, not bull my way out. I lay still and listened.

The earthen breastwork would have provided the mob with adequate protection from the attack, but it sounded as if the attackers were advancing on both flanks along the river. The sounds of the battle moved toward the river and beyond as if the Missourians had crossed Crooked River in retreat. The clanking of swords meant hand-to-hand combat, and derisive shouts began to issue from both sides.

It was fruitless to try and think my way out, so I put the bull method to work again. I pulled strenuously at the cords that bound my hands, heedless of the tearing flesh around my wrists. I stretched the cords enough to gain an inch at best between the backs of my hands. I tried to stand again, with the hope of running away from the fray. I just couldn't. I rolled over again and felt a lump under me that hadn't been there before. I groped until my hands touched the lump, and I immediately recognized my fanny pack, no doubt left there by my mysterious helper.

The front zippered pouch still contained my knife that was designed to be opened with one hand. The serrated blade passed through the hemp cords without effort, and the rest seemed to fall off by itself. My hands were free for the first time in two days. I ripped the sack off my head and cast it aside triumphantly.

My ears had not deceived me, and what I saw closely matched what I had heard. Encouraged at the accuracy of my senses, but unsure if my fatigued legs could carry me, I watched the melee for an opportunity to hobble safely away in the confusion. I checked the fanny pack for its contents and miraculously found everything accounted for.

Bogart's men had retreated across the river and were now running in panic through the fields to the south.

The fury of the battle passed by me quickly. The unearthly yells and pleas for mercy died slowly in the prairie on the far side of the river.

I straightened my legs with difficulty and pulled myself up precariously. When an opportunity presented itself, I ran awkwardly in painful lunges.

The rifle reports were intermittent now, but several men went down as stray rounds found targets in the confusion. One man was taken in the face by a bullet and fell instantly. Another was running awkwardly through two feet of river water in pursuit of a mobber. The Missourian reached the dry ground of the other side and turned suddenly, raised a pistol at his pursuer, and fired. One of my rescuers was lost.

I made my way cautiously toward the river and the safety of the tall rushes. I did not jump, but rolled over the steep banks of the river into the cold water.

I felt relatively safe huddled in the reeds along the river. Lacking the adrenaline that had rushed through my veins during the escape, I was now too sore to move on. At some point while I lay in the waist-deep water, the sounds of the battle turned into the sounds of the aftermath. Men sought comrades who had been lost in the confusion, and the soft murmurs of the injured could be heard on the breeze as they mingled with my own inner murmurs.

I hadn't planned my escape any further than just making it to the river, but I resolved to remain hidden and eventually make my way west on foot until I reached something akin to civilization. For the moment, however, I was content just to hide.

Still under the cover of the rushes, I pulled myself out of the water and drew my knees up to preserve warmth. I shivered softly as the dawn turned to midday. It was clear and bright, but the sun did little to take the chill from my body. At some point during the morning, I decided I had to move or succumb to hypothermia. The sounds of men along the riverbanks had long since ceased and I doubted if anyone was still around. The attacking party rallied soon after the charge, and marched north away from the river. Under the circumstances, it was impossible to tell who they were and what precipitated their hostilities. I considered surrendering to whomever attacked the camp, but I could take no more abuse from the miscreants in this forsaken part of northern Missouri.

A human noise, a voice softly calling a name, snapped me out of my stupor. I dropped my head and hugged my knees tighter, hoping I wouldn't be seen.

"Rolly?" the voice called. "Rolly." The voice sounded worried and insistent at the same time.

A protracted silence followed before a wearied voice answered. "It's me. John, is that you?"

"Rolly," answered a relieved voice.

They were close to me, moving slowly toward each other. They may have been within twenty yards. My only concealment was the vegetation along the riverbank.

"Rolly, I been lookin' for ya."

"I'm hurt, John. Real hurt. It's my arm and chest."

"You don't worry none, Rolly. I'll care for ya."

"Where'd they all go, John? I haven't heard a thing in hours."

"South, mostly. Some went east. I don't know. There's a group forming up river that's set on going east to Livingston County. There's talk of raiding that little mill place on Shoal Creek. Revenge, Rolly. We're gonna rid the county a Marmons, Rolly: men, women and children."

"Help me up, then."

I heard the two men rustle off upstream and I relaxed slightly as they left, wondering if Rolly would make it. I feared leaving the protection of the bank because I couldn't trust that other men weren't also hiding or recovering from their wounds nearby. I spent the rest of the morning sitting in the mud, curled in a ball. By mid-morning I was shivering. I was so cold. Eventually, I would have to move, if only to dry off and find better cover.

Just before the sun reached its zenith, I clawed my way up the bank of the river. The remnants of the militia camp were strewn all over the countryside. It looked as if an elephant stampede had charged right through the middle. *They'll be back.* The thought hit me suddenly. *Get moving, Owen.*

I stayed at the camp just long enough to drink water I found in a cup. I remembered the brownie in my fanny pack and I ate half of it. My teeth were sore.

My head felt like it was full of cobwebs, and every major joint was stiff. One of my eyes was partially shut and I could feel the swelling along my brow line. I tucked my thumb into my belt to take the weight off of my wounded shoulder. I limped perceptibly on both legs as I walked away from camp. The thought of the sight of me made me laugh; freedom was certainly liberating.

I have to go north, I thought, looking for the mountains to orient me. They weren't there. I needed my friend Mac's little geo satellite thingy-majig. He carried it everywhere with him. I wouldn't tease him anymore when I got back to work—if I got back to work. I thought, too, about Julianna's joke of telling directions by looking at the sun. Little did I know how apt her humor would turn out to be, or how intensely I would miss her and worry about her. With Julianna in mind, I set out again.

***

I estimated the path of the sun in the sky and made a crude guess at a northerly route. The terrain before me was unfamiliar, but it was not much different than what I'd seen so far in Missouri. The countryside swelled and was a patchwork quilt of open grassy areas and forests of various densities.

I faced the same tactical disadvantage as when I left Far West; I had to either move through open terrain past thick vegetation where an enemy could be concealed, or beat the bushes in the forested areas. Sacrificing time in favor of safety, I decided to make my way through the forested areas as much as possible.

My other challenge was the cold. I'd spent two nights without a blanket or coat and I was now wet. I was too weak and too sore to raise my body temperature through physical exertion. I limped, shivered, and looked over my shoulder.

Picking my way through the lifeless tree branches, I moved ungracefully in short bursts. I stopped often to listen, hoping to hear potential danger before walking headlong into it. During one of my rest-and-listen stops, I retrieved the leftover half of brownie from my fanny pack. I struggled with the front zipper, trying to grasp the small tag with my shivering fingers. I finally got the brownie in hand and stuffed it into my mouth, crumbling most of it onto the ground. My hands shook violently and I realized that I was dangerously cold and dehydrated. This realization sent a stream of adrenaline into my blood and I shook even more violently.

Movement was the only thing I could think about. I decided to chance it and move in the open areas. I hoped to find the help I desperately needed, but fatigue and self-doubt eroded my resolve. I should have stayed by the river, I told myself. I should have hailed someone during the attack and taken my chances that they were friendly forces. I shouldn't have gotten involved. I should have stayed in Salt Lake.

I set my course by establishing landmarks ahead of me, only to find that I couldn't keep a straight bearing. Each time I stopped to check my progress, I found that I didn't recognize my surroundings. I walked in large arcs and lost my sense of direction more than once. I was too cold.

I was barely conscious by the time I fell forward on the ground. I was shivering violently and a vicious headache prevented clear thought. I called out for Lewis but could only muster soft groans that faded into the blackness of what was either night or death. I couldn't tell and I didn't care.

**

"Mr. Richards." The sound in my ear was fraught with urgency and I wanted it to go away. "Mr. Richards."

It was several minutes before I realized that everything was shaking. Now what? *An earthquake*, I thought.

"Mr. Richards." The voice was near panic so I slowly fought for consciousness. The ground shook more vigorously, hurting my shoulder terribly.

"Mr. Richards. Please."

I realized that the ground wasn't really moving, but that a man with familiar eyes was shaking my shoulders trying to wake me. When he saw my eyes open, relief registered on his face and he stopped rousting me.

"Thank you, Elias," I whispered.

"I've been looking for you, Mr. Richards."

"I mean, thank you for stopping with the shake therapy."

"Oh, yes. Of course, Mr. Richards."

By the time I reached full awareness, Elias had a fire burning. It was dusk and the sky was just giving up its bright orange sunset. Elias had been dripping water into my mouth from a dirty piece of cloth. I wondered where the cloth had been, but I needed the water so I didn't make an issue of it.

"Mr. Richards. I thought you had been taken with the mob in the retreat."

"That was us? I mean, you? You attacked the camp?" I pushed the dripping cloth away for a moment.

"Not I. No, sir. Captain David Patten rallied the men and led the charge. I was with the rear guard. I made off in the confusion to look for you."

"How did you know I would be there?" I asked.

"I was not sure, but Brother LeJeune said you had been taken."

That rascal had had me followed, despite my attempts to shake the tail. I'd underestimated just about everyone in the county and I was getting sick of it.

"LeJeune knew? Where was he when I needed him?" I grumbled under my breath.

"Pardon me, Mr. Richards?" Elias asked innocently.

"Nothing," I groused.

"We had no way of rescuing you," Elias said, as if he'd heard my complaint. "We tracked you to Crooked River. Three other brethren were also hostages."

"The others," I whispered. "Did they escape?"

"Yes, sir," said Elias, straightening his jacket. "They were rescued."

"Good work Elias," I said. "I owe you one."

"On the contrary, Mr. Richards. I believe this makes us even."

"I suppose so," I said and changed the subject. "Have you seen Julianna, the woman I was with?"

"No, sir. I'm sorry. Brother LeJeune sent out a search party, but they came back when we raised the rescue party for you and the others."

"We've got to find her, Elias."

"Not yet. Meaning no disrespect, but you've got to get warm."

Elias helped me out of my wet clothes and propped me by the fire. When I finally got a good look at him, I saw a familiar face covered with purple, green, and yellow blotches; his bruises were healing and his smile mitigated the pity I felt for him. Besides, my face probably looked the same, or would in a few days.

I eventually pulled myself together mentally and took stock; I did an "appreciation," as the SWAT guys would say. Elias had enough food to get us back to Far West in fair shape. I had my pistol and could put up an adequate defense should the need arise, and if the other side stuck to muskets and primitive rifles. Elias was healing well and could help me along. I was worse for wear, and I could do nothing productive with my injured shoulder. But I could walk, given a few minutes to get to my feet.

"It's getting late," I said to Elias who was putting the remainder of his hard rolls and jerked beef in a small leather satchel. "I must have lost a day, somehow."

"You sleep," he said simply.

"We'll take turns. You get some shut-eye and I'll wake you when I'm tired." I knew we'd be better off if we both started fresh in the morning.

Elias looked at me with a grin. "You're a peculiar man, Mr. Richards."

"Owen," I said.

"Owen," he repeated and curled up by the trunk of a tree.

I was still tired, but not too sleepy. I spent some time trying to stretch sore muscles and test injured joints. My legs were merely bruised and would work loose in time. I thought about ways to immobilize my shoulder, and decided that the old thumb-in-the-belt loop trick was about as effective as anything. I didn't want to bother with a sling.

My face, in particular my jaw, was still tight and swollen, which made eating difficult. I moistened bread with water and sucked it down, and even this meager fare made me feel better. My body was starving for protein, but the jerked beef was too much for my injured jaw. I did, however, put a small piece on my tongue and sucked it. It tasted great.

I spent the next six hours breaking off little bits of jerky and savoring them in my mouth. I heard the usual night sounds, and occasionally my heart raced when I heard something close by. In each case, the sound turned out to be a passing animal, and after I learned to distinguish those sounds, I relaxed.

My watch said it was after midnight, and I was becoming sleepy. I nudged Elias awake and he graciously assumed night watch duty. I squirmed into a comfortable position and closed my eyes. I lay that way for several minutes before Elias's voice interrupted.

"Mr., uh, Owen? Are you still awake?"

"Uh huh."

"Forgive me for asking, but they say you are not to be completely trusted. I just wondered . . ."

"Who said that?" I asked.

"Brother LeJeune and some of the others. They mean no disrespect, I can assure you," he said defensively.

"None taken. I can't blame them."

"And, I would like to know more about you. They haven't asked me to spy on you. I'm just curious," Elias said meekly.

I answered, "I'm from Salt Lake City. I was out here visiting some historical sights with an old friend." The mention of her made me anxious. "I never dreamed anyone like you would be out here."

"Like me?"

"Yes, like all of you. What gives here? I mean, you guys act like you're not even part of the civilized world."

"Pardon me, Mr. Richards, the west is a rough place. In time, we'll settle this area. You'll see. Until then, it won't do any good complaining about it."

There was a long silence, during which I regretted having slighted Elias and his people.

"Where is Salt Lake City?" Elias asked, apparently forgiving me.

"In Utah. You ever hear of Utah?" I laughed.

"No, sir." Elias's face was without guile.

"You've never heard of Utah? The Great Salt Lake? Temple Square? The Jazz?"

Elias's face looked puzzled. "No, sir."

I shook my head and smiled. "I'm a police officer there. It's a fairly large city. It's kind of in the middle of the west, so it's a big hub. It has a big airport, universities, one of the best hospitals in the country, and a pro basketball team. The city used to be exclusively Mormons, in the early days. I'd say it's about twenty-five percent now, give or take, though it's still the center of Mormonism."

"Mormonism?" Elias asked.

"Sure, every Mormon on the planet knows where Salt Lake City is. Except you."

"How many Mormons?" he asked.

"Thousands," I said flatly, not really knowing how many Mormons lived in the valley.

Elias was quiet for a long time. He was a good kid, I could just tell. He was eager and loyal and had not an ounce of malice in his soul. I wondered what had brought him and his sister to this place, especially from Boston where Anna said they had come from. What had drawn them to such a forgotten part of Missouri?

"Elias," I said, "I really want to know what's going on with the people here. I'm a part of this, now. I feel like you owe me at least enough to tell me."

"Tell you what?"

I tried to lean up and grimaced. Elias moved closer to make it easier for me to see him.

"Tell me why you people are living out here like earth muffins and feuding like hillbillies. If you're having legal problems with your neighbors, call the police. Call the FBI." I thought about that for a moment and said, "On second thought, don't call the FBI."

"But we've sent emissaries to the state and federal governments and they ignore us. We have lobbied for peace. We've been chased from place to place. Some say now is the time to make our stand. Some say that we should answer bloodshed with bloodshed. Some say this is where we should stand or fall."

It occurred to me that this boy believed what he'd been telling me. I'd assumed that the lifestyle choices being made by these people were intentional, but I no longer thought that was the case. Something very different appeared to be going on in this part of Missouri. A chill tickled the hairs on the back of my neck as I considered the possible alternative explanations.

The most plausible explanation was also the most outlandish: brainwashing on an unheard-of scale. I didn't know enough about such things to rule it out, but it seemed highly unlikely that so many people engaged in a such a furious disagreement could be kept in this state of mind. Logically, pure emotions would eventually combat whatever brainwashing method was at work here. Yet, Elias showed no signs of wavering. And, it seemed, he enjoyed a great deal of freedom among the Mormons, a condition I considered unlikely if he were being controlled by an outside force; and, for what possible advantage? Any good cop would have told me to look for the money. Who had something to gain by causing an entire community to re-fight a war that was fought and forgotten over a hundred years ago? *Maybe I'm just sick in the head*, I thought.

"Are you well, Brother Owen?" Elias asked, giving me a worried once-over. "May I call you Brother?"

"What? Oh, yes. I was just thinking. And, yes you may."

"It's better if you sleep now," he said with some concern. "I'll keep the watch. Sleep well, Brother."

Not likely, I thought, but I instantly slipped off to sleep.

The next noise I heard was the panicked voice of Elias rousing me from a fitful sleep on the ground that had grown harder by the hour.

"Brother Owen, Brother Owen. Get up."

I made a guttural noise from deep in my throat and opened my eyes.

"Brother Richards." Elias's voice was lower and quieter but no less urgent. "Shh," he warned.

I heard the voices too.

CHAPTER 8

"Stay down," Elias ordered, his concentration firmly fixed on whatever lurked in the predawn darkness.

I heard the noise, too, and recognized it as voices, but I couldn't hear well enough to determine the identities or motives of the speakers. If they were simply a couple of farmers out to survey their fields, they would pass us by in the darkness, but how many local farmers would be out at such a time? Fearing the worst, I rolled up onto my knees and drew my pistol. The possibility of impending combat produced an intensity of purpose within me that momentarily displaced my pain and fatigue.

"Shh," Elias coaxed.

Until that moment I hadn't noticed that the ground was covered with dry leaves that crackled when I shifted my weight from one leg to the other.

Elias turned toward me and looked at the weapon in my hand; then we made eye contact. I could tell that he sensed my resolve, but all I could see in *his* eyes was trepidation. He glanced furtively toward the dense forest beyond the fringe where we stood, and motioned with his head. I shook mine. Perhaps in his condition, he could move quickly and quietly into the depths of the forest and disappear. I could not.

I was so dizzy I could hardly sit up, let alone stand. I gestured to my legs and hoped he understood what I meant. I was in no shape to travel; I would have to be firm.

I nodded to him, indicating that he should move into the woods. I made a semicircle with my free hand and hoped he would understand that I wanted him to flank. I thought his eyes registered under-standing, but it was difficult to tell in the darkness, and he didn't move right away. Instead, he took a deep breath. He was afraid; he was a bright boy.

He eventually moved into the woods in a suitable direction. He made less noise than I would have made moving through the trees and I didn't think he'd been heard. He didn't have a weapon, but he was well out of my field of fire and near enough to help me if I needed him.

I strained my ears toward the voices again. They were nearer now and I could hear them perfectly.

"Ye can't read sign in the dark, I tell ye. Yer a fool," said one of the voices from the clearing.

I recognized the voice of Fatface immediately. Of all the voices in Caldwell County, Missouri, his was the last I could have wished for.

"You were supposed to keep an eye on 'im, not me."

I assumed this was the voice of one of the cohorts who was with Fatface when they beat Elias half to death. I thought it might have been the tall one with the greasy mop of long, blondish hair.

"What d'ya see over there?" asked Fatface.

"Jist a minute. Come over here? Smell that?" asked a third voice.

I knew immediately what he smelled and I looked at our fire that had long since burned down, but was undoubtedly still smoldering enough to lead a good nose to us.

These were relentless, heartless people whom I'd consistently underestimated. I wouldn't let their antique rifles and their old-fash-ioned clothes fool me anymore. I was in a desperate fix with few options, and I had mere moments left to philosophize.

The sound of breaking branches and crackling leaves was very close. My little smoldering campfire would soon be surrounded. Instinctively, I scooted up against a tree, still on my knees, and raised my pistol to a low, ready position. The speed of my already-racing heart increased even more when I saw flashes of movement in front of me and to my left.

I took a deep breath to calm my nerves.

***

It was all over so fast. I'd never shot anyone before, although I'd been in situations where maybe I should have. When the first Missourian came into view, stalking carefully through the trees, he immediately drew his rifle into his shoulder and pointed it at me. I put two rounds into his chest and one in the center of his forehead in the same time it took for him to fire one wild round in my direction.

Even before he fell to the ground, I was assessing my next threat. Another Missourian, rifle ready, crashed through the brush into the small clearing. My pistol bucked twice more and his evil grin was covered by a crimson mask.

While all this must have occurred in mere seconds, it seemed infinitely longer. In times of intense stress, the mind races, yet events seem to occur in slow motion. Seconds seem like minutes, and minutes seem like hours.

It seemed like it was a long time later when I saw the third man skulking along the clearing, oblivious to me. He was whispering the names of his partners in a forlorn and lonely voice.

I let him walk until his back was to me. "Idiot City—population one, and that's you," I said under my breath just before bellowing a challenge. "Police. Don't move. Don't speak."

He stopped in his tracks and turned suddenly, locking his eyes on mine. Except for the malevolence apparently aimed at all things Mormon, his gaze was largely vacant. He looked from me to my gun and back, his upper lip curling like a snarling dog's. He held his rifle by the forestock in his left hand; I clearly had the drop on him.

He held his gaze long enough to try to intimidate me, then reluctantly tore it away to look at one of his dead companions resting in the fallen leaves. I held the sights of my pistol steady, aligned and aimed at the center of his chest. When he looked back at me, the depth of his hatred had intensified.

I recognized him right away. It was Fatface, the same filthy Missourian who'd administered the vicious and brutal beating to Elias. But he was alone now and in peril of hellfire if he made any move against me.

"Put the rifle on the ground," I said without emotion. "If you make a move, I'll kill you, too." I'd made many arrests at gunpoint, and I'd probably made that same threat once or twice in the heat of battle, but I'd never meant it with as much conviction as I did at that moment. I meant it for me and all I'd endured over the last week, for Elias and the beating he'd taken, for the Mormons who'd been severely abused at the hands of these Missourians, and especially for Lewis who had died unjustly because of scum like this.

He lowered his rifle and placed it gently on the ground at his feet. Then he turned to face me. Normally, I would have ordered him to face away and lie down. But when I looked him fully in the face, encountering once again his wide, evil grimace, I decided it was *my* turn to stare. His resolve weakened, and he began to make furtive eye movements as if he were going to run. I'd seen it before on the street. You could always tell when someone was going to run.

I could have killed him as he turned, but I let him go. He would probably kill again, or be killed trying. Fatface, the backwoods Missourian, and Raymond Hunt, my best friend's murderer—they were both alike. They killed when it suited them, with no thought for the loved ones left behind to mourn. Through some unimaginable deficiency of human virtue, life was not precious to their kind. I should have killed him, but I couldn't.

Elias appeared after Fatface's footfalls faded into the night. His face held a worried expression as he scanned the bodies of the dead Missourians. He looked at me and I indicated with a nod that I was all right.

"They will not let this rest," he said flatly. He picked up the rifles beside the dead men, and then retrieved the one placed on the ground by Fatface, and examined them.

He repeated what he'd said before. "They will not let this rest. More will come, and more after that. We cannot stay here."

My tired and sore body wanted to believe he was wrong, but my intellect told me he was right. "Help me up." I pointed at the bodies. "Anything we can use?" Elias searched through the men's pockets and pouches.

"Nothing of value, at least to us," he said.

Elias picked up the rifles and jammed the barrels into the wet Missouri dirt several times. Then he threw them into the brush where they wouldn't be found. He turned to me and helped me balance on my stiff legs.

"Thank you. I'll loosen up in a few minutes." I looked at what I thought was north and took a step.

"This way." Elias turned me by the shoulders.

Cursed flat land, I thought. *Where was Julianna's blazing sphere when I needed it?*

We walked until the rising sun began to warm the autumn air. Except for asking a couple of times about the state of my health and giving a few directions, Elias had been silent. I was walking quite well when he finally started talking. My mind had been more occupied with the dead bodies than with Elias's silence, so I welcomed the opportunity to get my mind on something new.

"That's an interesting weapon," Elias said cautiously.

"What weapon is that?" I asked.

"Your pistol. May I see it?"

I retrieved it from my fanny pack, unloaded it, and handed it to him, handle first. He stopped walking and gave the pistol his full attention, turning it all around in his hands and examining each side.

"Inspected by number fifty-four," I said.

"Pardon me?"

"You look like an inspector at a firearms plant. Inspector fifty-four." I laughed.

Elias didn't seem to get it but it didn't matter because he was far more intent on studying my pistol than worrying about my failing sense of humor.

"I would like to shoot it sometime. I have never seen its like."

"It's Austrian," I explained. "It's a little unique because it's made of plastic—polymer or something. It's top-rack safe."

"Pardon me?" he said again, this time showing real interest in what I was saying.

"You know, dishwasher safe. Top rack. That means it's pretty sturdy."

He shook his head slowly and shrugged.

"Never mind," I said. "The slide and barrel are steel. The parts are interchangeable, which makes sense for police departments and armies. There are better guns out there, smoother and more finely machined, but none better for the kind of work I do."

Elias nodded and looked inquisitively at the pistol.

"Let's rest a minute," I said. I took the gun from Elias and we sat down just inside the perimeter of a small grove of trees. "It comes apart really easily." I took the slide off the handle and dropped the barrel into Elias's hand. He ran his fingers across the smooth, machined surface and then took the handle from me for more inspection.

As best I could, I told him what each part did and how the pistol worked. Like a good student, he listened without speaking, waiting to ask his questions.

"Where do you put the powder in?"

I had assumed too much about his knowledge of modern firearms. I held one of the nine-millimeter rounds in my fingers and gave Elias another lesson: primer, powder, casing, bullet, cartridge.

Elias was a quick study and grasped each concept without much trouble.

"So," he said, "the force of the . . ." He thought for a moment.

"Recoil," I prompted.

". . . of the recoil makes the slide move backwards and allows another bullet . . ."

"Round," I corrected.

". . . round to come up from the magazine to be loaded into the chamber. Then it is ready to fire again." He looked up at me with a proud smile.

"Exactly."

"You fire eighteen times before you have to reload?"

"Give or take."

"And what is involved in making one of the rounds? How long does it take?" he asked.

"I don't know," I said. "I buy them at the store. Or, actually, these were supplied by the department. I haven't bought my own ammo since I was twenty-one."

Elias was toying with the magazine, taking rounds in and out like I'd shown him. I told him that I had a bunch of magazines in my truck, and an extra in the front zippered compartment of my fanny pack, and that it took about a second and a half to reload. He shook his head in amazement.

I had Elias put the weapon back together and showed him how to rack the slide to chamber a round. I holstered the pistol in my fanny pack and had Elias hoist me into a semierect position to resume our trip. We talked about police work in Salt Lake City and Elias didn't stop asking naive questions until well past noon.

The exploration into Elias's naivete kept me from thinking about the two men I had killed only hours before. My spirit, like my body, was injured beyond comprehension, and as I limped slowly alongside Elias, I tried to think about anything except the pain, both physical and emotional.

"I never really got to ask you how you found me, anyway." I pulled at Elias's shoulder and we both sat in the grass for a rest.

"I came with the rescue party," Elias said without further explanation.

I gave him a smile. "Yeah, but how did you find me? The rescue party left the area long before you happened by."

Elias frowned and looked a little embarrassed. "I was told to stay with the horses at the crossroads about a mile from the camp. When the main rescue party marched on the camp and the battle began to rage, I abandoned my post. When we rallied our troops after the battle, everyone was accounted for except you. My apologies, but you were somewhat of an afterthought in the rescue plan. Three of our brethren were prisoners and they were the primary object of the rescue mission."

I thought about that for a few minutes before I made a reply. "They were right to leave me behind," I said, offering Elias a way to save face. What Elias hadn't said and what I supposed was difficult for him to say was that he left the rescue party for no better reason than to find me. I changed the subject. "How far out are we?"

Elias let out a sigh of relief. "No less than seven, perhaps as many as nine, miles from Far West."

I'd limped and staggered over half the Missouri countryside. I didn't look forward to floundering over the rest of it. My shoulder was fine as long as I didn't move, or breathe heavily, but I was still dizzy at times and was frequently winded just from the exertion of walking.

"Do you think you could make it to Far West before sunrise?" I asked Elias.

"Certainly. Are you suggesting that I leave you here?"

"I can't go any farther." I had to be realistic. It was well past noon and I was holding up the train. "There are bound to be mobs around Far West. I underestimated the threat a couple of days ago and look what it cost me. You have a better chance of making it in alone."

Elias bristled, reacting as if I'd slapped him across the face with my gloves. He was already shaking his head. "I will not leave you," he said. "I simply will not."

As if on cue, I began to convulse as a cramping pain tied my stomach in a knot. Elias tried to put his arm around me but I brushed it off. I rolled up onto my elbows and knees and rocked gently back and forth to try to quell the pain.

"Brother Richards?" Elias tried to comfort me and I could feel his hand resting on my back.

I started to cough, and was soon vomiting bile and black blood. Elias still had his comforting hand on my back, but he turned his head and fought against his own case of dry heaves. Within moments, there was fresh blood that tasted metallic in my mouth.

By the time I stopped heaving, there was a fair amount of blood on the ground. Elias had gained control of his gag reflex, but he was looking away from the blood when I finally straightened up.

"It always looks like a lot more blood than it is," I said with as much of a smile as I could muster. Elias was pale. "Help me up?"

Elias pulled me to my feet and we walked to a clean spot of ground. I was dizzy and I would have fallen to the earth had it not been for Elias's grip on my shoulders. I was beyond caring about my shoulder injury anyway, so the pain of Elias's grasp only enhanced my surreal feelings. I faded in and out of consciousness, which was as good as a painkiller.

My coughing fit had occurred sometime in the afternoon, but it was dark by the time I could remember anything coherently.

Elias was still sitting beside me and he was softly singing.

"What are you singing?" I inquired as I tried to sit up.

He stopped singing abruptly. "Owen, be still."

"Either you need to hightail it to Far West, or we need to make some time together, my friend. I'm not going to last out here like this."

"Then we shall travel together," Elias said stubbornly, and hefted me to my feet. As far as he was concerned, I would walk with him whether I wanted to or not.

We made better time than I expected. My body alternated between chills and fever, but the cool October night air made the travel seem easier. Elias was practically dragging me when we saw the first signs of human life. Elias let me down gently behind a thicket and peered around to investigate. It was long after dark and Elias could afford a good look. After a lengthy silence, Elias crept back to where I lay.

"Sentries," he said under his breath. "Mob sentries."

***

Elias crouched by my feet. Lines of concern were visible across his forehead where small beads of sweat collected. I realized in that moment that I'd thought of him as an ignorant farm boy, but he was certainly in his element now and it showed in the sharpness of his vision. He'd been eluding mobs and maneuvering in enemy territory for months, and I trusted he would know exactly how to get us both into Far West safely.

"It's a small encampment. Two or possibly three men spelling each other on sentry," Elias whispered. "Two of the men are visible. I suspect the third is on his post. Far West is just on the other side of them."

"Is this a typical setup?" I asked.

"No," he answered, wiping his brow with the back of his hand. "Indeed, enemy numbers have increased in the last two days. I'll scout a way around."

I nodded. Elias put a reassuring hand on my arm and started to get up. I waved him back.

"What is it?" he asked.

"Take this." I unbuckled my fanny pack and pulled the nylon strap from around my waist. Elias's eyes grew wide as he accepted the pack. He put it on, fumbling with the buckle, and then tested the zipper on the hidden holster. He nodded once and disappeared quietly into the tall grass.

Elias returned a full two hours later to find me half-asleep. I'd thrown up more blood, but didn't have the energy to move. I imagined my mouth and chin were a sight.

Elias made a face at me and shook his head. He took a deep breath and sighed. "It is far worse than I thought. The enemy numbers are in the hundreds. I believe we can skirt the encampment, but there's no guarantee of what may lie ahead."

"You're going to have to find your way alone, Elias," I said flatly. "I'm not going to make it."

Elias didn't say anything. We both knew I was right. Elias's life was hard and he understood the harsh reality all too well. He sat down next to me and rested his chin on his palm as if to ponder his next move. I was impressed with his patience which was, I assumed, the result of firsthand knowledge of what happens to Mormons caught lurking in the fields. High stakes were not new to either of us, but the reality of failure was a keen memory for both.

Elias nodded to himself as if he was satisfied with whatever had been going on in that young mind of his. "I'll go," he said. "You stay hidden."

I didn't want him to leave me, despite what I'd told him, but we both knew I wasn't going to be any good hiking around on a detour. "I'll stay hidden," I promised.

Elias started to rise, wanting to get started under cover of darkness. He turned in the direction of the enemy camp and froze. He put up a hand to signal me to keep quiet and slowly lowered himself to his knees in the grass.

He held out two fingers and I couldn't even guess what he was trying to communicate. Two threats? Two minutes? Two points? A moment later I heard the voices and the footfalls of two men approaching. The scene was all too familiar.

I tried to force myself into a sitting position and I wished Elias would give back my pistol. I was going to ask him for it, but when I looked at him, I was astonished to see that he was kneeling with his head bowed and his arms folded. He was praying.

"Elias," I whispered hoarsely as the voices grew nearer. "Elias," I prodded.

Not only did he not respond, he didn't even move. He just kept praying. I wanted to crawl over and retrieve my pistol, but Elias was too far away. I held stock still, not even daring to breathe. Elias was still praying, seemingly unaware of the men who were almost upon us.

Two men, still talking quietly to each other, came into view, not more than ten feet away. I looked at them; they looked at me. Our eyes locked. I wanted to put up my arms in a gesture of surrender and plead for mercy. Something very subtle told me not to. The two men, although they'd looked right at us, kept on walking, still engaged in a personal conversation.

Elias finished his prayer, stood up and pulled me to my feet. I was able to stand without great discomfort, but I still held to Elias for support as we walked.

"We're walking right into them," I said in a panic. But, Elias calmly walked on. "Elias, we're walking right into them."

"Have you read the story of Elisha? In the Bible," he added when I just looked blankly at him.

"I guess not," I answered sheepishly.

"You should." We walked steadily on until we were literally in the midst of an enemy encampment. Elias was right, there were hundreds of men here who'd made what looked like a hasty camp for the night. Some walked here and there taking care of small camp errands, but none took notice of us.

I gripped Elias harder.

"Faith, Mr. Richards. Please," he urged.

My fears subsided as if they'd been washed away, and we continued walking. By the time we'd reached the far side of the encampment, I was walking under my own power and had let go of Elias's arm. I was at peace and a warm feeling flooded my heart. I recognized the feeling from what could have been a lifetime ago—Lewis's funeral. Was the source of my comfort the same now as it had been then? Suddenly I felt rejuvenated. Elias and I walked confidently and smiled at each other as we left the enemy camp behind and pushed on. We reached Far West before morning.

***

I remember walking into Far West, but only bits and pieces of what happened afterward. I was guided into a small cabin in the center of town. The interior was dark, even in the light of day, and the bedding smelled of smoke from the fire. Elias helped me out of my clothes and kept me conscious long enough to see to it that my wounds were cleaned.

"He's got a fever," I heard a voice say, but I couldn't tell who it was. "And he's been throwing up blood."

"Hmm, never a good sign, you understand," said another unfamiliar voice. "It's a wonder they made it here."

They hovered about until they'd tucked me comfortably in bed, given me water, and encouraged me to rest. That was perhaps my last lucid memory after entering Far West.

I was only semiconscious, but at one point I opened my eyes to see the faces of strangers staring down at me. And, I could hear voices, muffled and soft, moving in and out and about the room.

"Brother, please come in," said a voice as the rattle of the single door roused me. It was all I could do to listen.

"Good morning," answered my visitor. "We were to meet here, but I see I am early."

"Come in, please," said the host. "He is sleeping."

"I see." Footsteps shuffled on the plank floor near my bed. "Is he well?"

"Without speaking to our patient, it is hard to determine. Fever, numerous superficial injuries, perhaps serious injuries internally. One never knows."

"Indeed," answered our guest. "It truly remains in the hands of the Lord."

Responding to the genuine care I heard in the words of my visitor, I allowed myself to fade out again until a soft knock on the door disturbed me. I opened my eyes slightly and saw two men admitting a third man through the door. Before they turned around, I closed my eyes and settled back into semiconsciousness. I heard their voices through a muddled brain and made out just a few phrases.

"Our Brother, Owen Richards," a man said and touched me on the head.

Eventually another set of hands lay on my head and another prayer started. I had been around long enough to know that I was receiving a blessing. Lewis had explained the process to me.

". . . if it be thy will, that he should feel and recognize thy spirit, by which he has most recently been touched . . . And we ask, dear

Father, that inasmuch as this man is a faithful servant, that he will in due time recover his full physical faculties and proceed in a manner pleasing unto thee . . . And these things we say . . ." Nothing happened for a moment and the pressure of the two sets of hands remained on my head. "And, I am moved at this time," began the soothing voice again, "to ask that this brother receive comfort and understanding of his role as a righteous defender of souls, and that he be ever vigilant to resist the unrighteous temptation to seek vengeance. This we ask, Father, in the name of Jesus Christ. Amen."

Righteous, I thought. These men must not know that in the last two days I'd cursed the unseen faces of many adversaries and killed two people without flinching. Still, the fact that I'd been so well cared for and that someone had seen fit to say a prayer for me gave me comfort. I faded out and my next memory was of darkness.

I slept soundly for what seemed like hours. When I awoke, I was sore and stiff and still a little out of it. I examined my surroundings in the small cabin. The roof was low and the log walls were close and dark. The only window was covered by a quilt of the same design as the one covering me.

I craned my neck forward, which caused considerable pain, and looked around. The room held only a table with two mismatched chairs, and a bench, a cupboard, a large trunk, and the crude but comfortable bed in which I was resting. There was little room for anything else. I lay back and looked at the trunk. It was wooden with iron-like straps around it. It looked like a treasure chest from a pirate movie. I wondered idly what it contained—probably the personal belongings of whoever had given up the cabin for my convalescence. I would be ever thankful to whomever had been displaced in this city bursting with refugees; there had been a point during my captivity that I'd almost given up, and now finally I felt safe.

Gradually, I let the stress and pain of the last few days slowly drain out of my mind and body. I lay content for the moment in a semi-stupor and thought about the emotions I'd been repressing since my escape. I let go in stages, and reasoned that I'd passed through the worst of whatever was going to happen to me. I was hurt, but the pain was dulled by sheer exhaustion, and I was confident that in time my injuries would heal.

The physical hurt would eventually fade, but the emotional scars would take longer to heal. I'd never been truly victimized; I'd never drunk of the helpless rage. Of its own volition, my mind rehearsed the events of the last several days, playing segments repeatedly like movie trailers. Bogart's black eyes stared relentlessly into mine as he laughed and denied me the necessities of life—food, water, and warmth. My mind created the faces of the heartless men who'd beat and kicked me senseless while I was rendered blind. I kept hearing my own gun shots and seeing two men collapse into death. I knew that in time, the intensity of the events and images would fade, leaving me with unpleasant memories but without the horror of the emotions.

I missed seeing the glorious dawn, but I watched the rippled, wavy glass in the window brighten, and I was fully awake when LeJeune entered my little cabin without knocking and strolled to my bedside. He took off his hat and tossed it lightly on the end of the bed.

"I should have you flogged, Mr. Richards, and then beaten. Pity I'm too late." He spoke in such a cheery voice that I couldn't tell if he was serious or if, heaven forbid, the man had a sense of humor.

"I haven't been flogged yet," I put in, testing the waters.

He laughed merrily. "I'll see to it immediately," he quipped, producing a tin cup of water for me.

"Thanks," I said. "You're in good spirits."

"Well, someone has to be." LeJeune let go of a long sigh and shrugged his shoulders under his long slicker. "Truthfully, things are as dire as they have ever been. We get reports hourly of new atrocities being committed in the surrounding settlements. More enemy troops are sighted all the time, gathering in the east and on their way to Far West. It is even rumored that the governor himself, the dishonorable Lilburn W. Boggs, has issued an order that all Mormons are to be driven from the State of Missouri or exterminated."

"I can't believe any governor . . . You can't be taking that seriously."

"I haven't heard confirmation, but I have met the man, Boggs, and I have no reason to doubt the veracity of the reports." LeJeune pulled a chair from the table and placed it by the bed. He sat, ran his fingers through his hair, and looked at me. "But that is our problem. Not yours. How are you feeling? You appear to be recovering."

"I am, thank you. So, you visited yesterday?" I asked.

"Yes, and for two days before. You are a heavy sleeper."

"Two days," I blurted out. "So I've been laid up here for three days?"

"And part of a fourth," LeJeune added with a grin. "But don't fret, although you do look like the devil himself. I do not envy you." LeJeune got up and walked to the window. Looking out at the scene at Far West, he said, "I'd flog Elias if not for his innocent enthusiasm. When we counted heads after Crooked River and found him missing . . ." He didn't finish. He rubbed his temples with his thumb and middle finger.

"Speaking for myself, I'd like to kiss him." I smiled.

LeJeune turned on me with a look of horror. Seeing my face, he smiled as well. "You're joking. Oh, yes, I suppose." He looked embarrassed. "I'd like to talk with you about Elias," he said. "If you have no objection."

"Go ahead."

"He's a fine young man, independent, responsible, and quite a leader . . . yet he's taken to following you quite thoroughly."

I looked down. Now I was embarrassed.

LeJeune noticed and went on. "Not that I blame him. You saved his life—miraculously, it seems. You are from a far land, exotic, new, strange, brave. Any young man in his position would feel the same way." LeJeune paused and looked me in the eye. The look on his face told me nothing.

I nodded and returned his look.

"You see," he went on, "Elias and his sister are special to me, uh, to us, in Far West. Their coming here was a great personal sacrifice. Anna recently lost her husband and Elias has since played the role of father, brother, and caretaker to Anna."

I wondered if LeJeune wanted the latter role for himself. *Probably,* I thought, while he went on with this incredible prologue to whatever it was he wanted to say.

"So, you see, we consider Elias a special young man."

"I can understand that. And just what is it you want to tell me?" My tone must have given away my impatience because he came to his point.

"When I first saw you, I did not trust you. We have many enemies here. The mob stirs up the hearts of our people and many wish to fight a losing battle and let the Lord decide our destiny as a church and as a people. Where your sympathies lie is still a question."

"I feel for your people. I really do. I can't understand why you live like this and put up with it, but I feel terrible for what you're going through. I have no other sympathies, if that's what you're asking. You can't think I'm one of them. Not after this." I let him have a good look at my face.

"Of course not. I am not afraid of that. It is the evil within, Mr. Richards, that worries me more than anything the mob can do to us." He rubbed his temple again, walked back to his chair, and sat down. "It is always so. The evil within is the only evil that can really hurt us, as individuals, as a people, as a nation. The worst the mob can do is torture and kill us. Our own vices and weaknesses—they are our ultimate destruction."

I thought about the men I'd killed in the woods. They could have killed me; they would have killed me if I'd given them the chance. I wondered if I'd done something worse to myself by killing them first. LeJeune, who I'd thought was an arrogant bore when I met him, was giving me no reason to doubt his sincerity. What he said brought to the surface some of the emotions I'd been ignoring out of an instinct for self-preservation.

LeJeune kept talking. "You haven't been told. Brother Patten did not return from Crooked River alive. Elias has taken it rather hard."

My heart squeezed into a little ball for Elias's sake. "How many died?"

"Patten, a man named Gideon Carter, not a member of our church incidentally, several seriously injured, many hurt. It is unknown how many men were killed on the other side. One, at least."

"Add two more," I said slowly.

LeJeune nodded; he'd been told about the men I killed in the trees. He looked me over and, apparently seeing something of the guilt I felt, he said, "You may have saved those men from committing unpardonable sins, at your expense." The corners of his lips turned up slightly. "We do what must be done and if it is done by the will of the

Lord, we should not fear. Killing or being killed, it matters very little if it is the will of our Father. I have learned that through hard, hard experience. In fact," he said as an afterthought, "Brother Patten would tell you the same thing if he were standing in front of us at this moment."

I smiled. It was uncomfortable for both of us, but I averted my gaze first and LeJeune took care of changing the subject abruptly.

"I don't want Elias involved in any more resistance." It was a plea, strongly stated.

"Me neither," I agreed.

"I use young, unmarried brethren to communicate and gather intelligence of mob and militia activities in Caldwell County. When I learned that three of my men had been taken to Crooked River, I suspended all other missions. It is far too dangerous outside of Far West now."

"You got that right." I put on a mischievous grin. "So, what's so special about Elias, and his sister?"

"Elias and Anna are very important to me." LeJeune admitted, his face suggesting that there was more to say. "I was called to serve a mission in Canada as companion to Anna's husband. I esteemed him as one of the greatest men of his generation. He died of the fever soon after we left, not more than about six months ago. Under the circumstances, I was called back to Far West to serve our needs here. Before Anna's husband died, I made an oath to care for Anna, and Elias, until . . ."

"Until she remarried," I said, so he wouldn't have to.

"Yes." LeJeune struggled to regain some of his composure.

"But, she has been at the mill. Why so far away?" I asked.

"I suggested she stay at the mill until she could properly mourn her husband. I thought it was best."

"You're a good man. Does she know?"

"Know what?" he asked, knowing full well what I meant.

"Does she know how you feel about her?"

LeJeune pursed his lips, thinking about how to answer.

I upped the stakes. "Does Elias know?" I prodded.

"Certainly not," he said, giving me the and-you-better-keep-your-mouth-shut-or-else look.

Changing the subject, he said, "Since I assume you would like to leave us as soon as possible, I will do my best to arrange your departure. May you have better luck leaving this time."

I'd just been scolded, professionally and directly. If I hadn't deserved it, I might have taken offense. But LeJeune's heart was in the right place, and he was looking out for the men who would have to rescue me if I blundered again, so I accepted the reproach in the spirit it was given. "I would appreciate that, LeJeune. Thank you."

"Very well." LeJeune stood to leave and replaced the chair, slipping it neatly under the table. He picked up his wide brimmed fedora and flipped it onto his head. He opened the door to leave, but turned around on the threshold. "Your pistol is under the bed. Just as it was. And, if you see Elias, would you ask him to find me? I need to speak with him immediately." He turned on his heel and walked out of the cabin, shutting the door firmly behind him.

"Don't worry; I won't say a thing about you and Anna," I promised to the back of the door.

***

My pistol was under the bed secured in the secret holster in my fanny pack. It was just as I'd left it. I had a total of twenty-one rounds left in two magazines. I'd fired some when I first met Elias, and had used five in the woods.

I put thoughts of the dead men out of my head for the hundredth time and replaced my funny jammies with my own clothes that were neatly folded in a stack on the table. It felt good to be in clean clothes after days of filth. I had to work the shirt over my injured shoulder and I noticed that someone had repaired a rip in my jeans and several in my shirt.

My boots were in good repair and I reflected that I was lucky to have them. I'd seen some of the boots people around here wore and mine would have been easy to steal. Now if I could just get my three-hundred-dollar Gore-Tex jacket back, it would be a clean sweep and I could leave Caldwell County a happy man. *I'll be even happier when I find Julianna*, I thought.

Dressing tired me out but I couldn't take another minute of lying down. The bed sores from only three days, and part of a fourth according to my new friend LeJeune, were worse than the injuries that put me there. I sat for a few moments at the table and stretched my arms and legs.

The door to the cabin opened suddenly and slammed against the back wall. The loud crack startled me and I shot out of my chair.

LeJeune was standing in the doorway with an angry expression blackening his face. He started for the bed, but turned toward the table when he saw me standing there.

"What did you tell him?" he roared. His face was drained of color, and his eyes flamed with rage.

"What are you talking about?" I countered.

"What did you tell him?" LeJeune took a short breath. "What did you tell Elias?" he asked, obviously suppressing an urge to throw me around the cabin.

"Calm down. I haven't seen Elias. What is your problem?" I asked caustically.

LeJeune shook his head and turned his back on me so I wouldn't see the emotion running rampant over his face. "Elias left the city. I just got word. I thought you . . ." he couldn't finish.

"LeJeune," I said, taking him by the shoulders and turning him to face me. "I haven't spoken with Elias for days. Tell me what's happened."

His face softened, worry plainly visible. "I got word that he left the city to fetch Anna. I can't blame the boy. He tried to bring her here before. Her safety is my responsibility. I should have gone for her." LeJeune shook his head.

"LeJeune, get a grip, buddy." I was surprised to see a man as proud and stoic as LeJeune in such an emotional mess. I put a hand on his shoulder.

He dropped his head. "One of my men saw him leave and followed him."

"You've sent him on dangerous missions before. You must have some trust in him," I encouraged.

LeJeune looked up through fearful eyes, still shaking his head. "You don't understand, Mr. Richards. Elias has been captured, again."

CHAPTER 9

"Calm down, LeJeune. Let's take this one step at a time," I said, hoping I could control my nerves as well. "How long ago did he leave?"

LeJeune was getting his grip. He pulled himself together and said, "About half an hour ago. He was taken quickly by a small group of men, probably unorganized mobbers."

"Okay," I said strapping on my fanny pack. "I'm going to need something from you."

"Anything," LeJeune said with complete conviction.

***

"I must be completely nuts," I said under my breath. I'd now been captured by Missourians twice in the same week. I was being dragged by my arms (really only by my good arm) by two men in dirty clothes. Two additional men, similarly dressed, accompanied them.

I'd traded my clothes for an ill-fitting pair of knickers with a front flap. Not as comfortable as the jeans I was used to wearing, but I fit the part. I also wore a nifty little vest under a jacket that was a size too small—made me look just like a local.

It had been inevitable that Elias would get caught. The prairie around Far West was thick with mobbers. Since leaving the city, I'd seen several groups. They were all pretty much your standard mouth-breathing scum. No one seemed to care much about the five of us, except to stare and toss insults in my direction. I looked like any other captured Mormon being escorted away from Far West. What I feared most was running into an organized militia troop that might take a real interest in a captured local. So far, so good—only mouth breathers here.

The sentry who had seen Elias leave the city had followed him for as long as he could. When he saw Elias taken by the mob he followed until they made camp, then he ran back to Far West to get help. The group that had Elias was less than a mile from the city.

"Hallo the camp," yelled one of my captors when we were near enough to see half a dozen men sitting around a fire. A bound and gagged Elias sat nearby under a tree.

"Who is it?" answered an older man with a tooth missing and a week's growth of gray, scraggly beard.

"Got anothern," said my captor. "Pretty slippery devil, though. Can we share yer fire a spell?"

The mobbers seemed not at all surprised as I was pulled into their midst and dropped on the ground. I lay in a defeated slump while this group of rancid-smelling, lice-infested dregs eyed me and nudged me with their feet. One man kicked me in the ribs and nearly awakened the not-yet-dealt-with rage engendered by last week's beating. I suppressed it and closed my eyes.

"Found 'im wanderin' outside the city. Lookin' fur somethin', I figure," my captor explained.

"Uh huh," grunted one of the mobbers. "Let's see if he's as much fun as this one was," he said, gesturing at Elias.

Elias was on the ground, his eyes half shut, seemingly in a daze. He'd taken another brutal beating. Blood spilled from his nose and a severely cut lip, and his face was bright red and swollen with new bruises.

If I was headed for the same treatment, I wouldn't survive it. I opened my eyes just enough to take stock of my situation and to see that one of the mobbers, tall and slender with stringy blond hair, was wearing my coat. My three-hundred-dollar Gore-Tex coat. That mangy low-life, I thought.

"I know this man," said the tall blond. "That's the man what sprayed me in the eyes."

He sprang at me, his eyes burning with the memory of the pepper spray I'd coated his face with a little over a week ago.

"I'm gonna kill you, mister," he growled.

"I'd be more afraid of your sister," I said, opening my eyes wide.

My captors, three of Far West's best men and LeJeune himself, bolted into action. The six dizzy Missourian mobbers that had beaten, bound, and gagged Elias were overcome so quickly that none had a chance to fight back. I took on the blond man myself, grasping his arm and turning it over by the palm into a wicked gooseneck wristlock. He bent at the waist and let out a screech that made us all cringe.

My four compatriots searched and disarmed the rest of the band and had them on their knees in a group almost before I got the coat thief to the ground. Elias stared, in utter and complete confusion, until he saw my grinning face and LeJeune kneeling by his side. A slow crease developed on his face until his mouth turned upward into a broad smile.

"Hello, you foolish, foolish boy." I smiled at Elias. I still had the blond man by the wrist and he was whining softly.

"I had to try, Brother Richards, Brother LeJeune. I had to," he said.

"I know. We'll talk later." I let go of my prisoner and shoved him onto the others. My men, the ones LeJeune loaned me, were armed with pistols and kept a close guard. "Right now we need to move quickly."

"But what about Anna?" Elias objected.

I turned to face Elias to field his objection. As I did so, the blond man, still angry beyond the ability to control himself, lunged at the nearest guard, knocking him to the ground and taking his charged derringer.

Blondie took off at a dead run and had gone about thirty feet by the time pistols were raised in his direction.

"Don't shoot!" I screamed. "Don't!"

LeJeune's men turned their heads toward me in unison, like a choreographed dance movement, their eyes wide and questioning. Ol' Blondie was nearly as stunned as they were. He stopped in his tracks and turned, pointing the derringer at me.

I put a round from my Glock in the ground at his feet. He jerked as if hit and then, realizing that I'd missed him, he straightened his stance and got ready to shoot me at his leisure, thinking my weapon was now unloaded.

I put another round at his feet and watched the expression in his eyes go from fervor to fear. I put another eight rounds in a neat semicircle around his feet, kicking up sod in an even pattern. He literally danced. The shock was so complete that Blondie was making blubbering sounds through his quivering, slobbering lips.

"Take off my coat," I ordered coolly. "Do it now."

Blondie dropped the derringer and let the coat slide off his arms to the ground.

"Go away," I said calmly to him. His jaw hung wide open until he regained his composure, then he turned and ran off into the woods, wet pants and all, swinging his arms like a rag doll, his greasy hair trailing behind. "All of you," I said to the rest of them.

They took off into the forest, the most terrified Missourians of the day. A couple of LeJeune's men started to back away from me in utter wonderment. "Not you guys," I said, shaking my head.

I gathered our crew and we made a loose huddle.

"I'm going to have to have this dry-cleaned now," I said, picking up my coat. "And as for you guys," I looked at my partners, "you just about shot a hole through a three-hundred-dollar Gore-Tex coat." It took a second, but one nervous laugh followed another until our merry little band was snickering away joyfully and enjoying a happy reunion with Elias.

"We need to get back into Far West before it gets dark. There are more troops surrounding the place by the minute." Everyone nodded, except Elias.

"I'm going to the mill to get Anna. You can't stop me." Elias's face was stone serious. He looked from me to LeJeune and back.

"I'm not even going to try," I said, shaking my head. "Let's get these guys on their way back, though."

LeJeune nodded and took his men off a little way for a private conference.

I turned to Elias and said, "I'm going with you. We're going to have to travel fast. We'll go to the mill and bring back anyone who wants to come."

Elias nodded in agreement.

LeJeune's men said their good-byes and disappeared, leaving LeJeune with us.

"What's up?" I asked LeJeune before he left to accompany his men.

"Pardon me?" he said.

"Why aren't you going with your men?"

"I am," he said without explanation.

Elias and I just looked at LeJeune as he stood there.

"Well," I said impatiently.

"I am with my men," he said with a smile. "You aren't going to the mill without me. Anyway, I have something to tell Anna." He winked at me and then gave Elias a stern none-of-your-business glare.

"One for all, then," I said, and Elias, Bart and I made our way east to the mill with me in my reclaimed coat.

***

A clear morning sky presented the illusion of warmth, but it was brisk and wet in the brown grass of the prairie. However, by mid-morning, the prairie was dry, and I'd taken off my coat to prevent a heavy sweat from over-exertion.

We traveled slowly, partly from fatigue and mostly because we decided that as we neared the mill we would need to be more careful. Accordingly, we stopped often, like hunters, or more aptly like the hunted, to look and listen to our surroundings. I didn't think the mobs would have patrols this far out, but one never knew. There was a lot of militia traffic headed to Far West and we didn't want to run headlong into any of it. For that reason, we trekked several miles to the north, into wilder country, to avoid contact.

Because we altered our route, I relied heavily on Elias's sense of direction and knowledge of the area to keep us from getting lost. I never should have doubted; by midday we arrived at my truck, our energy almost completely expended.

My day pack was still sitting on the hood of my truck, just as I'd left it when I had to leave unexpectedly with Missourians on my heels. I smiled and jumped into the cab.

The engine turned over with a comforting rumble and I was feeling at home in the familiar surroundings. But this was not the case for Elias and Bart, who found my truck very difficult to wrap their brains around; Bart didn't appear up to wrapping his brain around anything. He stood in front of the truck, mouth agape, in a stupor.

"It's a machine for driving," I finally resorted to saying. "The engine is gasoline powered and it drives these four wheels which move the truck along. Well, at least they did before I got stuck in this blasted mud."

Elias didn't say much; he was too busy looking at the truck. He climbed inside and ran his hands over everything.

"This young man needs a truck of his own." I grinned.

Bart was still staring. "It's a wonder, a wonder," he kept saying.

We were famished and we thanked-goodness there was plenty of food and water amongst my gear for all three of us. After I taught them how to eat from little plastic bags, Elias and Bart joined me for dinner. I ate a hasty lunch of crackers and cheese, tuna noodle casserole, and a hard, dense brownie baked to military specs. They had identical ready-to-eat meals of meatballs in sauce. Their meals came with crackers and brownies, too.

I had only one MRE heater: a cellophane bag containing a mysterious iron, magnesium, sodium wafer that gets very, very hot when exposed to water. I placed the meatball meals in the cellophane bag with the heater and added a small amount of water from my canteen. I propped the bag against a nearby rock and let the heater do its work. I could force-feed myself a cold MRE but I wouldn't have subjected anyone else to a cold meatball and rice MRE.

I poured the contents of a packet of powdered orange drink into a field cup full of water, and washed everything down in three swallows. My dinner partners watched and did the same.

I changed into fresh underwear, clean socks, and dry fatigues, draping my wet "local" clothes over the seat where the heater could do some good. Bart had taken to waving his hand back and forth in front of the heater as if it were magical. I had to pull him away to get him to change into a spare set of fatigues. His old pants were wet to the knees and smelled like they hadn't been changed since spring . . . of the previous year. Elias was more than keen to jump into a pair of fatigues and, as it turned out, he replaced a pair of flimsy leather boots with two pair of thick wool socks and Lewis's Danner Go-devil boots.

As I was changing, I caught a glimpse of my face in the rearview mirror and hardly recognized the man I saw. My face was unshaven, a rarity, and one cheek and eye were still heavily swollen. I thought I could see almost every color of the rainbow in the bruises on my cheeks and around my eyes. Patches of skin were worn off like rug burns on my forehead. It was then that the full impact of this ongoing nightmare hit me.

I had been starved, beaten, and nearly killed in the last week and perhaps, worst of all, I had been forced to kill two human beings in self-defense. My body would eventually heal, but my mind would never give up the awful memory. The worst part was that it wasn't over. Anna needed our help and I had no idea where Julianna had gone. The sense of urgency that accompanied that last thought made my stomach turn and tighten. She was still out there in who knows what kind of trouble. I shook off the haunting memories of the past week, promising myself to revisit them when I had time. Now, it was time to go to work.

Lewis's handgun was still in the holster of his load-bearing vest. He carried a Glock 9mm identical to mine, but for the alignment of the sights. I drew it from the UM84 holster attached to his load bearing vest and held it at low ready. I examined it, checked to see if it was loaded and replaced the weapon in its holster.

"Here you go," I said, heaving Lewis's olive drab vest, full to the gills, to Bart. He caught it, nearly dropping it, and hefted it in the air in front of him. He wasn't expecting it to be so heavy.

He examined it for a moment, looking at the various Velcro enclosures and the contents of each. "What is this?" he asked.

"It's a load-bearing vest. I want you to wear it. For the pistol rig, mainly. And, there's some other stuff on it: a flashlight, a couple of light sticks, a smoke canister, CS gas, a good knife, a trauma first-aid kit, and extra ammunition for your rifle and pistol."

"But I have no rifle."

"You will," I promised.

It took some effort to explain what each item on the vest was. Some of the concepts seemed to be genuinely foreign to Bart and

Elias. They understood flashlights and light sticks after a quick demonstration. As for the smoke and CS tear gas grenades, they had to take it on faith that what I described would happen if they pulled the pins.

"Don't worry, you probably won't have to use any of this stuff. But, considering how things have gone, I'd like to be prepared." Both heads nodded.

I gave Bart the same kind of short course on the pistol that I'd given Elias during our escape from Crooked River. Bart was a quick study and grasped the concepts without difficulty. I gave Elias my pistol in the fanny pack and had them both dry-fire the weapons a couple of times to get used to the trigger pull. We didn't dare fire a live round for fear of attracting attention.

Since Bart was wearing the load-bearing vest with three thirty-round rifle magazines, I gave him Lewis's assault rifle and an extensive tour of that weapon.

"It's a gas-operated .223 caliber rifle," I explained. "The round is small and fast. It'll penetrate any of the board buildings in Far West. It may even penetrate the wall of a log cabin. Be careful of your back-stop." I felt like a firearms instructor. "Always keep your finger off the trigger until you're on target and ready to fire," I added.

"What are you putting in the bag?" asked Bart, as I stuffed four black cylinders in my daypack.

"Flash-bangs," I said.

"And what devious design have those sinister items?" asked Bart, enjoying himself.

"Loud noise, bright flash. A controlled explosion occurs within this metal body." I held up the device, which was just smaller than a pop can.

"For what purpose?"

"Well," I said, "the bang disorients your opponent, and the flash blinds him. The effects last five or ten seconds. It gives the attacker a bit of a head start. Great for assaulting a room full of mouth breathers, or whatever you call 'em."

"I don't prefer to call them any kind of derogatory names," Bart said piously, "But 'pukes' is an acceptable regional epitaph."

We all laughed at that.

"Eli, I'd like you to travel light. You're fast and quiet; you'll have the fanny pack and my pistol. Bart, you can provide fire support from a distance. You can shoot that rifle accurately from at least five hundred yards. That should give you a tremendous advantage over anyone shooting a black powder rifle."

"Five hundred yards?" asked Bart incredulously.

"If you can see it in the reticule, you can shoot at it. You may not hit it, but you can try. Remember, you're long-range support."

"Very good," he said in a very professional voice. For all their ignorance, neither Bart nor Elias misunderstood solid tactics.

"I have something a little different," I said, holding out Lewis's MP5 submachine gun by the forestock, "and I'll stay closer to Elias." Bart gave me a look of approval.

While Elias and Bart went through their gear again, identifying each item and reminding each other of their respective functions, I rummaged through my rig putting useful odds and ends in my daypack. I even went so far as to siphon some gas from the reserve tank of my truck into a few two-liter pop bottles which I kept in my tool box for water. I tied the pop bottles full of gas to my pack with parachute cord and tried it on. Bart and Elias had been watching with interest, especially when I'd siphoned the gas.

"To the mill, then?" asked Elias. Bart was nodding, anxious to be on his way.

"To the mill."

I secured my truck by remote. The horn made a short beep and the lights flashed. Bart and Elias got a kick out of it so I did it a couple of times before we started off.

"Oh, whoops," I said, stopping abruptly. "I forgot something." I jogged back to the truck and looked through the jockey box. I found what I wanted, put them in my pocket, and ran back to the guys. It was about three o'clock on a lovely fall afternoon.

We took nearly the same course to the mill that I'd taken with Anna and Elias, except this time we skipped the drudgery of dragging a man along the creek bottom and we approached from the high ground. We were well over a thousand yards away when we first saw the mill. Both Elias and Bart relaxed a little as we got closer to Anna's proximity, both sharing a look of relief that the settlement was still in one piece.

"I gotta set this down for a minute," I said, dropping my daypack and massaging my sore shoulder.

Elias nodded and stopped with me. Bart was more than happy to take a breather. The vest he was wearing was heavy and took some getting used to.

"Do you wear this often, Brother Owen?" he asked.

"You get used to it."

His sense of honor prevented him from taking the vest off, but he stood and squirmed, trying to redistribute the weight where it was cutting into his shoulders.

I winked at Elias. He winked back, trying to keep Bart from seeing him. I gave my shoulder another quick massage as I gazed at the countryside.

Shoal Creek, which cut its way along the south side of the settlement, meandered lazily east to meet the Grand River in Livingston County. The banks were covered in an undergrowth of hazel amidst scattered trees that had dropped their last kaleidoscopic leaves in the river, letting them drift at a leisurely pace toward the Grand, then ultimately to the Missouri River. I thought about the leaves as they floated east, wondering if they would reach the mighty Mississippi and then the Gulf of Mexico on their lazy journey.

North of the creek stretched a rolling prairie broken occasionally by stands of trees and low shrubs. The mill, owned by Jacob Haun I was told, sat near the creek, backed by a working blacksmith shop. Behind the shop, a low meadow was dotted with the tents and wagons of recent arrivals to Haun's Mill, mostly from the East Coast.

"It's a beautiful place," I said to no one in particular as I donned my pack again. Bart and Elias were raring to go, and we set off down the hill.

A figure in light-colored clothes sat atop a small knoll overlooking the settlement a couple of hundred yards from us, no doubt on guard duty. He waved an arm casually at us as we neared. We'd gone no more than ten yards in his direction when he jumped to his feet, yelling, and broke into a frantic run toward the settlement. People at the mill stopped in their tracks, heads turned first toward their frantic watchman and then towards the river where men on horseback were

spurring their horses up the creek bed and emerging into the settlement from the cover of the trees.

The horsemen formed into a three-square formation with a
trailing vanguard. The watchman was nearly lost in the tall grass as he
ran down the hill, waving his hat and screaming, "Peace. Peace." His
entreaty was ignored by the leading horseman who fired one thun-
derous rifle shot into the settlement and then reigned up to give the
crisp order to fire that resulted in a hundred smoking rifles breaking
the peace of Jacob Haun's Mill.

We were too far away.

"Don't do it," I ordered as Elias bolted ahead. I was afraid he
would run headlong into trouble and get hurt.

"Anna," he screamed.

Bart was heavily burdened but stomped recklessly after Elias, a
horrified look on his face. I stopped to raise the machine gun, but I
was out of range. I broke into a run after them, scrambling and stumbling. I was sore and stiff. I fell once, driving my injured shoulder
into the ground. Stars shot across the landscape of my tightly closed
eyes. A wave of nausea made me vomit; I spit furiously and struggled
back to my feet.

Men, women, and children ran screaming for safety from the hail
of bullets passing through the settlement. Some did not make it and
fell in their bloodied tracks. Some of the lucky ones fled into the
woods. Even if the settlers had been standing at arms, they wouldn't
have been able to repel the attack that had come upon them with
such sudden ferocity. Without weapons, their only hope was to find
cover from the demonic horsemen still pouring into the settlement. A
hopeful few fled for the solid-walled blacksmith's shop.

The mob, hundreds of men with faces painted in horrifying
black, advanced on the blacksmith's shop like a band of Lucifer's
angels, and shot volley after volley into the log-walled building.

At a dead run, I went for the settlement. Children ran for the
woods, followed by frantic mothers; the bodies of those not quick
enough to get away lay lifeless amidst the rush of the mob. Spinning
horses and running feet churned the earth from the ground.

I was winded before I was halfway there. Five hundred yards was
still too far away for a good shot with the MP5. Elias was closer, but

with only a pistol, he was too far away as well. Bart was close behind Elias, still running. I slowed my pace and tried to suck air into my burning lungs. I was coughing up blood and bile and spitting the bitter residue as I ran. I was running much slower than I wanted to now, although the scene in front of me was getting more and more dire.

An elderly man stood at the front of one of the more substantial cabins, arms stretched wide, pleading with members of the mob. He was shot in his tracks and fell limply to the ground. One of the mobbers barbarically thrust a corn sickle at his once proud body.

At just less than two hundred yards from the horsemen, I dropped to a knee and braced my short weapon for a shot. I was gasping violently for air and I struggled to steady the weapon as I pulled the trigger. The sound of my MP5 spitting round after round was swallowed in the noise and confusion, and the rounds flew harmlessly into oblivion. I got up and ran closer, still gasping as I reached the settlement.

I didn't see many of the settlers. Most were either gone or lying lifeless on the ground. The slowest of the Mormons were being followed into the woods.

There was a congregation of mobbers, now dismounted, exiting the door of a large building by the mill. They were throwing their heads back and laughing. Whoever had been inside was surely dead.

"Police," I yelled like an idiot. Some habits were hard to break.

They turned as one and looked at me, stunned to see someone defying them. One man raised a rifle in my direction. By raw instinct I snapped the machine gun to my waist and put a string of rounds in his chest and a group of three in his forehead. The small crowd dispersed into the creek bottom and disappeared.

Most of the mob was by now outside the settlement in the woods, searching for the weak and slow. I could hear the terrified screams of women and children being pursued.

I followed the sounds, walking to calm my lungs so I could shoot from a steady platform. I saw a filthy creature bent over a young girl and pulling at her dress. I steadied my weapon and fired another three-round burst. The man fell into a heap. I didn't stop to examine my work, but scanned the forest for more mobbers.

They weren't hard to find. Another man, his face painted like an Indian warrior's, was beating his fist into the face of a small boy. The boy's tiny body lay relaxed and lifeless on the ground. I fired a string of rounds into the painted head and moved on, not thinking, not feeling.

The screams of the helpless got farther away as I searched the woods. I heard the moaning of a woman, but I couldn't see her. I was focused on the sound when I was surprised by another painted mobber off to my side. I turned and fired, missing the man and driving multiple rounds into a tree. He smiled and showed me a large, fixed-blade knife. He took one step toward me and I fired again. His face showed only shock as his body slowly relaxed into a pile on the ground. Robotically, I released an empty magazine on the ground and inserted a fresh one.

I didn't realize it until some of my own shock wore off, but I was crying. At least, tears were running down my cheeks. I walked in ever-widening circles around the settlement but found no one else. There were still mobbers at the mill; they were busy pillaging the settlement, taking everything from food to feather mattresses. I resisted the temptation to walk back into the mill and kill every lice-ridden one of them. Instead, I focused on the survivors in the woods who needed my help.

I was scouring the brush when I heard a soft murmur behind me.

"Elias." I turned to see him writhing slowly on the ground. I'd completely lost track of Bart and Elias during the melee.

"Owen," he murmured. "Owen. Help."

I went to him, thinking back to the first time I'd come to his aid not far from here. He didn't look seriously hurt, thank goodness. Over his right eye was a deep cut, the blood from which covered his face.

"It's okay, Eli. Stay down." He tried to sit up, but I coaxed him back to the ground. "Where's Bart?" I asked.

"Anna," he coughed.

"Did you find her? Is Bart with her?" I looked around in vain, seeing nothing but barren trees and underbrush.

"Anna," Elias whispered. "Bart went to help her, to help Anna." His whisper turned to sobs as he said, "Owen, the mob has her."

CHAPTER 10

I helped Elias to his feet. "Where did they go?" I asked in a panic. "Where are they?"

"I don't know," he said through tears.

"How long ago?" I asked. "Come on, Elias, get a grip."

He shook away the tears and wiped his face. "Just before you came. It all happened just a few moments ago. They took them both—Anna and Sarah."

"Who?"

"Sarah," he said, without explanation.

Sarah was the girl who visited Elias when I brought him to the mill after his first beating, I remembered. "Which way?"

He pointed away from the settlement. I looked and saw only the lightly forested prairie. I sprinted into the woods in the direction where Elias had pointed, listening for a scream or call for help from Bart or Anna. I slowed only when I realized I might miss something by rushing. I looked hard at the ground as I walked, but found no discernable sign. I listened and heard nothing but the distant noise of a community being destroyed. They were gone.

I wasn't close to tears; I was beyond. The sunken feeling in the pit of my gut was intense and unyielding. I wanted to throw up, but I'd done that already. I sat on the hollow end of a fallen log, face in my hands, heart in my throat, unable to feel much of anything. For the moment, I was numb. Guilt and panic soon snapped me out of my stupor and an unstoppable tide of emotion swelled in me until I could think of nothing but a catalog of my problems. Lewis is gone. Julianna is gone. Anna is gone.

"Please God," I whispered, not knowing exactly what I was doing. I felt awkward, as if I couldn't do this. I let myself drop forward onto my knees, as I'd seen Lewis do numerous times while praying. Just tell the truth, Lewis had said. "Heavenly Father," I tried with more conviction, more faith, "thank you for sparing my life. Please help me to help my friends. Please help me find a way. Amen."

I could hear nothing of the mill settlement now. It had been decimated by the mob. The survivors had been scattered.

Did I really believe in the unseen God? I did; He was somewhere. I knew at that moment that He was real. All at once, as if the sky had broken apart, I felt His comfort. I wanted to see Him with my own eyes, but gentle emotion told me that the conviction I would feel about His presence would be stronger than sight. He was with me.

"Owen," a voice said quietly.

I was startled. I turned to see who was talking.

"Elias," I said, letting out a gasp. He was walking slowly toward me. His face was caked with dried blood and smeared with mud.

"All is lost," he moaned. "All is lost."

I stood up and picked up my weapon. I checked the action to make sure a round was chambered and the magazine was full.

"Buck up, Eli. We've got work to do."

He looked at me through bloodshot eyes. I wished I could do for him what had just been done for me.

"What shall we do?" he asked.

"We shall do," I said with renewed hope, "what needs to be done. Tell me what happened."

"I ran into the settlement," Elias said, giving me a blow by blow accounting. "Anna was running for the woods toward me. I waited for her near the edge of the settlement. I hoped we could run together from there." Elias rubbed his eyes, willing the images to fade from his memory. "She stopped," his voice cracked, "and ran back. Back toward the settlement. Sarah was crying, on the ground. Maybe she was hurt, or scared. Anna bent over to help Sarah off the ground." He stopped.

"Go on, Elias. It's okay," I prodded.

"A man on horseback stopped over them. I tried to shoot but I missed and then the pistol wouldn't work. It just didn't work."

Elias had jerked the trigger, interfering with the recoil of the pistol. The gun had jammed, I was sure. "What happened then, Elias?"

"I yelled at them. The man shot at me. Two or three others suddenly surrounded Anna and Sarah too. They took them away. Out of the settlement." Elias let his head hang, obviously feeling responsible.

"Where was Bart?"

"I don't know. He was there, somewhere. He saw what happened and he was firing into the settlement. He ran after them. He disappeared." Elias felt the crown of his head with his fingers. "I must have been hit. I fell down." He looked at me, pleading for forgiveness. "And I failed them," he whispered.

The image of Lewis dying in the dirt at the oil refinery flashed before me. He was so much like Elias. I had been helpless at the refinery, too, and I felt responsible.

I wanted to explain to Elias that it wasn't his fault. I wanted to sit him down and convince him, but there wasn't time. There never was.

"Let's go, Eli. Let me see your pistol." He drew it and handed it to me. The slide was partially locked back, an empty shell casing stuck sideways in the ejection port. I cleared the jam and racked another round in the chamber. I checked the magazine. Only one round had been fired. I gave the gun back to Elias.

"Where are we going?" asked Elias.

"North," I said, "to find Anna and Sarah."

***

We skirted the settlement, where some members of the mob were still milling about, and walked north. The residual effect of my Heavenly Father's answer to my prayer was still affecting both my mood and my intellect. I prioritized what needed to be done, and I was comforted in my decisions as if I was being fed confidence and wisdom by some unseen conduit.

First, we had to find Bart: I was certain that he felt as desperate as both Elias and I did. Then, we could all liberate Anna and Sarah from captivity. And last, but not least, I had to find Julianna. But what could I possibly do about her after so long? I couldn't do anything right now, and I had to trust that Julianna would be taken care of.

"Anna's boot prints in the ground should be very easy to follow," Elias said, pulling a long straight branch off a tree and trimming the twigs off of it.

"You're a tracker, too?"

"When necessary."

The trail of horses' hoof prints leading away from the mill was easy to pick up. There in the midst of them were two sets of women's boot prints. Both women were wearing boots with heels, which made their sign obvious. Elias put his stick on the ground and measured the stride of each woman, scratching a tick mark on his stick for each one.

"I don't know which set of marks goes to which person," he said, "but this will help us when the sign fades." Elias sounded confident.

"Oh, really?" I said.

"When we run out of sign, we use the stick to pick up the trail again by looking where a footprint should be. Have faith." It seemed plausible to me, so I didn't argue.

The trail we were following was faint but consistent. "Where does this lead?" I asked Elias, pointing to a cow trail.

"I don't know. My assignments with the Spy Company never took me farther north than the mill."

"Spy Company?"

"Yes, we're Brother LeJeune's men. Organized by the Prophet, under the direction of General Hinkle, and under the supervision of Brother LeJeune."

"Well, if that don't beat all," I drawled.

Our trail led us roughly along the river. I let Elias lead, since he seemed familiar with the concepts of tracking people. I stayed back and off to the side, carrying my rifle at port arms in case Elias needed covering fire. I wanted to be able to see the big picture while he was occupied looking at the ground for sign. Several times the trail ran out and Elias put his stick to use. He put one end of the stick on the last bit of sign he could see on the ground and then fanned the stick in an arc. He closely examined the ground near where he'd measured the women's strides and invariably he found what he was looking for.

Ingenious, I thought. Rather like Dirk Pitt. I wondered if it would work through parking lots. It just might.

After a couple of hard, slow miles, Elias was temporarily stumped by the sudden end of the trail at the side of the creek. He examined the moist ground carefully, but turned to shrug at me several times, pointing up the creek to suggest that the mobbers had hidden their trail in the creek bottom.

I was about forty yards from Elias and had taken a defensive position along an eyebrow of the hill where I could see a good stretch of the creek.

We didn't have to worry about finding Bart, because he found us. He must have watched us pass him because he emerged from the creek bank from our rear.

He wore a smile of relief, but the dread of what had happened was evident on his face. Elias saw him and abandoned his work to come over.

"Brother LeJeune," Elias greeted Bart.

Bart returned the greeting, haggard and dirty. He still wore the vest and carried the rifle I'd given him.

"They are just ahead. I was praying you'd come," Bart said.

"Man, was I praying I would find you," I blurted out sincerely.

Elias and Bart both smiled approvingly.

Feeling suddenly vulnerable, I cleared my throat and said, "Let's get off the trail." I waved them both up to the brush cover on the hillside. "What do you know, Bart?"

"They have stopped for the night, I assume. They're in a cabin not far from here. So far, the women have not been abused, except they have been made to walk."

"How many men?" I asked.

"Five. All on horseback."

"What kind of weapons?"

"Each one has a rifle. Some or all have pistols; I couldn't discern. At least two have swords."

"Rifles?" I asked. "What kind? Your kind or my kind?"

"Just rifles," he said, shaking his head. "Most definitely not like yours."

"Good." I looked at Elias and then at Bart. They were both sorry sights. Elias was still covered in dried blood and looked like the walking dead. Bart had been trying to keep pace with the mobbers and was physically exhausted. "We will get them back," I said. And then I smiled.

I asked Bart to take Elias to the creek and wash him up. Armed with a supply of butterfly bandages, I turned my attention to the wide gash in the crown of Elias's head.

"You have a pretty smart part in your hair now," I told him. "Do you think Sarah will approve?"

Bart would have laughed, if not for the seriousness of our circumstances. He smiled, though, and gave Elias a knowing look. Elias's face turned crimson.

"You've no room to rib, Bart buddy. You lovesick pup," I taunted. It was Bart's turn to get wide-eyed and grow red-faced. Elias laughed and Bart tried unsuccessfully to suppress a growing smile.

"Let's get our women back then," Bart said.

***

The initial plan was rudimentary; I hadn't seen the layout of the cabin where Anna and Sarah were being held.

"Let's get some eyes on it while it's still light," I suggested. "If we have to move on this place, the best time is dusk." Both nodded their heads. Bart and Elias may have been completely ignorant to the modern world, but they understood tactical language. "It's almost dark now," I said, looking into the twilight.

"I'll get my eye on it," Bart stammered, using my vernacular awkwardly. "You," he nodded in my direction, "come with me and take stock."

Taking stock was what I called doing reconnaissance. I went with him, and Elias followed at a distance as a rear guard.

Bart led me up a short draw and through a thicket to a crest overlooking a small valley. We stayed low to the ground, crawling as we neared the edge of the woods. From our position, slightly higher in elevation than the valley, we had a perfect view of a small log cabin, a barn, and an outhouse nestled comfortably in a natural draw that eventually led to Shoal Creek.

The small farm sat on a couple of acres of cleared farmland. Most of the crops had been harvested, except for a pumpkin patch near the cabin that still bore green vines. Even in the poor light, twilight fading to blackness, I could see a trail of smoke curling out of the rock chimney.

There was one lookout, a mangey-looking character who walked back and forth in front of the cabin before sitting down on the steps leading up to the small porch, and leaning back on one of the roof supports.

Elias crept up from behind, eager to be with us. Once we were together, Bart spoke. "With our newfound weaponry, it should pose no problem in a pitched battle. I suggest we call them out, using our few numbers as bait. Unbeknownst to them, we will have a great advantage."

"They will all be dead," said Elias. I looked at the boy, surprised at his bluntness. I couldn't tell whether he made the comment out of misplaced zeal or dread. Bart said nothing. He obviously meant to form a line, charge the cabin, and exchange gunfire in obedience to a long forgotten code of warfare. That wasn't for me. I didn't want to insult Bart's honor, but I didn't want to play tin soldiers.

I thought about the faces of the people I'd already killed. No doubt my actions were justified, yet I didn't necessarily want any more of that.

"I have a better idea," I said.

***

I posted Bart at the scouting site and gave him more encouragement on the assault rifle.

"Hardly any recoil," I told him. "Nothing like those beasts you're used to."

"Very well," he said.

"You are the great equalizer, Bart. If we get in trouble down there, you take up the slack. Got it?"

"Very well," he said, running his hand over the smooth composite stock of the weapon.

"Elias, you come with me." We crept away from the valley and skirted the farm well outside of the perimeter. The trees surrounding the farm were closest to the cabin on the northwest side, nearest the rear of the cabin. The windows of the cabin were covered with wooden shutters, and scant light shone through one left slightly open.

I stalked quickly and quietly to the building, Elias watching for the guard out front. When I got there, I could hear voices inside.

"I'm not a lyin' to ya, boys. Them Marmons got harns an' all. Why his rifle was a spittin' lead ball faster'n you could say"—he had to think a minute—"wull, faster'n you could say spit." That was the voice of my friend, Fatface. I couldn't mistake that idiot's blather. I should have known I'd find him here.

Laughter followed the inane comment and then another voice said, "I didn't see nary a harned Marmon, though I looked throughout the place. I think yer a liar."

More laughter, then Fatface driveled on. "Ya callin' me a liar, ya devil?" he asked heatedly.

A third voice interrupted. "Shut up, you two." This was the voice of a more cultured speaker and he had the presence to shut both the other men down. "We have more immediate concerns. Sit down," he ordered. With their voices lowered, it was more difficult to tell what was being said. I strained at the small window, but I could only pick up single words that meant nothing to me. I didn't hear a female voice, nor did I hear evidence of the women being hurt. But what I did hear gave me a sudden chill.

"The woman, with child. You know she will birth soon. She is having labor pains." The voice was one I hadn't heard before.

"Looky here, we have us a midwife," said the voice of Fatface.

The voice in charge said, "I told you to shut up."

I heard nothing else so I eased back out to the tree line where Elias was waiting.

"Men's voices. Nothing from the women," I said to Elias. I told him I wanted to look at the barn, and he gave me a worried cringe. The barn was located closer to the front of the cabin and presented a greater risk from the sentry.

I couldn't see Bart on the slope above, but I knew he was watching us. I moved slowly in a direction that would take me to the barn, but allowed me to walk directly toward the sentry. The less lateral movement I made in sight of the sentry, the better my chances. I made it to the back of the barn. Staying close to the walls, I moved to the big front door. It was ajar, so I stepped inside. There was a man sleeping directly under my feet. I was stepping on his coat tails.

I slowly moved away from the man, but my presence in the barn woke him. It was much lighter outside and near the door, so I moved quickly past him into the darkness as he stirred.

"Who is it?" he mumbled.

I moved further into the barn, testing each step so as not to stumble or kick something noisy. I sidestepped down the center alley and nimbly backed into an empty stall. Softly, softly, I willed my feet to tread lightly. At the back wall my foot struck something solid, and a bucket tumbled over on the dirt floor. The wooden bucket made a soft thud, just enough sound to raise suspicion. I froze, and tried to control my breathing and the thunder in my chest.

"Who is that?" demanded the sleepy man. It sounded like he was still lying down.

The horses in the barn shifted restlessly and made gentle noises that I hoped would cover my breathing.

I heard some scuffling from the man's direction. He was coming to investigate. The age-old question was: Do I sit still and hope he passes me over in the dark or do I attack while he's unaware of my location?

"Who is it?" his voice sounded suspicious now. "Who's that there?"

Attack or hide; I was still deliberating, coming no closer to a decision. Without warning, the barn door opened and then closed completely, leaving the interior of the barn even darker than before. Peachy, now he had help. O.K., that settled it. I'd attack.

I could hear the man slowly coming closer, scuffling straw across the dirt floor. I used his noise to cover my own movement. I backed up against the wall of my stall and edged toward the door. Shooting the MP5 machine gun would bring me all kinds of trouble, so I slung the weapon and readied my fists to do hand-to-hand combat.

The man was close enough now that I could hear him breathing.

"There you are," he said quietly.

I hung in there, fists firm and teeth clenched. I hoped he wasn't pointing a gun or carrying a knife. Why did I have to look in the barn, anyway?

He stepped closer. I could see the outline of his shape moving toward me.

Another form followed him down the alleyway and I could make out that the second person had something raised over his head. I pulled back into the stall and waited.

The next thing I heard was a hollow thud, followed by the sound of a body dropping limply onto hard dirt. And then the second figure entered the stall.

"Owen, are you well?" asked Elias, holding a thick, dark object over his shoulder that turned out to be an axe handle.

I let about six cubic feet of air out of my burning lungs and thanked my rescuer.

"Where did you get that?" I asked.

"By the door," he said casually. "Ill conceived plan, Brother Richards," he added. "You shouldn't have come in here alone."

"Bad idea?"

"All to pieces."

"Right. From now on, I'll stay in sight of my cover guys. You're a good man, Eli. Now, what do we do with that?" I pointed at the limp mass on the ground.

"Bind him?" suggested Elias.

"That only works in the movies," I said.

"Move ease?"

"Never mind." I put a finger to my lips and pointed in the direction of the sentry outside.

"Asleep," Elias announced. "Sitting up." He went to the door, looked, and nodded. I went to work with a roll of ninety-mile-an-hour tape—black duct tape I carried in my day pack. By the time the bludgeoned Missourian came to, he was taped to an upright support in the barn and was breathing loudly through his nose, owing to the tape over his mouth.

"Not a mouth breather anymore." I chuckled at my own wittiness. "And then there were four," I said, when I'd finished.

Elias didn't hear my humor. He was busy saddling horses, letting them nicker softly to him as he worked. Four were ready. I picked up the remaining saddle and walked toward the last horse. Elias shook his head and made a sour face.

"Skittish and wild-eyed," he said. "More hindrance than help. I have a sense about these things." He smiled.

There was a side door to the barn and we used that to lead our horses out and away from the clearing. As far as we knew, the sentry still slept soundly.

"Just a minute," I said to Elias. "I need to do something else." I untied the pop bottles from my pack and skulked back into the hollow toward the cabin. Elias held the horses until I returned without the bottles. We took the horses back to Bart's position above the valley where we picketed them.

Bart was a little miffed when we got back. "I truly believed you were caught," said Bart, scolding us.

"The sentry is fast asleep," said Elias. "I could hear him snoring."

Bart was still skeptical. "I cannot tell well enough from here," he apologized.

"Are you looking through the scope?" I asked, getting only a mystified look in return. I showed him the scope, a piece of equipment I thought he'd understood from the beginning, and watched as he scoured the valley in three power detail.

"This is fantastic," he said with renewed vigor. "The sentry is still asleep."

And this was my sniper, I thought cynically.

"Oh, before I forget. These," I said, pulling a box of .223 caliber ammunition from my pocket, "are tracers." I smiled, but no one smiled in return. "Tracers," I said, "are cool. They have a phosphorous tip and they look really cool at night. Reload your mags so you shoot one every fifth round," I said, dropping the box by Bart. "You'll like the results if you hit the bottles I set around the yard."

Bart picked up the box, nodded, and set them down.

I'd had a good look at the farm and decided to act before someone in the cabin took a head count. I turned to Elias. "How do you feel about Mormons with horns, Eli?" He looked at me quizzically. I took three light sticks from my daypack and turned to Bart. "When you hear a loud boom, the party's begun."

Bart nodded and went back on lookout.

I put the light sticks in my pocket and walked back to the valley. Elias followed and Bart remained at his post, studying the darkening valley through the scope.

Stopping and turning, I smiled and said, "Lessens yer chicken."

"Pardon," said Bart, looking up from his rifle.

"Nothing. Wish us luck?"

"Farewell," he said.

Elias and I made our way back to the edge of the brush and stopped.

I took the gas mask out of Elias's carrier and showed him how to strap on the device and make a seal by plugging the in-valve and sucking the whole thing tight to his face. Like all SWAT dogs, Eli was thrilled with the new and exciting gear, but he didn't have a clue what the mask was for.

"You cover me. Understand?" I asked.

Elias nodded, wide-eyed. He was breathing heavily under the mask, but he hadn't yet asked why he was wearing it.

"When we enter the cabin, you just protect my back," I told him.

In Elias's eyes, I could read the seriousness with which he took his assignment.

"Now, hold still," I said. I withdrew the light sticks from my pocket and activated them one by one. As they lit up, Elias' big eyes grew even bigger under his mask. He'd never seen anything like it. I cut the end off of each one and poured the luminous liquid in my bare hands. I made Elias kneel and went to work massaging the sticky stuff into his hair. After I was done, I rubbed as much of the bright-green film off my hands as I could and put gloves over the glowing residue. *What's old Bart going to think?* I wondered.

After a final briefing, all done in whispers, Elias and I were ready to perform our stunt. Elias was going to start the action. I deftly donned my own gas mask and gave Eli the thumbs up, which he eagerly returned.

Keeping the cabin between himself and the sentry, Elias made his way into the clearing. He paused at the corner of the cabin and waved me up. I moved next, in turn, to the back of the cabin near the window where I'd been before, and waited.

I'd asked Elias to give me a count to one hundred before he moved. I had four grenades to manage and I wanted time to get them straight before things got out of hand.

I placed all four on the ground in front of me. I removed the tape I'd used to secure the spoons to the sides of the body and straightened the cotter pins that kept the spoons in place. Then, I waited for Elias to get to a hundred.

When he did, no one in the valley could have missed the blood-chilling scream. I imagined the heart-skipping panic induced when the sentry awoke to the sight of Elias, dressed in camouflage fatigues, wearing a black rubber gas mask, and sporting bright green fluorescing Mormon "horns" on his head. The sentry literally burst open the door of the cabin in his panic to get inside. At that very moment, I pulled the pin on a flash-bang, dropped it through the open shutter, and followed that closely by a burning tear gas grenade that wasn't supposed to be used in structures—I made an exception, just this once.

The resultant ear-shattering explosion, brilliant flash of vision-destroying light, and billowing smoke created just the diversion we needed to make an unforgettable entry. I tore around the cabin in time to meet Elias at the front door.

It's common to get tunnel vision under such circumstances, but I took the time, a few scant seconds, to take in the faces of the people inside the cabin. By the time their eyesight returned to normal, all they could see through the haze of CS tear gas was a lunatic, horned amphibian-looking creature ravaging through the cabin. Anna and Sarah were as affected by the diversion as their captors, and fought valiantly not to be taken by the swamp thing. I set another canister of gas and a smoke grenade on the steps of the cabin to cover our escape. The CS would be carried nicely by the smoke and add to its irritating effects. Discovering I would have to help Elias drag the women kicking and screaming, I bolted inside the cabin door. Mucus was already running from their noses, but the men were coming to their senses and grabbing for their weapons through tears and fits of coughing. Elias needed a couple of seconds to convince Anna to leave with him.

I swung my MP5 machine gun into position and put twenty rounds, give or take, into the plank floor. Everyone stopped, except Elias. He was yelling through his mask, "It's me, it's me," loud enough for the people of Nebraska to hear. He had a handful of

Anna's dress in his fist and was swinging her to the door. Sarah was flailing at the end of Anna's free arm, trying to save her.

Elias nearly had her out of the door when she caught hold of the frame with both hands. Normally I would have struck her knuckles with the hardest object handy, probably the end of my firearm. In this case though, I ripped off my mask and showed her my face. Recognition dawned, and with a wave of my arm, we were off, Sarah dragging behind and trusting to Anna's good sense. Unfortunately, I took a deep breath of tear gas and had to brace for the stinging in my lungs.

By the time we were off the front porch, the four remaining men from the cabin had cleared their heads and had taken up the chase. A couple of rifles poured out the door in the hands of coughing, crying, angry Missourians. Elias, with Anna and Sarah, ran for the brush. I turned, knelt, and pulled the machine gun firmly into my shoulder. I was going to have to kill again.

One man, seeing me ready with my weapon, turned and ran the other way. The next man around the corner of the cabin was Fatface. In his eyes loomed the aggravation of days of enmity between us. He didn't run, but pulled up with his rifle and aimed. Through teary eyes, I made the decision to fire. I squeezed the trigger, taking up the slack.

Before the hammer of my weapon dropped, a hail of bullets from the ridgeline rained down on the valley in rapid succession. Every fifth round left a bright, acrid line through the darkness. As if this wasn't enough, Bart managed to hit two of the three plastic pop bottles with the tracers, and the night was shattered by the sound of gasoline vapors exploding into bright mushrooms between the cabin and barn.

Fatface recoiled at the explosions and lowered his rifle. I held my shot. His eyes went wide, and the orange glow of the fire reflected off the greasy sheen on his face. Looking at me through eyes filled with hostility, he raised the rifle in both hands above his head in a gesture of surrender. I was in no position to take hostages, and our survival depended on our escape. After the things he'd done at the mill, I would have been more than justified in killing the vile beast.

But instead, I backed toward the tree line with my pistol still aimed at the center of his chest. Fatface was shaking. I thought it was fear, until I saw the edges of his wide mouth start to turn up into a smile. The dirt bag was laughing.

I stopped at the tree line where Elias and the women were waiting. My heart was raging with the fire of revenge, and I raised the MP5 to my shoulder.

"Owen, please don't," coughed a voice from behind me. It was Anna struggling to speak to me between tear gas induced gasps. "Owen, please."

I lowered the weapon and took another step back into the brush, still looking at Fatface as he laughed.

Just before I turned to run into the woods with the others, Fatface made his move. He swung the rifle down and threw it up on his shoulder, aimed directly at me; but he never got the shot off. From the bluff overlooking the valley, one shot rang out and Fatface dropped on his face. I wasn't going to lose any sleep over it.

I looked over the valley into the orange haze of smoke and tear gas, wondering at the events that had brought me to this place.

"We must go," urged Elias.

I turned my back on the small farm, and the four of us made our way safely out of the valley and deeper into the woods.

Elias got a whiff of the tear gas when he pulled his mask off and he coughed violently for a few minutes, shaking his head as we ran. Anna and Sarah were both still feeling the effects of the gas and had to be led through the forest with tears streaming from their tightly shut eyes.

Bart, bringing the horses, met us on the run near the creek, and we enjoyed a short reunion and caught a breather while Elias tightened the saddles.

"What was that awful smoke?" Anna asked.

"Just a little 'Marmon' skunk spray," I said proudly.

***

We were all in good spirits, five lively faces in the night, although some of the faces were livelier than others. Elias in particular was elated. He and Bart explained the wonders that I'd shown them, not making much sense to the two women who were just plain glad to be rescued and not much interested in the means of their escape.

After the euphoria of success wore off, Bart looked a little shaken. I understood his conflicting emotions about what he'd been through and what he'd done, but I also understood that Bart LeJeune was a professional soldier and he understood his responsibilities as well as I did. When our eyes met, so did our minds; I needed his reassurance as much as he needed my thanks. All that needed to be said was said in that glance.

Elias pranced around in his horns as Anna and Sarah looked on, partly amused and partly bewildered.

Our celebration was cut short, though, when Anna wrapped both arms around her belly and doubled over with a gasp.

Elias got a sick look on his face. "What have we done?" he moaned.

"She's in labor," said Sarah.

"All that commotion," Bart said. "We've summoned the child early."

"Brother LeJeune," said Sarah, "she's been this way for nearly two days now. Blame the mobs if you must." She put a hand on his shoulder and he relaxed. "But, she was ready anyway."

All eyes turned to Sarah who, because of a collective gender bias, was conferred the role of birthing expert.

"She mustn't ride a horse," she said in a matter-of-fact tone. She examined each of us and asked Bart and me for our coats. We provided them, wondering for what purpose. "Brother LeJeune, would you please build me a travois? Use the coats."

I felt relatively safe using the flashlights to find poles. Elias watched for unwanted company and Sarah had all her attention on Anna.

Bart was a good horseman and was able to secure the poles through the stirrups of the saddle. Our two coats made a thin, but sufficient bed on which Anna could be transported.

We stopped often in the first couple of miles to resecure the travois and tend to Anna's needs. Though I knew next to nothing about childbirth, I knew that Anna's contractions were strong and consistent.

"She isn't going to make it much farther," Sarah said quietly to Bart.

"We can push on to Owen's truck, then perhaps we can stop there."

"That is not what I mean. She is not going to deliver this baby. She's ready, and has been ready for two days. The baby will not come."

I let out a long breath. "Let's pick up the pace," I said.

Elias and I watched carefully for stray mobbers. Bart was attentive to Anna. Often he lifted the travois over obstacles to smooth Anna's ride. It was slow travel, and I was relieved to reach the truck.

We unhooked the travois from the horse, letting Anna down gently.

Anna let out a tremendous rasping moan and Sarah fought to her side, pushing Elias out of the way.

Sarah brushed a moist lock of hair from Anna's forehead and looked at Elias. Sarah, who had held up well until now, turned away and began to cry quietly. "It will not come. It simply will not come. We will lose them both."

Bart looked downcast and Elias allowed a tear to run the length of his face.

"What exactly is the problem, Sarah?" I asked, going to Anna and kneeling at her side.

"The baby is not positioned correctly," she said, wiping beads of perspiration from Anna's forehead.

Bart shook his head. Elias was silent.

I felt for a pulse; it was barely there. Anna was burning with fever. Her breathing was shallow and slow. She was dying, and with her, the baby.

"Can you do something?" asked Bart.

I stood up and looked at him vacantly. The only baby I'd ever had anything to do with was born between the photoelectric doors of University Hospital in Salt Lake City. I'd pulled over a speeding and desperate father, and then, realizing that I'd much rather the baby be born in the hospital than on the sidewalk beside my patrol car, I'd let the father and mother-to-be go, and followed them. The baby crowned, a term I'd learned from the frantic hospital receptionist, between two sets of sliding doors at the hospital entrance and was born into the capable hands of the emergency room staff to a chorus of cheers from the hospital lobby. I'd ended my shift that night in awe, but I knew I couldn't deliver a baby, especially under these conditions.

I also knew that Caesarean section births had been performed for hundreds, even thousands of years. I even had the equipment to perform such a feat. Lewis's field surgery kit contained iodine, morphine, scalpels, and sutures. I actually had seen the procedure performed twice—once by a paramedic at an accident scene under even worse conditions than we were in now and once on the Discovery Channel under ideal conditions. The procedure itself was the same, and amazingly simple. Even so, it was beyond me.

"I . . . I don't know," I stammered, closing my eyes to avoid Bart's helpless stare. "No, there's nothing I can do."

I eventually looked at Bart as he knelt over Anna. His gaze was fixed on Anna's face, and tears were forming in the corners of his eyes. I watched him until a solitary tear ran the length of his face and dropped onto his collar. I turned away, not only out of respect, but because I didn't have the guts to look at him.

I was sure he had developed feelings for Anna since the death of her husband and had been tormented by his growing love. Out of propriety, he'd probably said nothing about it to her. And now, he was losing her and his best friend's child.

"I sent you to the mill to live," Bart said softly to Anna, wiping his tears off her cheek. "What have I done . . . oh, my love, what have I done?"

Anna made another moan and Sarah and Elias both knelt at her side. I stepped away as the others tried to lend her comfort.

Anna looked up past the caring faces hovering over her and caught my eye. For an instant, I saw only the sea green eyes of my best friend Lewis McCray as he lay dying. They were fearless eyes, confident eyes—they were Julianna's eyes, too.

I backed away from Anna's pleading eyes and withdrew to the privacy of the woods at the edge of the clearing. Eyes blurry and legs shaking, I dropped to my knees. Tears flowed freely as I poured out my thoughts and feelings in humble prayer. I spoke in my heart, not as a man speaks to an unknowable god, but as a son talks to his Father. I sought and pled not only for the understanding to help

Anna, but to understand the life and death of my friend Lewis, to understand the confident testimony of my new friend Julianna, and mostly to understand the stirrings of my heart and the purpose of my life. Never before had I uttered such simple words with such power and conviction.

I don't know how long I knelt, but when I stood, I was smiling through tears. I felt that peace, that comfortable peace, which I'd felt before, but this time it was accompanied by a clear and abiding understanding of its source and its meaning.

I strode from the forest into the meadow where Anna still lay. Elias, Bart, and Sarah were standing in a small circle above Anna, huddled together. When they saw me coming, Sarah turned to face me, her face streaked with tears. In her arms she held a swaddled form.

"It's a boy," said Sarah, pulling back the corner of my Gore-Tex coat to reveal the red, blotchy mug of a newborn baby. "Is he not beautiful? He turned in the womb and was born minutes after you left. It was truly a miracle."

"I know," I said. "And I especially like that baby blanket."

"We used your coat, Brother Richards," she said. "I believe it's ruined."

"I cut it in half," Bart said sheepishly. Elias nudged him, grinning, and Bart retorted, "It was tied to the travois. I cut it up."

At Bart's feet lay the other half of my camouflaged raincoat.

"You owe me three hundred dollars," I said matter-of-factly. Bart's eyes widened to two times their normal size and I had to suppress a grin. It took a few seconds, but he soon realized I was joking after I shook my head and gripped him by the shoulder.

"Where did you go?" asked Elias.

I didn't really have an answer, so I was glad when the baby began to cry, drawing the attention away from Elias's question. Anna, lying restfully on the ground, held out her arms and accepted the baby from Sarah, who then folded up the remaining half of my coat and placed it under Anna's head as a pillow. Anna looked radiant, fussing over her new son.

Bart, Elias, and I cleaned out my truck and we gently moved mother and baby to a more comfortable bed on the front seat.

"Anna?" I said when we had a moment alone. "I know you and your people are going through some extremely difficult times, and it's going to get worse before it gets better, but it won't last forever."

"I don't know whether that makes me feel better or worse, Owen."

"Well, whatever happens, I can tell you that it all turns out okay in the end. You know, life isn't very long compared to eternity."

"Spoken like a true Saint, Mister Richards."

"If you don't tell the others, you can call me Brother Richards," I said with a wink. Her smile turned me into pudding. It made me think of Julianna.

Elias approached the truck. "You need to rest now," he told Anna.

She was about to object when I interrupted. "Listen to the man. He seems to know what he's talking about. After all, he saw me coming a mile away." Anna gave me another killer smile—it was the perfect photo op.

"But first, how about a picture of the happy family?" I suggested, getting my camera from the floorboard. "Bart, you slide in next to Anna there and Sarah, why don't you just hold Elias's hand and get it over with." Elias gave me a warning glance that could have frozen peas, but he warmed right up when Sarah took his hand. Bart was ever so glad to sidle up next to Anna and even put his hand under the baby.

I leveled the camera at them. "Look at me, everyone." They didn't necessarily know what I was doing, but they'd trusted me this far, so they went right along. "Okay, say . . ." I lowered the camera. "Hey, what are we gonna name that thing?"

Anna smiled. "That's easy," she said. "After his father. His name will be Lewis."

A lump rose in my throat.

Anna went on, "And after the man who gave him life—Owen."

I was honored.

"Lewis Owen McCray," she said proudly, caressing the baby's small, pink forehead.

I should have known, but then again, maybe I did. I aimed the camera again and adjusted the focus. "Okay, say Lewis Owen McCray."

"Lewis . . ." they began in chorus.

***

"Owen," she sang out. "Owen. Are you going to take the picture or stand there with your mouth open catching flies?

I closed my mouth self-consciously and lowered my camera until I saw Julianna's beautiful form standing in front of me.

"Julianna, is that you?" I stammered, looking around for Bart, Elias, Anna, and Sarah. They were gone.

"What did you say? Of course it's me. Who did you expect, Ann Margaret?"

"I said . . . I mean . . . umm, well, what I said is that is *sooo* you. Hold that pose."

"Captivated by my beauty?" she asked, and held her coy pose.

She was slightly silhouetted in the golden autumn sunset, her honeyed auburn hair gently fluttering in the breeze. Her smile was slightly mischievous and more than a little alluring. Even from a distance, her green McCray eyes reached out like beams and pierced my soul. "Captivated indeed, Sister McCray. Captivated indeed," I whispered.

"Hey Anna . . . uh, Julianna. Let's go look for your great, great, great, grandfather's birthplace." I took her by the hand and we walked up the slight incline to the clearing.

Julianna melted me with a smile. "Owen?"

"Yes."

"I know you might not really understand how important these kinds of things are for me, you know, traipsing around looking for something we'll never find, but I appreciate your company and your patience, especially after everything you've been through lately."

I understood better than Julianna would ever know. "Hey, it's no problem. Besides, I think we will find what we're looking for."

EPILOGUE

"Oh no, not again," lamented Julianna, putting her hands over her face.

"Oh yes," I exclaimed, doing a clumsy cabbage patch dance in the aisle in front of thousands of spectators.

And that's another Seahawk first down, bellowed a deep voice over the public address system at Arrowhead Stadium in Kansas City.

"You're gonna lose, Julianna. You're gonna lose."

"I told you before, I don't bet," proclaimed Julianna.

"I can see why. Uh oh, wait a minute," I said, watching another play unfold on the field. "Yes!" I screamed. "Touchdown!" I threw my arms into the air and spilled Julianna's peanuts all over the bleachers.

Julianna dealt me a wicked blow on the shoulder.

"Ohh," I grunted, grasping my arm. A shot of pain seared through the joint and I thought about Bart and Elias—and of course, Anna.

"Poor boy," Julianna reached over and put her arm around me in mock tenderness. "Let me kiss it and make it better."

Didi who?

ABOUT THE AUTHOR

Willard, a Senior Police Officer with the Pullman, Washington, Police Department, is an avid reader of both fiction and nonfiction, and loves to write. He is dedicated to the idea of providing LDS readers with wholesome entertainment. "I wanted to write a man's action-adventure novel that my sisters could buy for their sons and husbands."

Eleven years as a police officer and member of an inter-local SWAT team served as his research for the modern police material in this book. On an extended SWAT mission, one of his teammates asked him what it would be like if their SWAT team were suddenly transported back in time with all of their modern equipment. The idea of having a modern-day police officer travel back into Mormon history evolved from there.

Willard loves to play softball in the summer, soccer in the fall, and racquetball with his (nationally ranked!) eighty-four-year-old father. He and his wife, Diana, stay in shape by weightlifting, running, biking, and keeping pace with their two young daughters. They love living in Washington state, and are loyal Seattle Mariner fans.

I'LL FIND YOU

by CLAIR M. POULSON

Squeals of little children's laughter mingled with a warm summer breeze before floating cheerfully through the second-story window of Mindy Egan's home. She smiled and looked up from her cleaning. Through the large window of her son's bedroom, she caught sight of an older model green car moving very slowly down the street toward their house. Her eyes lingered longer than seemed reasonable to Mindy; and for reasons she could not fathom, she felt a sharp twist in the pit of her stomach.

Instinctively, she stepped closer to the window where she quickly spotted Rusty in the neighbor's front yard as he played with his constant playmate, Jeri Satch. Both almost six, both with tousled hair, both in blue shorts, and both barefoot, they squealed in delight as they chased a bright red ball across the lawn. Reassured, Mindy smiled and turned from the window as her infant daughter began to fuss in the room across the hall.

Mindy spoke softly to the baby and as she rocked the crib, she thought about how close Rusty and Jeri were as friends; yet they looked so different. Rusty was light-complexioned, with intensely blue eyes and sandy hair—and in spite of being constantly outside in the summer sunshine, he didn't tan easily. Jeri, on the other hand, had dark brown hair, and skin that seemed to tan instantly with the first appearance of the summer sun. Mindy sighed as she reached for the baby whose cries had intensified. But before her hands had touched her daughter, a terrifying scream from outside penetrated the house. Mindy whirled, and tore through the door, across the hall, and to the window of Rusty's room. Jeri was screaming, Rusty was nowhere to be seen, and an old green car was leaving a trail of blue smoke as it hurtled away from the curb.

"I'll find you!" Jeri screamed as Rusty's head popped up in the front seat of the old sedan and then was shoved roughly back down by the driver.

Mindy realized instantly what was happening, and fled in terror toward the stairs. She ran outside, stumbled, fell down the steps, picked herself up, and rushed across the lawn to where Jeri continued to scream and call Rusty's name.

"Mindy, what's happening?" Katherine Satch yelled from her porch.

"Call 911! He took Rusty!" she shouted.

"Who took . . . ?"

"Just call!" Mindy screamed.

Katherine dialed. Jeri cried. Mindy stared in horror as the green car carrying her son turned a corner two blocks away and disappeared. The mild breeze that only moments before had carried the laughter of children now dispersed the blue exhaust.

When the cops arrived minutes later, Mindy described the green car. She tried to describe the driver, but all she could recall was a black baseball cap.

Little Jeri finally calmed down enough to be of some help. "I told Rusty to stay away from the man in the car," she sobbed.

"What did he say to you kids when he stopped?" Officer Howard Green asked.

"He wanted to know where somebody lived."

"Where who lived?"

"I don't remember." Jeri started to cry again.

"Mrs. Egan says he was wearing a black hat. Can you think of anything else about the man that will help us recognize him when we find him?" the officer asked.

"You've got to find him. You've got to get Rusty back," Jeri sobbed. "He's my best friend ever."

"We will, Jeri, but we need your help," he assured her. "What else can you remember?"

Jeri was thoughtful for a moment. "His hands were dirty," she said at last.

"Like with dirt from the ground, or spilled food, or maybe grease?" the officer asked.

Her face brightened momentarily. "Yeah. Like when Dad works on the car," she agreed.

"Good," Officer Green said. "He must be a mechanic."

"He wasn't a mechanic," Mindy said firmly.

The officer looked at her. "Why do you say that?"

"His car smoked. Mechanics have cars that run well," she reasoned.

"Maybe," the officer said, "but not necessarily. What else can either of you recall about either the man or the car? Did it have Utah plates?"

Mindy thought hard. She had no idea. Neither did little Jeri, but she remembered something else. Brightening, Jeri said, "He smokes."

"He smokes," the officer repeated. "And how do you know that?"

"A cigarette fell out of his mouth when he grabbed Rusty," she revealed.

A look from Officer Green to his partner sent the other officer scurrying across the yard. "Marlboro," he said when he returned a minute later carrying the partially burned cigarette in a plastic bag.

More police came. Mindy was assured that the department was doing everything that could be done to locate the suspect's car. Thirty tense minutes passed. Mindy's husband, Patrick, rushed in. He embraced his wife who started crying again. The terrible story of the kidnapping of his son was recounted for his benefit.

Jeri, whose eyes were red, sat tentatively on her mother's lap. "I'll find you, Rusty," she said softly and then, before her mother realized what was happening, Jeri was off her lap and racing for the door.

"Come back here, Jeri!" her mother ordered.

Jeri paid no attention, and in a moment she was outside and

running up the street in the direction where the green car had taken her best friend forty minutes earlier. Her mother caught her and carried her kicking and screaming back to the Egans' house.

"The police will find him," she assured her daughter, but Jeri was not buying it.

"It's my fault he's gone. I should have grabbed his hand," she agonized. "I've got to find him and tell him I'm sorry."

"It's not your fault," Officer Green said. "It's the bad man's fault, and we will find him."

They found his car.

They did not find the man with greasy hands who wore a black baseball cap and smoked Marlboro cigarettes, or the little sandy-haired, barefoot boy wearing a bright yellow shirt and blue shorts.

The car had been stolen from a garage in Salt Lake City several weeks earlier. The plates on it were Utah plates but belonged to a 1998 Buick. They too were stolen. The car was only about a mile from town, abandoned in a small grove of trees beside the road. Tire tracks indicated another car had been parked in the grove as well. It appeared that the abductor had left another car there for the very purpose of switching. Now the police had no description to work from.

Rusty Egan, a sweet boy, a well-behaved boy—Jeri Satch's best friend—was in serious trouble. Rusty Egan was gone.